APPALACHIAN OVERTHROW

APPALACHIAN OVERTHROW

A NOVEL OF
THE VAMPIRE EARTH

E. E. KNIGHT

A ROC BOOK

ROC
Published by the Penguin Group
Penguin Group (USA) Inc., 375 Hudson Street,
New York, New York 10014, USA

USA / Canada / UK / Ireland / Australia / New Zealand / India / South Africa / China

Penguin Books Ltd., Registered Offices: 80 Strand, London WC2R 0RL, England
For more information about the Penguin Group visit penguin.com.

First published by Roc, an imprint of New American Library,
a division of Penguin Group (USA) Inc.

First Printing, April 2013
10   9   8   7   6   5   4   3   2   1

 REGISTERED TRADEMARK—MARCA REGISTRADA

LIBRARY OF CONGRESS CATALOGING-IN-PUBLICATION DATA:
Knight, E. E.
    Appalachian overthrow: a novel of the Vampire Earth/E. E. Knight.
        p.   cm.
    ISBN 978-0-451-41444-1 (hardback)
    1. Valentine, David (Fictitious character)—Fiction. 2. Vampires—Fiction. 3. Human-alien encounters—
Fiction. 4. Appalachian Region—Fiction. I. Title.
    PS3611.N564A67 2013
    813'.6—dc23   2012040814

Set in Granjon Roman

Printed in the United States of America

I have been a stranger in a strange land.

—Exodus 2:22

All great deeds and all great thoughts have a ridiculous beginning.

—Albert Camus

APPALACHIAN OVERTHROW

An Account of the Coal Country Revolt 2073–2079

(as excerpted from Volume 2 of
THE FALL OF THE KURIAN ORDER:
A XENO MEMOIR)

PART I

USEFUL TO THE ORDER

THE CURTAIN RISES

I gave myself up for dead when the bullets ripped out the back of our fleeing four-wheel drive. They cut through the back panel, glass, and my flesh with the ease you'd expect of steel-jacketed high-velocity rounds.

I would draw my last breath on the traditional human holiday of Halloween, having seen forty-two years. The Kentucky soil of the Ohio Basin would absorb my blood, and I would join my mate, our children, and the ancestors after a brief period of suffering.

I have been told to begin this account in medias res.

Were it up to me, I would open this memoir with a brief account of my background as a Xeno, a species foreign to this earth, yet born here nevertheless, and, as I noted, the first of my family born on our new homeworld. I would name myself the son of a people lied into war and rewarded for their losses with poisoned land and broken treaties.

I'm told I came into life in the year 2031 in the normal manner for a Golden One, letting out healthy yapping cries and covered in fine, translucent hair, born in the house of my father and uncles on the banks of the Missouri River, the old state designation of Nebraska. A prophecy of the stains of my birth said I would make my mark among men in strange lands. Some account of my early years as a trader and then later as a speaker for my people would explain my ability with English, the most common tongue of the humans of my region. My rise into the Golden Ones' councils at a young age might give you some reason to accept the facility of my senses and judgment.

My scars in the war against the Kurian Order remain for all to see, even if they are faded and camouflaged by an old Grog's sags and wrinkles. The lies endured, the losses suffered by my people, including the murder of my beloved and our family, would explain my affiliation with our common cause, when this extraordinary world's even more extraordinary people rose and rid us of those who treated us as livestock.

We think, though I have reason to wonder. But that takes me beyond this narrative.

I would speak briefly of my meeting David Valentine, a man I am proud to call my seshance,* who found me wounded and revived me in body and spirit. I would conclude that sketch with a mention that our endeavors are chronicled elsewhere with the usual mild omissions and exaggerations that inevitably cloud reality when a biographer is asked to weave, telling the colorful oft-told tales and disclosing the sometimes-disappointing truth.

Without those particulars of my life, how is the reader to judge the value of this reminiscence? It would be like weighing the goose by extrapolation from a single feather.

But my publisher has requested that I begin with the wild

---

* friend-as-important-as-family

flight across the Ohio River and into Kentucky on Halloween night.

There were seven of us in that big black high-riding utility vehicle that crashed through the bridge barrier, fleeing like Eliza across the Ohio with a far worse master than Simon Legree behind, though southbound rather than north. We had escaped a no-longer-secret installation of the Kurian Order called Xanadu with a pregnant woman, a patient there who had once been married to my David's friend William Post. I was rearmost, filling the back of the truck, squatting uncomfortably on some tools, tow chains, and a spare battery. A bag of groceries hastily thrown in as provision had spilled, so there were apples rolling back and forth on the floor as we took hard turns.

Our intention was to race into the Kentucky hills and lose ourselves among the legworm ranchers there. Kentucky was a wild land, thinly held by the Kurian Overlords even then, and the legworm ranchers enjoyed a measure of independence required by the needs of their voracious herds.

A spray of bullets from the surprised sentries ended that hope, at least for me. Three bullets and a piece of what I believe was glass struck me across the abdomen and neck. Worse, the pursuit started almost instantly, suggestive of expectation on our enemy's part.

I suspected I would not last much longer in the chase, so I volunteered to take the wheel and lead the pursuit away from the others.

With an approaching column of Ohio vehicles filled with soldiers, I did not mention my injuries or the inevitable outcome of the chase. It was the sort of moment that would take an entire night to say what needed to be said.

We had to act while the pursuers were still far enough away not to notice a ruse, so at a thickly covered hillside I took the wheel from my David. My David has never had much confidence behind the wheel of such machines—to this day he is an atrocious driver even if one allows for his bad eye. Though one of our party was a doctor and saw to it that my injuries would not immediately bleed me out, I would only slow them on a foot pursuit. Everyone saw the necessity of the action, and we parted with regret and brevity, though my David took some convincing. Our farewells are not something I can remember without much emotion, and I will not slow this narrative with sentiments recorded elsewhere.[*]

Before squeezing behind the wheel, I took the precaution of putting some of the chains and locks and hitches in the forward passenger seat.

Determined to lead the Ohio forces on as merry a chase as possible so that my friends might escape safely, I pulled away. I avoided looking back at the trees where my friend of many years disappeared with his party, not unmoved by emotion or unwetted by tears.

I drove perhaps two more miles and then stopped at the other side of a crossroads long enough to smash the taillights of the "Lincoln" (an odd moniker for so vast a vehicle, considering the former president's narrow frame and thin features).

The act was harder than you might think. Despite the bullet holes, the well-preserved vintage Lincoln was a beautiful piece of machinery. It offered an almost supernaturally smooth ride, yet transmitted a good feel up to the driver for what the tires were doing;

---

[*] Knight, *Valentine's Exile* (Renaissance Press: 2129).

it was also responsive, quick to accelerate or break. The onboard computer system automatically worked the power to the wheels and brakes in turns, making it more difficult to roll. You can literally say of such machines: they don't make 'em like they used to. The superb machine's performance was buying precious extra time for the escape of my friends, and I was grateful for it.

I failed to destroy one brake light, however, and I believe that proved to be my undoing. Or perhaps there was some kind of tracking device on the vehicle. Though I drove as fast as I dared, not using the vehicle's forward floodlights, I saw my pursuers closing, a remorseless snake of vehicles following the hare-trail I was tearing through the overgrown Kentucky highway, grasses, shrubs, and bits of branch clinging to my vehicle's grille and mirrors as though fighting to keep me from further destruction of the road's plant life.

My pursuers had large, high-clearance vehicles and, it seemed, a better knowledge of the terrain. Twice I had hopes that I'd lost them, only to see them coming at me from my quarter via a shortcut through the hills only they knew existed.

Only one gambit remained, it seemed; the one I had planned for when I placed the chains beside me.

Most humans have a tendency to fill in blanks in their education with a set of less-reliable associations born of their own experiences and prejudices. Because we are larger than even the biggest men, until recently alien to their world, hairy, big-eared and sharp-toothed in a manner similar to the Gray Grogs, most humans will assume my intelligence and understanding operate at the more rudimentary level of my distant relations, though we are as dissimilar in our mental abilities as man is to the chimpanzee. This category error has worked to my advantage before.

I drove a few more minutes until I saw my opportunity. A downed limb partially blocked the road bordered now on either side by forest. I swerved around the heavy limb and aimed the big four-wheel at a thick trunk. Though I braced myself for the impact, I can still feel the collision in my neck when I remember that night.

In my remaining moments I wound the chains around my seat and, with some fumbling, locked and hitched them behind me. Long arms and a dexterous set of feet have their advantages.

My pursuers deployed their vehicles as well as the trees and over-grown roadside allowed, using their doors as shields and rests for their weapons.

They shouted at me to show my hands out the window. Instead, I pounded on the still-functioning horn until they fanned out to one side to approach, boots crunching the fall leaves, carbines and shot-guns held to their shoulders.

Of the possibilities for my immediate future, none looked par-ticularly promising. A straightforward execution in the form of a bullet to some quarter of my head seemed the most likely, especially when they saw my wounds. I could meet death calmly, perhaps wel-come it. Ever since the loss of my beloved, I have waited for death's misted portal to open, sometimes taking chances that might hasten it, for after a soul-purging tour of the hells I've missed in this life, I'm sure my soul would be judged worthy of ascension. And there, she would be waiting. We would set teeth to ear as we had at our pairing and never be parted again. I've kept the honor of my father's name and labored for the betterment of my people and, I suspect, even made a difference in a human life or two. I'm confident that's worth something when my acts are calculated and will avoid the humiliation of a reincarnation. At least I hope so.

The pain of my wounds waxed. Our vet had been fairly certain that my vitals were untouched, but that didn't stop the throbbing, warming sensation rapidly escalating into a burn. Enough pain, and you become resigned to your fate; your one hope is that it is over with quickly. I wasn't there yet, but I feared I soon would be.

An early death would be a kindness. My beloved hates to be kept waiting. Nothing in this patch of Kentucky woods would mark my death, save for a scar the roadside tree would bear for the rest of its life. Maybe someday my David would piece it together; I could rely on him to place a small memorial.

"I told you it was riding higher," were the first words I heard through something other than an amplifying speaker.

"That's a Grog," another said.

I hit the horn again and offered blubbering noises. It was no stage performance for police-vehicle limelight. The grief over the damage to the Lincoln was very real.

The next thing I knew, the barrel of a pistol was pointed at my head from over the rearview mirror. I could follow the foresight back to a steady eye, glinting in the darkness. What looked like lieutenant bars were stitched onto his collar, gray against black. He'd crept up as silently as my David, though my blasts on the horn had helped.

More men came around the front, and powerful flashlight beams lanced into my eyes. I gave a very real whimper and a pained yip.

"Yo!" the lieutenant said. "They got him chained in the driver's seat. That's why he didn't run. Get a bomb-dog up here, now!"

"Keep those hands up," a voice ordered. I'd been trying to shield my eyes from the flashlights with my forearm.

"Yeah, Corp, it'd be just like those bastards to blow up some poor dumb Grog to try to get us," another, younger voice said.

Not just one dog came forward, but three. After the first, a good-natured yellow pot roast of a birder sniffed around beneath the car and behind my seat, pausing with interest over my wounds; other yelping hounds smelled the upholstery and started running in and out of the surrounding woods, trying to locate a trail.

They removed my chains with bolt cutters and kept their guns on me.

The lieutenant had an aged, battered face, but kindly eyes. He looked like the sort of man you'd send into the brush after an escapee from a sensitive institution. I wondered what sin lay in his past, that the Kurian Order did not let him rise above his original commissioned rank.

"That's those guerillas for you," an Ohio backing up his lieutenant said. "Take some poor dumb hurt animal and chain him behind a wheel. Fuckers. I bet they told him home and bed were just down the road. Poor dumb Grog."

Since they seemed in no hurry to effect my ticket for the hells I've missed in this life, I fell out of the door and decided to vocalize. Maybe it would draw the hounds' attention. Every minute counted. Eventually they'd backtrack, but if I could delay things here . . .

I lay on my face, hiking my butt up as though expecting a deserved kick, arms extended toward the lieutenant with the pistol. "Me drive. Me drive good," I gabbled. "No go wrong way. No carelessnessish! Not see tree beside road. Only see tree on road."

"Wow, this one's a regular J. Edger Proofcock," a soldier to my right said, with the youthful voice I'd heard earlier.

I looked at the front of the car and let out a wailing cry of horror. "You fix? Please you fix? Scrap, no, not scrap! Oh, oh, oh! Drive good no!" I finished, summoning the rest of this season's allotment of tears. I crawled for the wreck, patted the hood of the Lincoln, threw myself against a tire under the hostile guns, weeping like bereft Niobe herself. Human culture is so rich in emotional exhibitions. Not the Golden One way—we only howl to frighten enemies—but over a lifetime among men I've now learned to appreciate the benefit of a good teary purge.

"He's worried we'll shitcan him for wrecking that Xanadu ride," the man with the bolt cutters said. "He doesn't know guerillas from churchmen."

"Whaddya say, Lieutenant? End the laments?" the man with the shotgun said, bringing it to his shoulder again.

Coming your way, beloved. Tell the children.

"Top, hold up," the youthful-sounding one who'd expressed sympathy for the poor dumb animal said. "Let me take him. I can find a buyer in Lex. Ought to be worth a couple thou. Big healthy Grog like that."

"Healthy? You see he's bleeding, Frisky?" bolt cutters said.

"C'mon. Grog's clean their teeth with grenades," my new guardian said. "If he's still yappin', he'll live, probably longer than any of us. Thirty percent for you, Lieutenant, twenty for the Top. I'll take him to Lexington with a pass and see what I can get for him."

"Forty percent for me," the lieutenant said.

"And thirty for me," the shotgun-wielding Top added.

"You'll take ten," the lieutenant said. "Eager to please, muscles like that. And can drive, too. Ought to be worth four or five thou if he speaks and savvies and is intact below the belt. Schmuck." He took a breath, looking at the anxious dogs, still running back and forth sniffing for scent fifteen miles behind. "This night's going to suck hard, and six gets you a Kewpie doll that the damn legworm ranchers will be peeing in the wells before we use them. Might as well take a bonus."

"That's being on the righteous side, sir," Frisky said.

"I'll want a receipt, Frisky. I don't want any of my forty rolled up some whore's ass so her pimp don't find it. Buy him a decent labor-belt to hide those bandages."

"Sir yes sir," Frisky said.

Frisky went to work securing the detail's investment in me. They didn't have handcuffs big enough for my wrists, so they settled for leg irons.

If I'd known what was to be endured over the next few months, I might have been tempted to rush the top sergeant. A shotgun blast, a brief caress of hot air and lead before the end of this trying world; that would be nothing compared to the evil awaiting me in the Coal Country.

I visited Lexington by a slow and bumpy route, my injuries were sorry to say.

The only light shining into the gloom of my captivity came from the busy flurry of radio traffic squelching over the vehicular and personal radios. That the search was continuing, reinforced by more forces from Ohio, was a sign that my David had made it away.

They put me in a badly sprung vehicle with a Truck 2Go logo somewhat visible under rust streaks and a thin coat of flaking green Ordnance paint.

I saw a quick glimpse of the Ordnance field headquarters as the truck carrying me passed through it: lines of men and horses and vehicles being fed and serviced, dispatched and received. The truck carrying me was metal sided, but someone had punched a peephole; though the tiny opening was at a tiresome height for me, I couldn't resist making use of it despite the cramping. A few legworm ranchers even wandered through camp, as did an assortment of ill-favored individuals with the fresh-from-the-rat-pit look of the bounty hunters we'd met on the banks of the Tennessee earlier that year.

They studied a new set of wanted posters pasted on the bowed side of a collapsing wooden barn with patient, hungry eyes.

The continuation of the search assured me that my David, Gail Post, and the quick little Alessa Duvalier had vanished into the Kentucky thickets. If they had not been taken in three days, I counted them safe. Still, it was strange that there were this many called out into the field for such a small party of escapees. Or had the Ordnance lost something of exceptional value?

Frisky picked up a boy with a face like a field of red wildflowers to help him in handling me. The teen, who still hadn't grown into his Ordnance uniform, fed and watered me and allowed me to wash with a bucket of water and a rag. For the first leg of the journey, the truck carried search dogs to some quarter of grazing land where the search had flared up again. We were delayed half a day because of the dogs, but apparently once they'd been dropped off in a field near a spaghetti-like mass of wintering legworms, we were on our own at last.

It was amusing to hear Frisky sounding like Polonius advising his young associate.

"Any time you get a chance to operate here in the Kantuck, you jump on it quick as hot skeet. All sorts of chances to pick stuff up. The legworm clans leave you alone, long as you leave them alone. Don't mess with their women or their worms and you'll be fine."

During the drive to Lexington, a zigzag along an old highway with cuts to fords circumventing ruined bridges, with only rudimentary signage remaining to mark the way, I considered again how attractive this land could be. Lush but open, defensible but still livable, mild and well-watered, it seemed to have Nebraska beat by many horizons. Perhaps the legworm ranchers chafed among themselves, even fought over grazing rights and ownership of new-hatched worms, but they kept their land bandit-free. Here we were, riding in an undefended truck loaded with valuable fuel and spares, with every expectation of being able to cross sixty or seventy miles of country unmolested. On the plains and in parts of Missouri, unless the Kurians rule an area, travel in this manner is most unwise. You're almost sure to be bushwhacked. But here was this Frisky, moaning only about the number of detours he had to take around blockages in the road.

Still, Frisky kept his carbine handy next to him in the cabin, and his ruddy assistant had a heavy pistol and a drum-fed shotgun. When I gently explored the limits of the ringbolt chaining me, he had the boy point the weapon at me.

"Relax," Frisky called through the grate separating me and the smell of soggy dog from the driver's cabin.

"Me drive. Me drive good. Yes?" I asked, miming working a steering wheel.

"Not this trip, strawberry," Frisky said.

The roads suddenly improved, the truck picked up speed, and moments later we were entering Lexington. I knew little of it, save that it was the sole Kurian-controlled city in the heart of Kentucky.

I saw little of it through my peephole, except for a tall burned-out building the locals called "the chimney," now home only to hawks and civil-defense loudspeakers. Kurian carbuncles topped a couple of the others, some formed into elegant spires and minarets, whelks clinging to others thickly formed, like bulges of clamshell growing along a building's side, glistening wet no matter how fine the weather. One was black and dead, a little shriveled like a rotting berry. I could hear trains coupling and uncoupling as we passed a rail yard.

Upon arriving in town, the first thing Frisky did was go to a Grog outfitter and purchase a laborer's belt. It's a fairly simple girdle of leather with rings for the attachment of securing hardware, tool pouches, or safety line snap-rings. He studied the injury on my neck and decided it was healing well enough that it could be passed off as a minor work injury.

I made whimpering noises and plucked at my waist, but Frisky ignored me. The dressing at my waist really could have used a replacement and a fresh dusting of iodoform powder, but that would have added to his expenses. He even denied his companion the tiny amount it would cost to go to an eatery and enjoy a hot meal.

I decided that if it came down to an auction, I'd look as sickly and dispirited as possible, both to hear Frisky's explanations and to chop the price intended to be shared among mine enemies.

Frisky stopped and questioned some doubtful-looking boys standing on the street corner, swathed in voluminous clothing that concealed who-knew-what in various pockets. I heard him inquire after someone called "the Young Turk" and another individual called "Blue Yo-Yo."

He eventually located this "Blue Yo-Yo," so the Turk missed his chance, but that's no one's business but the Turk's.

Blue Yo-Yo, who had no toy in evidence but wore a gleaming, diamond-studded ring on every finger along with a few extras pierced into one shaved eyebrow, took a look at me. He held a scented handkerchief over his nose, keeping five feet of airspace between himself and the back door of the truck.

"He's fucking big, yo. How the fuck old is he?"

"Just turned twenty, according to these papers," Frisky said, waving some Ordnance forms full of lies holding hands in block print. "He can drive, too."

"Drive? Are you fucking kidding, yo?" Blue Yo-Yo said.

I put on my best accommodating Grog grin, pulling back my lips. If this Yo-Yo knew anything about my kind, he'd know how to age me by gum line and the length of my pointed prominents and dishonor Frisky as a liar. And forger. When he found time to create documentation on me I do not know; we weren't at that headquarters more than the fifteen or twenty minutes it took to load the dogs. "No, it's true."

Blue Yo-Yo waggled his key-studded fingers. "Let's fucking see it, then."

Frisky gave me the fucking keys and I put on a fucking exhibition with the fucking truck. Blue Yo-Yo must have been fucking impressed, because he managed to put a subject and verb together without an expletive.

"Leather Hog needs new wheel man, but he won't cog Grogs. Take him to the Trapdoor, ducks. Shanghai Mike's always looking for strong backs for the mines in the Coal Country. I'll expect a cut out of both of you. I'm not a free fucking church dinner–and-lecture, yo."

Some humans have a tendency to talk among themselves as though any of my kind nearby are statuary. I sat cross-legged and sniffed at an empty snack-food bag left under the truck's seat.

"Crap, I should have thought of that," Frisky said. "I've heard of Shanghai Mike. Mining. He'd be good at mining."

"It's that fucking uniform, ducks. Kills brain cells. The old gang isn't the same without you, you know. Why you left Our Lady of Lexington, I'll never know."

"Ambition, Yo-Yo. Self-improvement. You should try it sometime. There's more to the world than nose lightning."

"Tough life is my life, yo."

"I'll throw a couple of bills your way if Shanghai meets my price."

Yo-Yo shrugged. "Ain't enough money to buy what I want."

"You just don't get the right catalogues. See you in a couple hours. We'll have a slice and a juice, just like old times."

They exchanged an elaborate set of pats and touches, hands fisting, opening, and hooking too fast for the eye to easily follow. Then we were off again.

The truck paused, with my eyehole revealing nothing but a dirty alley smelling of cats and garbage, for some minutes while Frisky and the boy dragged something out of the way. I tested my bonds once more, but they were secure as ever. I felt rather bloodless and sapped.

The truck inched forward another block, and I felt it bump over an obstruction. Then we were in some kind of empty back lot, with brick buildings of various heights presenting their unadorned backsides to us. We pulled up at a loading dock.

There we waited for some time, Frisky and the boy taking turns going in through a small back door. Once I heard the boy warn off a vagrant asking for a drop of change, then some kittens mewing as they passed under the truck.

Finally, Frisky, flanked by two big men in blue woolen overcoats, opened the truck.

"Good big Grog, right?" one asked me.

I grinned. "Good big Grog. No trouble."

"That's the spirit," Frisky said. "Stand up, King. Check out that thumping pole, guys. You might sell him to the zoo in Chicago."

I stood, and after some more words they released me, still shackled at the hands, my legs in irons. But it felt good to be out of the truck, even if my only vista was of a dirty back lot in Lexington.

I took care with my footfalls as I was led around to the stairs leading up to the loading dock and back door; it seemed sewage service was sporadic in Lexington. A noisome stream of goo ran down a gutter flanking the building. It washed around a dead cat.

I'm told I really missed something at Shanghai Mike's, kept to the back "tanks" on my visit. The vintage signage, the art glass, the vast selection of beers and liquors, and the plump, companionable females, the cheerful serving staff with their famously long hair and white teeth. But it was a honey trap, designed to catch young, unwary legworm ranchers and refugees dazzled by the bright lights after a long stretch in open country. All the bar's well-groomed workers and paraphernalia were there to put unwary customers at ease, and ease likely candidates into one of the bare little "tanks" in back.

A woman with half her hair shaved off, and also missing an eyebrow opposite the shaving, took my temperature (after wiping the thermometer on her dirty plastic apron) and tried to assess my blood pressure, but she did not have the kind of cuff that would go around my arm. I savored the small victory against the system here.

"I'm not sure what's normal for this color Grog," she told Shanghai Mike when he came in, followed by Frisky.

Shanghai Mike wore a robe of gleaming silk, elaborately stitched with fantastic-looking creatures, and odd wooden platform shoes that clattered on the floor.

He looked at my neck and pulled back the laborer's belt. "Fris, Fris. Are you kidding me? What happened to him?"

Nothing shamed Frisky, who snapped his fingers and tugged at an ear. "I was hoping you wouldn't get close up. Lots of guys are afraid of him. I'm not altogether sure about the injuries, but he's healthy enough and healing."

"He's big all right. I've seen a few of his kind over the years but never dealt with one. They're a cut above. The ones I did see were doing bodyguard work."

"Tell him, King," Frisky said. "Tell him what you can do."

"Yes," I said. "Me strong. Me smart, obey all. Drive good. Clean good. Make good. Me can some assembly required. All diagram good."

"Memorize good, more like," Shangahi Mike said. "What the heck. He looks sound enough, and I've heard these guys are good diggers and builders. A thou, and another thou if I can sell him over the phone. I hate greasing up buyers. Get a picture, Tongue."

The woman with half a head of hair extracted a tiny silvery camera, and the flash popped, lighting up a room better left dark.

"Five thou and spare me the details," Frisky said.

"For a wounded Grog? Tell it to the Golems, Fris."

After more haggling, Shanghai Mike finally had a small leather case brought in. He handed it to me with an order to put it together. I opened it and found a musical instrument inside, in four pieces. Luckily it was a fairly obvious vertical horn, and I had little difficulty telling which end the bell went on and where the mouthpiece capped it. It was the sort of test an inexperienced Gray One would spend an hour doing, if he could maintain interest.

"What did I tell you? King's smart!"

"So he can put together a clarinet. Three thousand five, with a five-hundred bonus for a quick sale."

"I can't wait around. Gotta get back to my unit."

"Go grab a bite in the club. Act like a regular down from Ohio who never misses the joint when visiting Lex and I'll think about thirty-eight flat, though if he croaks on me, you'd better never come home again."

It turned out I was sold to a West Virginia company by the time Frisky's sandwich left the grill.

"And there's an extra thou for the boy," Shanghai Mike said as Frisky handed over the key to my chain, as though I were a parked automobile.

So, the kid in the ill-fitting uniform wouldn't be returning north of the Ohio. Hopefully he'd learn a lesson about trusting Frisky.

"I want a separate receipt for him, okay?"

"Of course," Mike said, scribbling on a yellow pad.

Frisky looked down the corridor of tanks. "Dumb kid. Deserting on me like that. His CO's going to be so disappointed. He'll wise up in that turpentine camp."

"You did him a big favor, Fris," Shangahi Mike said. "He'll come out of it sharper."

"I like to think I do my part in seasoning the raw. Pleasure doing business with you, Mike. Bye, King. Say hello to the coal for me."

So my stay in Lexington was but brief. Evidently my size and weight made a full load for one of the slave transports, and I was bundled along with several other lost souls, protesting or weeping, onto a wire-cage flatbed and put under a canvas cover that reeked of assorted molds and droppings.

I've noticed that most of the Kurian Order propaganda posters talk about the dignity and advancement of man. A photo of this transport would make a fine rebuttal if it were attached.

The appeals to authority of my companions provided some mild interest. Those from north of the Ohio mostly threatened some form of official action from the Ordnance. It was just possible. The Ordnance was one of the better-run Kurian organizations stretching across much of what I'm told used to be called the "rust belt" between the Ohio River and the Great Lakes. Those from Tennessee on south vowed a more private or familial revenge. I suspect Shanghai Mike had heard many such threats over the years.

I liked one Ohioan in particular, formerly a young civilian assistant on some general's staff, his face polished with soap and his soft, full hair that of a human who hadn't seen his twentieth winter. I shall refer to him for a while as Mr. Vernabie. He seemed to understand his predicament better than most, or perhaps the nature of his captors. He continually shouted to Shanghai Mike's men that if they would just get in touch with his family, the Vernabies, they would pay double whatever they were getting for his back from our purchaser.

Only once we were bumping up into the mountains did Mr. Vernabie break his cool: "My father and uncle both won brass rings. So did their fathers before them! Pre-'twenty-two service to Kur runs in my family!"

If the drivers even heard him, they showed no sign of it.

One of the other prisoners made a comment about trying Mr. Vernabie's pinky ring and reached for him. He shifted quickly to the opposite corner and was quiet for the rest of the trip.

I passed up an escape opportunity on the truck ride into the mountains. Our consumptive diesel had to have a tire changed, and they took us out of the cage and shackled us together in a long line. I was sure that if I could get my foot on the chain, the pin holding the chain end to my hands would part easily enough. Instead, I made myself useful by putting stones behind the wheels of the truck so it would not roll as the drivers changed the tire.

"Me cop trucks all same, help!" I told the drivers, grinning and licking my lips while scratching at the earth in front of their feet in the manner of a submissive, pleading Grog. "Help good. Help all time."

Two men and a muzzled dog watched over the prisoners. Both wore pistols at their belts and one carried a shotgun. If my fellow prisoners had been a little more spirited, we might have taken them and used the tools to free ourselves, but my companions were as conditioned to authority as the truck's transmission.

We bumped up mountainsides and bumped down them. The roads improved slightly and I heard the driver say we'd passed out of Kentucky. Finally we arrived at a long, redbrick building.

Consolidated Mines
A Maynes Conglomerate Resource Holding

The words read in two-meter-high letters painted on the brick, and over windows in some cases.

They let us walk and stretch in a big parking lot out back between the office and another building with grinding and tapping noises; a workshop of some kind. While the guard visited the door marked RECRUITING OFFICE, we could pace between the buildings. A cold wind blew out of the north, and we limited our milling to pockets out of the wind. A man with overalls and a tool belt with various cleaning products and implements brought us hearty sandwiches. He was a kindly man, and he gave me three.

"Big boy like you must have a big appetite," he said.

After a couple hours' delay, a white-red-and-black bus, layered in color like a cake and bearing the Consolidated Mines logo, pulled into the lot. Four more men shuffled from the workshop. One had healing bruises all over his face.

A man with hair like a brush emerged from the recruiting office, his tie continually flapping over his shoulder in the breeze. The guards formed us into a line and arranged themselves behind us.

"Welcome to Consolidated," he said. "My name's Stackworth and I'm the director of requisitioned labor. Most of my men call me Boss. I don't care where you came from—"

At this, Mr. Vernabie tried to speak up: "Mr. Stackworth, I'm—"

I heard a quick step, a buzz, and I smelled ozone. Mr. Vernabie crumbled to the ground, wetting himself.

"As I said, I don't care where you came from. You work for Consolidated now, and we keep discipline. You're lucky you ended up here. As far as we're concerned, you're reborn. You'll find you've got a new chance here. We pride ourselves on our fairness and pro-moting from within. I myself arrived here wearing a pair of hand-cuffs; now I report directly to the White Palace. We'll work you hard, but you'll be paid. Give an extra effort and it'll be noticed and rewarded. Do your job, obey policy, and let the company take care of you. As your young associate just learned, the first policy is to listen when orders are being given. Are we networking?"

"Yes, sir," most of the men mumbled.

They gave the men some crisp new overalls—I received a gray woolen blanket that I fashioned into a poncho or tunic, belted with some cording. By the time I was done dressing myself, it was my turn for a brief medical examination. The nurse, who spent the whole examination twitching despite the happy, soothing coos I offered as she did her inspection, finally wrote a few vitals down in a shaking longhand.

"I don't suppose you know what's normal for your kind," she said, taking my temperature by sticking a probe in my ear.

"No injections! No injections," I said.

"Don't worry; we're not injecting you. No injections."

They put me through some basic cognitive tests. I found it interesting that in this little Kurian Zone, they tried to find out a little about your capabilities. I'd heard of plantations where they worked you, young or old, skilled or not, until your body broke down, and then they handed you over to the Reapers. I sorted a tray full of different-shaped objects into matching slots. Then they had me identify road signs. They watched me load and then use a simple bolt-action .22, and, satisfied with that, gave me an auto-loading pistol, one of the Atlanta Gunworks copies of a Glock, I believe. Luckily it had an oversized trigger guard. A man in a navy blue uniform and shiny black shoes set down a wooden tool carrier filled with rags, gun oil, and muzzle swabs.

"Strip and clean," he said.

"Strip! Clean!" I repeated, smiling as widely as I could. I examined the weapon for a moment from a variety of angles, set it down, and pretended to think; then I picked it up and checked to make sure it wasn't loaded. It wasn't. I broke down the weapon and went to work with the swabs.

"Not bad," the man who'd given me the pistol said to Stackworth, when he looked in on my progress. The others who had arrived with me had long since been filtered through the system; I had heard them say something about having lunch once they were on the way to their final destinations. . . . "Had a slow start. Grogs keep skills pretty well, as long as they can practice. Their memory's more or less muscle-based, you might say. Like riding a bicycle, you couldn't tell me how to do it, at least not so's I could, but once you get your feet on the pedals, your body remembers the skill. They're like that with everything."

While I will admit that is a serviceable description of how the Gray Ones build and retain skills, my kind work at a higher level of thought and retention. Though even I appreciate mnemonics. Anything from a matchbook to a day-pass to revisiting a bit of road will bring back memories that were lost to me—which is one of the reasons much of this was written contemporaneously in Golden One notation.

After the physical and mental tests, Stackworth came around and clipped a blue plastic tag to my improvised covering. He had an assistant with him bearing a ledgerlike book, much wider than it was high. "You're just right for bodyguard work, Groggie. Impressive size and muscle mass. Mechanical skills. They say you can drive and if you don't, we can teach you. You got a name?"

I thumped my chest. "King."

Stackworth looked at the assistant's clipboard. "What do you think? Might do for muscle in Bone's detail. They told me to keep an eye out for someone unusually big and eager. Furry here exceeds specifications by miles."

"Yeah," the assistant said. "An ape's just the wheel that won't squeak. Won't mind Bone's habits. He'd clean up unpleasant leftovers."

Stackworth took a deep breath. "Okay, ship him to the White Palace." Then he carefully rested his hand on my back, judging my reaction. "You're in luck—King. You're heading for the garden spot of the coal pits. Good food sitting on clean dishes. Work hard and make me look good, now."

"Who's going to take him over?" the assistant asked.

"I will," Stackworth said. "It's an excuse. I might even get some family liquor out of it. Order us something from the motor pool to haul him."

THE BLACK PRINCE
OF THE WHITE PALACE

The roads in the Appalachian Virginias are not maintained particularly well, so officials get around in high-clearance vehicles. Pickups and sport utilities converted into passenger carriers called shuttles are common sights, all painted a gray-black color the locals call "company shale" where they will be heard and "pissant primer" where they're sure of their company. The Maynes Conglomerate does not issue personal transport to any but its highest functionaries. Ordinary workers take a bus. Foremen and other low-level supervisors typically travel about in a shuttle. Should you pass out of the perdition of lower management and graduate to middle grades, you have use of a driver pool, but you still have to justify each trip. Then should you reach the executive level, you are issued your own vehicle, driver, and assistant.

Being a Grog, and a sizable one at that, I was put into a company shale pickup, open to the elements, for my trip away from the mine headquarters. I made myself as comfortable as I could on a spool of electrical cable and hung on with some cargo netting clipped into the bed. A man in a subdued, vertically patterned forest camouflage uniform rode with me. I would learn it was the uniform of the Coal Country Troopers, sort of a state police. He had a racking cough that brought up phlegm, and he seemed to take pride in timing his expectorations for aerial distance, launching them off the side on turns and out the back on lengths of good-road straightaway.

"That was a good one, stoop," he'd say whenever one hung in the air for several seconds before landing, or travelled an unusually long parabola. Rather than the more common term "Grog," "stoop" seemed to be in use to refer to my kind in the Virginias, when they did not use the more offensive "ape." They did not appear to differentiate me from the wider, shorter Gray Ones, and I had no reason to correct anyone—yet.

The driver bounced us all the way to one of the Maynes family holdings, a monumental white edifice that I learned was a pre-Kurian hotel outside White Sulphur Springs. Stackworth reknotted his tie and checked his zipper after stepping out of the transport.

It was a rambling, multistory structure in a clean Federal style, white as a solitary cumulous cloud on a fair summer day. Gardens, a golf course, and bridle trails surrounded it, with encompassing picturesque, thickly forested blue hills. In layout, it was staggered with several similarly styled buildings linked together over the vast grounds, not very different from the buzzing human hives in the bigger cities.

"Welcome to the White Palace," the shuttle driver said as we pulled up.

Stackworth spent a few moments talking to a man in a granite uniform with large, shining black buttons and a captain's bars. "This is the Grog I called about. For Maynes."

"You should be more specific. We have about sixty of the Maynes name here, not counting wives and first cousins."

"You know I mean Joshua Maynes the Third," Stackworth said. "Bone."

And that is how I learned the name of the most troubling, and troubled, man I ever served.

We dropped the soldier with the cough at a door with a medical cross on it, then shuttle parked around a lesser projection jutting out of the back of the white wall of the palace. They brought me in what I presume had been the staff entrance. I was met by an attendant with the inevitable clipboard.

"No luggage?" he asked the driver.

"Fresh out of the woods, I'm told," Stackworth said.

I waited, idle—there is a great deal of idle waiting in any Kurian Zone—while the attendant phoned the security administrative office and they sent someone up to get me. Once again, this woman was incredulous that I had no luggage. I decided to acquire a toothbrush at my first opportunity, just so whatever they needed checked off about my luggage could be checked off.

The security office, or at least the part that handled new employees, was located in the basement. They took me down three flights of stairs, the first having a polished wood balustrade, the second having no-slip utility strips, and the third being just three broken steps down under a sign that read WATCH YOUR HEAD. The hallway my escort took me down was narrow, and I wondered what would happen if we met someone coming the other way. I heard the muted roar of a boiler coming from nowhere in particular. As the sound faded, I was brought into a sort of office with a big whiteboard with a permanent black grid with names and shift information. "Maynes" showed up repeatedly on the grid along with names of those detailed to each.

Two men in granite-colored canvas uniform pants and creased light woolen shirts with silver snaps sat in chairs sorting documents into bins labeled "file" and "shred." A third, wearing a jacket and tie over a denim shirt, sat at a desk, sipping water out of one of those oversized tumblers you sometimes see bedside in hospitals.

"This is the Wonder Grog," my escort said, shutting the door behind her. "No sign language or icon books; he talks."

"Uh-huh," the man in the suit jacket grunted.

Rather relieved to finally meet someone who wasn't worried about my luggage, I stared at his water and smacked my lips. I was thirsty after the ride.

"You drive?" he asked. I liked that he didn't call me a stoop.

"Yes! Drive!" I said, mimicking the operation of a steering wheel and floor shift.

He imitated my syntax. "You fight? Know subdue. Subdue?"

I rubbed my forehead and looked at the floor. "What—who—not—me teach? You me teach? You teach me subdue?"

He nodded. "Mean not kill. Hold."

"Hold! Wrasslin'!" I said. I hoped they wouldn't put me on collection runs, or whatever they called them here, gathering victims for the Reapers.

"Yes, wrestling, exactly," shirt-and-tie said, throwing a look at the men sorting. I noticed he had an orange earplug in his ear. It wasn't attached to a wire, so communication or a personal sound system was out.

"Wrasslin', know. Wrasslin' do," I said, on my guard now.

"Do now," he said, nodding at the escort at the door.

The lights went out and the two men who were sorting papers flew at me like aimed arrows. I heard handcuffs open and felt the hard bar of a baton lever against my elbow.

They fought dirty. One stomped my instep, hard, with his bootheel as he worked the baton and the other fired a deafening air horn. I felt the force of it on my fur, but my ears had already closed and twisted back as soon as the lights turned off. Do not be impressed; this was more reflex than intention. Golden One ears go flat during a tooth-and-claw whether we want them to or not.

Wrasslin' he wanted and wrasslin' he got. My two attackers, so lively and aggressive in their opening moves, like inexperienced chess players, relaxed considerably once I had the blades of my forearms up against their windpipes. I hugged them tight until they went limp.

The lights went on about the same time that I smelled urine.

"Drop 'em!" the man in the suit and tie shouted, white faced. He reached for a phone on his desk, but he looked a little better as soon as my wrestling partners took deep wheezing breaths.

My escort had backed into a corner and held a canister of pepper spray in a shaking hand, pointed at me. I turned my head away, just in case. "Last time they kicked the shit out of that poor ape, Marko."

"I figured it was just Stackworth trying to snoot another security-hire bonus for himself," this Marko said.

"What the hell happened?" one of my attackers said, working his jaw experimentally. It was already swelling up a little; he'd have a decentish bruise by dinner.

"Good wrasslin'?" I asked, cringing a little before Marko.

"Have the vet give him the once-over; then send him to the kennels for an evaluation," Marko said to the woman who'd finally lowered her canister. "If he checks out, we'll start him off with Maynes Version Three. He's always complaining that Gus and Lightning look too old to intimidate anyone."

"Home has peed himself. Still sleeping like a baby." The guard rubbing his jaw stood up. "You know, we could all save ourselves by just using the big boy here to intimidate Version Three. Maybe if that little cocksucker would tone it down, we wouldn't be so busy bagging his dumps when he goes out for walkies."

He toed his partner and the man groaned. To be honest, I was a little relieved, though under most circumstances I don't pity the regime's armed lackeys.

"If I want you to have an opinion, I'll issue you one," Marko said. "Better get Home to the infirmary. And you, ape, are going to go get your kidneys prodded by the vet."

"He's hard as a piece of hickory, that one," MacTierney said.

My new master, Joshua Maynes the Third, didn't greet me on my first day. Or my second. Or even in the course of my first week.

I fell under the supervision of the barn staff, who also oversaw a few Gray Ones who did manual labor with the livestock and helped out whenever the groundskeepers or maintenance people needed strong backs.

I never learned what happened to "the Second," but Joshua "Version Three" Maynes was an important part of the Maynes family. The Conglomerate still exists in the Coal Country; indeed, I believe it thrives, and I would like to know if the same withered, grasping hand still remains at the nexus of the puppet strings. Few others share my curiosity about just who controls Maynes Consolidated these days; that scarred section of West Virginia is still something of a mountainous backwater.

The Maynes family, unquestionably the most powerful in West Virginia though there were others of import, maintained the White Palace as a combination residence, government center, and citadel near the road and rail line coming out of Virginia (and the main highway coming down from Maryland and Pennsylvania).

Though I hid it, I was thrilled with the appointment to the security detail of Joshua Maynes the Third. The assignment entailed everything I desired at that moment: access to weapons, a daily job that involved use of a vehicle, and presumably some sort of uniform or insignia indicating my proximity to those in power.

Those who have never lived within a Kurian Zone rarely appreciate just how far the trappings of power may carry you. The epaulettes and stick of the local patrolman, the overcoat and briefcase of the investigator, the simple black twill and orders of precious-metal clerical collar tabs of the New Universal Church—these and scores of others like them give the power of life and death. And I don't mean an easy movie death, either, where the villain takes out a small pistol and shoots his powerless victim in the head, clearing an obstacle the way one might brush off a fly.

Officialdom has the weight of documentation. The Kurian Zones were great keepers of records. Like a chicken within a coop, each egg produced is documented. Similarly, a careless phrase or a burst of temper could mark one as a troublemaker, and troublemakers tended to disappear in the night. The ability to place a note in a file, or worse, "card it" so it moved to a different, security-related department (at least in the Atlanta Kurian Zone and those affiliated with its internal policing arrangements, as we had in the Virginias) could change, and perhaps shorten, the course of your life. The ordinary people knew that what went in their file was more important than what went in their bodies; you were your file, to put it to a philosophical point, much more than you were a collection of cells processing proteins, carbohydrates, and fats.

If Joshua Maynes Version Three had been a modern product such as a pocket concierge, customers would have wondered why the Version Three did so much less than the first generation. It was his grandfather who put the Coal Country back together after 2022 and got a proud people back into something that resembled a civilization, despite being more than seventy when worldwide disaster struck. But I find that is often the case with the Children of Titans. In the shadow of such monoliths, who can find the sun to grow?

Having expressed sympathy for the man, I'm now free to describe him as I knew him for that tiresome seven months. Of all the humans I've known well, he was remarkable in that he exhibited fewer virtues than any other individual I've met.

We have a saying among our people, which I'll translate, taking some liberty with the phraseology:

When missing one, may just mean fun;

Take two away, adds spice they say;

When lacking three, thy purse keep to thee;

Four or more, show him the door.

In other words, those missing one virtue will probably be more companionable, for who can spend much time in the companionship of a saint without growing bored? Those without two will be fascinating to know, but I'd recommend not becoming too close to them. Those who show no signs of three virtues, never trust with money, and you're better off entirely avoiding those missing four or more.

The Golden One virtues share some similarities with human ones. For those interested, I will list them; the rest should skip ahead a page or two. In short, these virtues are empathy, truth, justness, reason, courage, fortitude, industry, salubrity, and generosity.

> Empathy—This virtue is usually called the first, because it is what separates the Golden One from the salbal.* Being able to put oneself upon the path of another, understand pain and desire to mitigate it, even knowing nothing of what challenges came behind and what obstacles stand before, is the bright shining line between sentience and bestiality. Unlike all the other virtues, its place is specifically listed in the Rhapsodies as the one that makes civilization possible. Empathy is a

---

* A sort of baboon-like creature from the Golden One's home planet. Some think they are a common evolutionary link between the Golden Ones and Gray Ones. They hunt in a mob, are socialized to an extent, have a rudimentary set of signals that pass for a vocabulary, and are notorious for infanticide during famines and eating their own wounded and aged regardless of season.

good place to start on one's ascent, for it takes no money or skill—we each have all the tools in our minds and hearts already to practice this virtue.

Truth—This virtue is at the heart of all others. While young, we're often taught that one must always tell the truth. But that comes at the end of the path of this virtue, not the beginning. One must be able to look at oneself, others, and the world with clear eyes. Once one has trained himself to see the truth, then he can begin to attempt to speak it. The final step on the Ascent to Truth is teaching others how to see and speak it.

Justness—Those who have gained some knowledge of truth, reason, and empathy may use it to pursue an ascent in justice. Without the three preceding virtues, justice would be nothing but chance-of-the-moment emotion.

Reason—The Ascent to Reason is more challenging than it appears, at least for our kind. In the Golden One definition, the first step of the ascent is control of temper. We can be subject to blind furies when the animal brain reawakens in response to what may or may not be a threat. The smell of blood, for example—I know many men who are indifferent or barely aware of the odor, but it sets a Golden One on edge, ready for what your behaviorists call "fight-or-flight." Humans seldom appreciate how quickly this can turn even the best Golden One dangerous. Under certain stimulus, our response is as quick as a leg-kick to a tap on the patella for a human. Reason must intercede, and quickly, or a tragedy may happen.

Courage—Too many of my kind consider only the physical side of courage to matter. Of course, when the Reapers are shrieking on the other side of the door, it takes physical courage to kick it open and throw in the gasoline bomb. For those who've seen much battle in the fight against the Kur, they know there is also an ethical component to courage. A general must be able to order his men to die and be able to move on to the next decision, letting go of his own failure if necessary, as long as he learned by it.

Fortitude—Life does not favor us all equally. A good deal of chance determines one's fate. I have seen enough of life and battle to have a soldier's realism about happy endings and just outcomes. The practice of the Virtue of Fortitude in adversity means keeping your other virtues even when it seems fate itself fights against you. Nothing inspires admiration more than seeing an impoverished man carefully scrubbing the stains out of his one shirt with a toothbrush and a bit of soap, or an exhausted charwoman taking a laboratory skills class.

Salubrity—This is another collection of good habits, a very big barn that holds many different species of animal. It can mean personal hygiene, appropriate dress, physical fitness, attention to care of one's teeth and hair, and proper grooming of the feet. Even getting enough sleep in an environment conducive to restoration and repose is part of Salubrity. While I have been filthy and tired many, many times in my life, I restore myself at the first reasonable opportunity. Appearance is deceptive, true, and the cleanliness of one's hair reveals nothing about the quality of the thoughts passing beneath, but I have found more often than not that how one presents oneself is self-fulfilling. It aids one's ascent like a mountaineer's stick or can hasten a descent as well. Present yourself to the world as what you wish to be, whatever you are. I have been long among men and for much of that time those I met thought of our kind as bloodthirsty savages. By keeping my hair trimmed, my teeth and nails polished, my dress neat and orderly, my speech minimal, brief, and to the point, I was able to begin changing a lifetime's prejudice and ignorance in a matter of moments. English is difficult, but, with practice, you can learn to speak better than most of the people you meet.

Industry—This is a virtue that can mean both quality and quantity of your work. Part of this is how your work affects others: a Golden One who keeps an estate that supports nine families will benefit from extra respect for making it possible for others to honestly earn their bread and trade their butter. Industry can also mean accumulating the necessary skills to take your role in family and society.

Generosity—This is the final virtue. Full exercise of this virtue's path is possible only if the others are practiced and a few perfected. Generosity can mean hospitality to friends and visitors, the practice of charity, spending time and skill in helping others, acting as an example and mentor to the next generation. It is the virtue that gives the most satisfaction of all of them. A day spent in practicing generosity is a day you will look back on with pride.

These are in my own order, though there are Golden One philosophies that place them in different groupings of thirds. There are the "at all times" virtues; the "daily" group; and finally the "endeavor" group, which includes those that rise to prominence above the others when carrying out a great duty to yourself or others. Sometimes, sadly, it is necessary to lie or become a coward to survive. I do not believe in self-immolation to keep to a philosophical principle. Some human philosophers have researched our Rhapsodies and drawn their own conclusions, recasting them as mind, body, and spirit. If it makes their life better and allows them to avoid or ease an ache, I certainly do not object.

I apologize to anyone whom I've offended with this digression. I've no wish to proselytize. The Golden One Rhapsodies have found some human adherents and followers among those who work closely with us. To my mind, this is a positive sign for our future. I'm impressed with the human Judeo-Christian ethical system and have done my best to read a little of its major contributors. I see nothing in the Rhapsodies that prevents harmony between our strains of sentience beyond a few home-planet death rituals that humans may find distasteful.

The less said about the rest of my introduction to the palace, the better. It turned out that the vet mostly worked with horses, and the "kennels" housed a mix of dogs and Gray Ones who rotated between landscaping work, family farm duties, and nearby road maintenance, depending on the season. The vet had to look me up in a *Xenoguide* to determine normal blood pressure and heartbeat. His issue was badly out-of-date, and it had some bordering-on-laughable illustrations. It seemed not many Golden Ones made it to the other side of the Appalachians.

They installed me behind the White Palace in the kennels—you could call it a barn or stable, divided into dog runs, chicken coops, and a few stalls for horses. In the white-painted basement, which still smelled faintly of pigs, there was some aged milking machinery along with a few partitions about the size of a mechanic's bay where the other Xenos slept and recreated.

The Gray Ones of the White Palace loved their work and their life. There were three of them, just enough to set up a small tribal hierarchy of a chief and two followers. They were all well into maturity, so the burning need to prove themselves and court females had faded into comradeship of long standing. They had easy labor and superb food and a comfortable dwelling—they were probably the happiest residents of the White Palace.

When I first saw them, I had thought I might be able to impress myself on them enough to take over the role of chief, as escape would be easier in a small group. Perhaps if I had worked with them every day, we would have jelled, but my schedule and theirs differed. They always worked with daylight; my schedule was irregular and required frequent overnights.

They did give me some training, mostly on special rules of the road for the Coal Country, signal flare notations, and a few military hand signals.

The most interesting of the road rules was the practice of following the firemen on calls. When a group of firemen in one of their vehicles had their whirling, blinking signal lights on, armed men of the Kurian Order in vehicles were to drop everything and follow behind and offer assistance, unless they were waved off by one of the firemen. I thought this a very strange rule until I learned the real role of the Coal Country firemen.

As for the signal flares, it was a useful way of communicating in the mountains for divided parties with no radio. They were visible in all but the heaviest weather and loud enough to attract attention for miles. I learned the signals for "objective sighted" and "assistance required" and "return to base." Any of the paramilitary commanders in the field had a corporal or two trailing him with a box of signal flares and a special small mortar for firing them.

They must not have expected much of me tactically, for I only learned the hand signals for "Wait here" and "Follow me," although it is true that a good deal of military activity can be said to boil down to one or the other. But then, if the Coal Country was employing three perfectly healthy Gray Ones shifting bales of straw, spreading gravel, pulling up scrub brush, and painting fencing, they must not have been experienced with just how effective they could be as scouts, snipers, and trackers.

They didn't have a uniform that fit me. The best they could manage was a cap.

Much of the lower level of the White Palace was filled with workshops. There was an electronics shop, a machinist-cum-locksmith, a gunsmith, a cobbler's area for shoes and boots, and a corner filled with tools for working leather. One of the larger working rooms was devoted just to reclaiming and recycling clothing and material.

While my fur serves to keep me warm and dry, I have found through long years of association with humans that being dressed in a manner similar to them turns our interactions into sentient-to-sentient, rather than those of a man interacting with a dancing bear. Also, I'm less likely to get a bullet fired into me by an overzealous hunter.

I found some cargo netting and fashioned a long tunic undershirt out of it, so my fur would have some airflow around it. I closed it with carabiner clips, one of the handiest things to have on you in the wilderness. It never hurts to have some netting handy, either, when you need to make a bag or shelter.

Next I fixed a knee-length kilt, using a woolen blanket. I found a discarded set of chaps and took one to fashion into a girdle when I had more time to work with it. I rooted through a huge old bureau filled with tiny drawers and found some studs, spring-closed hook-and-eye loops such as you find on a dog leash, and tough thread for the leather. There were many beautiful pieces of furnishings tucked down here showing the craft that went into each drawer pull and beveled edge, still gorgeous despite the battering of heavy use. Upstairs the Maynes family preferred clean, utilitarian lines and the atrocity of enamel paints over wood grain.

Gloves that fit would be out of the question, but an old leather doctor's bag had some wonderful lined leather that could be used for improvising a fingerless set, and I could put a protective iron band across the knuckles. A little extra heft and protection to a blow never hurt.

I wear hats and helmets only in extremes, preferring to give my ears full play to sweep my surroundings (I'm often asked whether the rotations and angles are deliberate. They aren't, unless I'm concentrating on listening to a specific noise).

I have found through long experience that truck tires make excellent footwear once properly fitted to a moccasin—another project for idle hours.

A land shapes (if not makes) its people, Hok-Tkrah* tells us.

The people of the Coal Country lived in a manner as timeless as their hills, at times as secretive as their forests.

The Coal Country people believed in some sense of natural rights in the Declaration of Independence sense. I heard the phrase "You can't do this to me" several times during my years there. There was a sense that as long as you stayed out of trouble, you were safe. In some of the more remote areas, they perhaps even felt free to start trouble with the knowledge that the Order would not spend the resources to hunt them down.

I have spent time in Kurian Zones where everyone acted, and often looked, like a convict with a noose around his neck waiting for

---

* A Golden One philosopher, famous for arguing against a clan-based society and building one around the individual and larger society.

the trapdoor to be pulled. In the Coal Country, the people walked with something of the swagger I recognized from the freeholds west of the Mississippi.

For example, once while waiting for Maynes to return from some grotty room above a bar with one of his press-gang victims of the day, I watched two women walking arm in arm along the sidewalk back from the market, lightly laden. A pair of firemen coming in the other direction made room for the ladies. Both very pointedly spat on the sidewalk in front of the firemen. They were good-sized, burly men. An insult such as that could have been met with violence; it would have in New Orleans (in Atlanta at the very least they would have been arrested and had their friends and family investigated).

Minor vandalism sometimes hampered, or just irritated, the firemen, troopers, and Maynes security forces. Tires would be flattened or punctured; locks would be disabled. The New Universal Church rarely had such difficulties; either the locals believed they were an innocuous part of the regime—they might have felt differently had they known that the Church kept more detailed records of the individuals in a community than the security services—or they saw the churchmen as being of some benefit to the community.

Of course, in the Coal Country, the Kurian Order ruled with a lighter hand. Which leads to a chicken-or-the-egg argument over whether the obstinacy and, at times, violence of the people forced the Order to tread lightly, or the easy treatment by the rules gave the average person a little more courage in asserting himself.

From what I have been able to learn, the people of Virginia, home to so many political philosophers of the United States' founding, were much like those in every other Kurian Zone.

I suppose I should outline the larger situation in the eastern half of North America in the 2070s. Living memory is brief, after all, and I suspect I do not have many years left as I recompile this diary.

The most powerful faction of the Kurian Order in Eastern North America was the Georgia Control. It had a skilled and creative populace, a professional technocratic class acting as intermediaries between the Kurian overlords and the populace, and an ecclesiastical hierarchy that was constantly nudged to improve its social role. They had an arms industry unmatched in North America, and one of the best equipped military forces in the world at the time.* The broad seacoast allowed trade. There were even flights out of the old Atlanta airport to South America, Europe, and Africa for the desultory trade and diplomacy the Kurians practiced when the mood struck.

Its strength was also its weakness: so much of its power flowed through channels of long use that it had become calcified and cirrhotic, lacking the ability to imagine consequences that could threaten its position.

On paper, the Northwest Ordnance looked powerful, stretching from Pennsylvania to the borders of friendly Chicago, with trade coming in from the Great Lakes and the New England patchwork of principalities, but it was actually a rather ramshackle construct, a poor imitation of the Georgia Control.

The eastern seaboard had a similar network of Kurian fiefdoms, but without even the appearance of a unified political structure, only

---

* Recent research has shown that the Georgia Control's military was much smaller than first estimated. They maintained roughly a dozen brigades, dividing their time between short deployments and rests in rather luxurious military reserves. Their mobility and skill at concentrating quickly made the Control forces seem much larger to the analysts of the time. Like most Kurian Zones, the Control had difficulty trusting their populace with arms, so every soldier had to pass through long periods of training and indoctrination through the Church and other institutions before joining the elite of the Control's military.

the Church and a few able administrators kept the jealous and grasp-ing Kurians from executing their endless vendettas and feuds in a manner that was too harmful to the populace. I never made it to the formerly great metropolis-states of Boston or New York or Philadel-phia, but I am told that the humans there showed an amazing resil-ience, with little neighborhoods getting on with their lives and ignoring the Kurians as best as they could. From what I heard from those who'd grown up there and left for the green of the Coal Coun-try mountains, your loyalty toward those of your neighborhood was absolute, with outsiders picked out and turned over so the rest of the neighborhood remained untroubled. In that region there was a very lucrative trade in "substitutions"—dealers in warm bodies who would trade one aura for another if a family had the money to re-deem a member picked up by the Order for a minor offense. West Virginia, like much of the Appalachian Trail, was hunting ground for those who supplied the substitutions.

In this environment, the oddities of the east were Kentucky and the Coal Country. Kentucky was ranching country for the fleshy legworms that provided ample, if unappetizing, protein that was ground up, flavored, and packaged into any number of premade meals (WHAM! being the most famous, still available for those who've developed a taste for its rather chewy blend of protein and fiber), and the Coal Country made energy. Of the two, the Kentucky legworm clans were the more independent; the nature of their herds meant they had a certain amount of independence, as they had to follow their voracious beasts, chewing up sod at one long end and depositing a rich mixture of fertilized, aerated soil at the other.

The Coal Country was, as you've read, for the most part left in the hands of the Maynes clan and the Church. Trouble with the other Kurian Zones started only once the coal shipments began to fail.

There were dozens of smaller Kurian states east of the Mississippi, of course. Many in the border areas, Memphis for example, were under constant attack from the Free Territory to one side, and attentively watched by larger predatory Kurian Zones at the other, like a lion watching a herd of gazelle in the hope of detecting a limp.

The employment I was given had one of the three things I needed to make an escape: access to a vehicle.

The second was some familiarity with the area. That would come, in time, driving around with the Maynes bodyguard.

The third required more judgment. I needed an opportunity—an event that diverted the security forces' attention or made it harder for them to operate. Ideally, a new Kurian arriving or an old one departing would create enough of a shake-up atmosphere that escape would be easier, if for no other reason than that men nervous about being eliminated would be trying to make it to a new territory before they could be selected for destruction.

The payoff for patience would be the opportunity for a clean getaway and knowledge that would make escape more certain.

There was danger in patience, however. Kurian Zones did not communicate much with one another about sappers and guerillas. While they sought them within their own territory, if they happened to move to a neighboring zone, the Kurians saw it as a win-win. They would be causing trouble for a rival, upsetting whatever designs were no doubt being drawn against their neighbor. Their neighbor might also kill the enemy. The elimination of a threat with no effort had its own kind of sweetness, too.

I finally met my employer during my brief stint of vehicular training. I stood in the Maynes motor pool, a sort of evolutionary chart of a graveled lot, with the functioning automobiles and trucks at one end, lines of machines either being worked on or stripped behind, and then component parts, tires, and glass stacked about rusting racks with blackbirds hanging about as though it were a graveyard.

A motor pool mechanic was taking half the morning briefing me about gasoline pumps and how to get a gas cap off—to tell the truth, I found it a little insulting and tried to cut it short with my "Know how! I do!" routine, but he would not be dissuaded from repeating three times that the gas cap spun one way to take it off, and ("This is very important, son") turns a different way to put it back on!

Two junkyard dogs added a comical note by chasing after and trying to mount a third, all three of them snapping out their sexual frustration at one another in brief, snarling quarrels. The Maynes family guarded everything, even its garbage heap.

My schoolmarmish instructor went silent as I put the cap back on for the third time. I smelled a burning cigarette.

"So, this is my new block and tackle?" said a voice like a bow saw drawn through soft wood, as if it were the result of too much tobacco on not enough sleep.

"Sure is, Mr. Maynes," my instructor said, anxiously eyeing the lighted butt. "He's still being oriented to the White Palace."

"What's his name?"

"King, Mr. Maynes."

"I don't care for that," Maynes said. "MacTierney's been calling him 'Hickory'; says he's solid as a walking stick. How about we call him King Hickory?"

"He answers to a lot of names." The instructor smiled. "Ape. Stoop. Dickface."

Maynes grimaced. "I'd say you're lucky he didn't pop your head off like a milk cap."

"Dunno. He might be fixed. They fix Grogs in Ohio, right, to keep them calm?"

"I wouldn't know. But he looks like he might be interesting, or at least fun," Maynes said. He held up his hand, palm out, and I returned the gesture, smelling alcohol-sweat under his arm. "See you on the bus."

Maynes was small for a human; most of his family was a little undersized.

In appearance Maynes was what my people would term "wild," what we call someone so fleshless, his bones are exaggerated. He had high, prominent cheeks, a broad forehead, and a heavy brow; yet he had a smallish, drawn-in chin, and had he been born with a larger nose, some say he would have looked very much like the American president Abraham Lincoln. I only rarely could see the resemblance, as I am not particularly attuned to human physiognomy. He had black hair, a little grizzled about the temples and very curly, like much of his family.

He was frequently dirty out of unavoidable circumstance, being on the road constantly while making his rounds of Maynes holdings under the Conglomerate emblem—the coal mines in particular. He shaved every three or four days unless he was spending a few days lazing around the palace and seemed to believe that a bed-rumpled and road-worn appearance suited him, but I've found that the odder the features on a human, the more important it is that he dress neatly with hair growth controlled. He almost always wore a whitish straw hat with a rather broad brim and black band—I am told the style is often called a "Panama."

His dietary habits were also strange. Like many of his habits, there was an internal logic to it. He ate only whole items: whole tomatoes, whole apples including the core, whole fish (he preferred smallish smelt-sized varieties). He would scrape corn off its cob with a knife and then have the cob ground into powder and placed in his drink. He put either horseradish or vinegar on everything he ate, including hard-boiled eggs still in their shells. He never suffered a bowel complaint.

My employer must have been something of a disappointment to his parents, or perhaps his grandfather, for despite being named for the organizational juggernaut that was his grandsire, he developed into some mixture of health and temperament that made him unsuitable for a dominant role in the Maynes palace. I'm told the brother who followed him and his sister, she being the fourth of seven, are the true heads of the Maynes household now.

So as not to openly disgrace the family, they gave him what you could call a sinecure. He held the title of "appellate judge" at a court of last appeal for those who ran afoul of the Kurian Order as it existed in the Coal Country at the time. His powers seemed chiefly reserved for functionaries of the Maynes empire, but this may have been unavoidable since the Maynes clan had a finger, if not both scooping hands, in every important business in the Coal Country.

My first time out with Maynes was a run to a lumberyard. The two other members of his security team, my "wrasslin'" partners Home and MacTierney, rode with Maynes between them in the cab of a heavy-duty truck. I rode in the back on an old, partly deframed love seat attached to the back of the cab.

Home drove and managed to strike every pothole and rut on the way to the lumberyard. To test me, they had me open the chain-link gate before driving into the wood-filled lot. I managed to swing the gate without knocking myself unconscious or scraping the truck, so MacTierney offered a "Thanks, King" out of the rolled-down truck window.

I grinned and did a quick back-and-forth hop, hoping I wasn't overplaying the "happy helpful Grog" bit.

Piles of plywood paneling and two-bys and posts filled the gravel-covered lot. Half of the supply was just sitting on the ground, rotting from the bottom up. One would think that the owners of a business calling itself Renaissance Lumber would know better.

The workers came out to greet us, tucking in their pants and rolling down their sleeves to look presentable. Most of them eyed me. A boy still in his teens who was playing with a tape measure gaped openly.

Every business in the Coal Country has a "director," and at Renaissance Lumber he was a firmly fat pencil chewer and spoke with Maynes as they reviewed a folder full of papers on the hood of the truck. Home leaned against the driver's-side door, hand on his gun belt like a movie-Western tough. (The White Palace had several television-viewing rooms and its own "channel" I suppose you should call it. They showed movies from a century ago alternating with New Universal Church educational programming—and *Noonside Passions*, of course.)

"Here's the thing, Mr. Maynes," the director said. "We have a lot of spare wood and scraps around. I let everyone help themselves to scrap. Fick and Nathaniel are good men. They both support families. They just got carried away with the lumber duels—and, well, Hammy being knocked out and getting his neck broke was an accident. No bad blood, not here, sir. I get rid of troublemakers right away. It was an accident, not murder. Don't I have a clean record? Never lost a man to an accident before, and when you think about all the saws around here and the shape they're in and what we have to do to keep them running, it's practically a miracle."

Maynes waved him off. "I understand accidents, Jorge. That time that radial blade took off on you and cut off that long-haired guy's hand—"

"Despre, his name was," the director cut in.

"It's making weapons that's more the problem than anything."

"You could . . . You could think of them as sporting gear."

Maynes chucked for a moment and scratched the day's growth on his chin. I would prefer someone holding decisions about my life in his hands to look clean and not hung over, but if there was one thing I learned quickly in the Coal Country, it was that you made do and found happiness where you could. Maynes was infinitely preferable to a Reaper. "I suppose I could."

He looked over the faces of the other workers. They were standing, hats in hands. He walked around the circle of workers. A few tried to put in a good word for their coworkers, currently absent somewhere in jeopardy of their lives, I supposed. "We're really sorry, Mr. Maynes." "The stick fighting got carried away." "We weren't betting or nothing, just a few pals having some fun after work." "We thought it was no big deal—a couple of the firemen liked to come to the fights."

Maynes finished his circuit of the employees and glanced at Mac-Tierney and Home. Home was still modeling as a waiting gunfighter still life. MacTierney shrugged and smiled.

"Right, Jorge," Maynes finally said. "I'll get your men out of the cage."

The lumberyard broke into applause and cheers. Maynes and MacTierney looked pleased; Home simply rested his hand on his holstered pistol.

The Maynes clan was shrewd to choose this specimen of humanity for the task. He had a sentimental streak that made him outright pardon roughly a third of those who came before him. Personal stories brimming with pathos brought tears to his eyes. I have seen him dash off a pardon and reach into his own wallet to hand over currency for clothes to replace prison uniforms, purchase a half steer to feed a hungry family, or otherwise provide comfort to those affected by what Maynes determined to be an injustice.

In another Kurian Zone, newspapers and church bulletins would place the charitable nature of the collaborators just under the masthead. But the Maynes family knew its locals. Those pardoned by Maynes were quietly released back to their loved ones. They knew word that spread across backyard laundry lines and in corner taverns would be much more convincing—and perhaps even be exaggerated.

A much smaller proportion simply had their sentences confirmed.

Then there were those to whom Maynes offered some manner of deal in order to get them out of the forage bag, as it were. There was a good deal of outright corruption in these deals; wealth and holdings were transferred to the Maynes business empire.

Temptation would come any man's way in such a position. Maynes succumbed easily to temptations of all sorts, but in particular he was a ravenous consumer of females. With these, he had the most distressing taste and habits, but examples of that will come farther into this narrative.

For all that, he had little interest in personal wealth. Bribes and so on went into the family banks and vaults—down to pairs of pearl earrings and single gold coins. He spent freely, held lavish dinners at the conclusion of business visits, and would drop in on parties and shower the hosts with gifts of food and drink.

Once, I held down a guard—he'd been caught sleeping on duty— while Maynes rubbed horseradish in his eyes. The poor fellow howled while I held him down and Home handled the head.

Whippings held a special place in his brand of justice. Maynes considered a good horsewhipping an honorable way to atone for fault. More often than not, once those who'd been whipped on Maynes's orders found themselves restored to their former positions, and with objective evidence of increased diligence and effort, a promotion would be given. Maynes, more than once, said to his travel team, "The lash draws the bad out."

My wrasslin' partner, Home, was not good company. He is not pleasant to remember, and even less pleasant to write about, but I am assured, my reader, that there is interest in what sort of person carried the everyday dirty work of the Kurian Order.

Home frequently spoke of the future, once he'd been ten years carrying a gun.

This requires some explanation. Like much of the Southeast and Mid-Atlantic East of that time, the Georgia Control system was utilized for ease of organizing the patchwork of Kurian principalities. In order to be an organ of the Kurian Order, one had to be permitted to carry and handle firearms, a difficult matter in the Kurian Zone (in the free territories, by contrast, it was a matter of basic survival; only fairly powerful rifles or automatic weapons gave one a chance against a Reaper). Once an individual passed the testing, obtained three letters of recommendation, and presented a clean work record, the procedure for the temporary permit began through the local police or New Universal Church organization (I understand in some places this also involved a substantial payoff, at least as far as the police were concerned, but most of the churchmen were too terrified of their thoughts being read to become corrupt in this pedestrian manner). For a year the individual remained on the provisional permit, and the authorities watched him, judged his marksmanship and firearm security, and of course made sure he returned expended cartridge casings. In my days as a guerilla, expended brass was almost like being handed fresh ammunition.

After obtaining the provisional permit, the holder received a renewal every five years, though of course it could be revoked for neglect.

Why was a gun permit so important? Jobs in the security services, the military and paramilitary organizations, even teaching and transport and broadcasting and field utility work, required weapons to be carried while on duty. The Kurian Order had vulnerable points everywhere and enemies both "domestic" and "foreign"—if not the resistance forces, a fellow Kurian might decide to tamper with his neighbor's territory in the hope of acquiring control over it. I am convinced that roughly half of the attacks and deaths in the Georgia Control were caused by Kurians warring on other Kurians and scapegoating resistance forces in doing so.

But back to Home. He had his life all planned out. He was in his third year of armed service and looking forward to his first renewal.

Here's a sample of his talk. I heard many variations, but it kept to this basic rhythm.

"I won't go independent until I've ten years under my belt. Sure, I can take off at five, but chances are I'll just get shuffled back to the bottom of the deck. With ten years armed service, I'll be in a position to negotiate. Of course, fifteen might be better, or twenty—now that's a man who can be trusted—but the way I figure, fifteen years, they might look at me and decide I've lost ambition, I'm getting set in my ways, just looking for somewhere where I can make myself comfortable and keep out of the way. At ten, they'll be thinking, 'He's still young. Ambitious. Let's give him the ball and see how far he runs.' That's what I've been waiting for, the chance to be given the ball. I'll be doing broken-field running all the way to that brass ring.

"Now, where will I try for? One of those zones where they let the AS* have multiple wives. I'll find me some big-hipped Ohio gal for

---

* Armed Specialists

the babies, maybe get a little Asian to do my hair and keep the place organized, and a Latin for the cooking. A little salsa on the kitchen table and in the bedroom. Figure on a baby every two years for the white girl, then the others maybe only two kids each. *That's* what the old squids like to see, just as much as a good service record. Lots of kids. They look at me, yeah, good work record, but a lot of guys have a good work record. A good work record and ten or eleven kids, they're going to want to make an example out of me, mention me in the church bulletins and newscasts. Look at all the good stuff that happens to this kind of citizen."

Home was conscientious enough with his firearms (he carried his pistol and a shotgun every day, with two full reloads of ammunition for each; his father had served armed and told him every time he'd fired his weapon it had been at a range of fifteen feet or less). He didn't brandish them in the aggressive manner of some Coal Country security I'd seen, or make a show of setting the shotgun where it could instantly be picked up everywhere he went. Maynes seemed to enjoy his presence and I suspect gave him regular positive reviews and increases in salary. He stayed strictly sober and did not spend much, even though he was frequently admitted with Maynes to the few special stores for privileged citizens.

As for MacTierney, he came from just the kind of large family Home dreamt of starting.

He did not speak much of his parents or siblings, but I can make a few guesses based on what he did tell me. The family strategy was to survive by placing the kids in several different careers important to the Coal Country, so there would be numerous avenues of influence. MacTierney wanted to be a railroad man. He had loved trains since he was a child, and that seemed to be in the cards until his eldest brother, who had gone into the security services, died behind the wheel in a training accident. The family demanded that he step into his brother's place (it seemed the other alternative offered to him was the Church, but he found the strict discipline and rituals off-putting, and he disliked working with blood and filth, which many clerical novitiates end up handling when involved with hospital and poverty-relief work).

I believe MacTierney's father, in his earlier life, erred in some grave manner and believed himself to be on a list for R & R* as soon as all his children were on their own. He perhaps intended his progeny to alter the general opinion by going into the Kurian Order and excelling in their positions. They all tried very hard for places in the Youth Vanguard and half of them made it. MacTierney spoke of having no fewer than three sisters enter the Church (one became a foster womb for one of Maynes's married cousins; she dwelled in the White Palace and could be seen in her white New Universal Church habit, heavily pregnant—she was always giving MacTierney tidbits from the rich diet she enjoyed during pregnancy).

MacTierney did not much care for his job, but he was levelheaded for his age, not easily riled, and seemed to form an instant sympathy with the locals of all classes. I saw him calm more troublesome situations, and he frequently did Maynes's job for him, handling the confidential paperwork Maynes did not have time to read. I believe he was assigned to Maynes more to protect the locals from Maynes than to protect Maynes from the locals. He was always stepping in before a situation would get out of control.

---

* Relocation and repurposing, often a euphemism for the last ride in the collection van.

For example, we were dispatched to a motorized vehicle scrap-yard on a call. The owner of the yard, whose wife had recently run off with a wealthy liquor distributor, had been caught stripping copper wire out and selling it on the black market and his business was being taken away (though he would be allowed to work there as the assistant for the new director for an indeterminate amount of time). The scrapyard had a small gas tank where fuel from wrecks and whatnot was drained and preserved, and he'd climbed up on the tank, opened the cap, and stood there with dynamite shoved in his belt and a butane cigarette lighter, threatening suicide.

We'd driven down a small hill. The scrapyard, covering several acres, yawned beneath.

"Crapaheenie, we're all going to end up smelling like gas," Maynes said. "Hickory, better back the van up the hill."

MacTierney had a word with one of the employees, grabbed the keys to the van, and hurried off to the adjacent town. He returned in less than ten minutes with the director's children from the care center.

"Clement, your kids need you; you know that. You're their whole world, and nobody in this yard wants to see them have their whole world go up in a big orange-and-black ball. Mr. Maynes is here, he'll see to it that these kids don't lose their father, too."

As for Maynes, I could understand why the family didn't want him lounging around the White Palace. One moment, he was lively and pleasant; an hour later, he could be depressed and despondent. He was often like a depressing philosophical maxim brought to life: if it existed, he could find some fault worthy of complaint.

He believed he had the worst job in all the Coal Country (an interesting claim in a land where about ten to fifteen percent of the men worked underground, choking on coal dust and squinting through eyes swollen from conjunctivitis, particularly from a man being chauffeured around the land in a comfortable converted bus stocked with Kentucky bourbon and Canadian whiskey).

Maynes's usual transport was known at the White Palace as "the Short Bus," but Maynes called it the Trekker. It had begun life as one of those smaller people-transports I've come across disabled at airports and large convention centers, designed for a driver and perhaps a dozen people comfortably riding in the back.

It had been retrofitted into a rather amazing conveyance for a dignitary and his team. The driver now had a spacious (luckily for me, for I was often behind the wheel) compartment with its own hatch for entering, with the passenger area turned into a comfortable lounge, with a sofa large enough for sleeping, a tiny kitchen cubby, a captain's chair and three more fold-down models, and a little toilet closet in back. A water tank on the roof fed the hygiene closet's sink-toilet (which flushed, disgustingly, right onto the road) and kitchen basin.

To cope with the mountainous, indifferently maintained roads, heavy-duty tires and an off-road suspension raised the minibus an extra foot off the ground. What had been storage space beneath the passenger area was expanded slightly and filled with emergency food, water, blankets, and medicines, a small generator and hand-pumped water filter so the vehicle could, if necessary, serve as an ambulance or provide a day's meals for a few dozen mouths, given an interruption of normal services. There was a standard gun cabinet that could securely store five long-guns and several pistols, plus ammunition, though Maynes personally never showed much interest in the firearms he carried ("I got sick of shooting in my first year with the Youth Vanguard," he told MacTierney).

I shall describe a typical town in the Coal Country in this era, so you, my reader, will have some idea of the conditions of the average person under the Kurian Order.

Most of the pre-2022 smaller towns were "repurposed" by this time. The Kurians preferred their humans living in moderately sized towns of two or three thousand. At that size, you needed just one of everything, making supervision easier. More than that and the town became a city. There were villages with populations ranging from a few families to several hundred people, usually near a resource site like a mine or an industrial center or other remote-but-important location that required servicing—the "village" that provided staff to the White Palace was an example.

Small family farms existed in the better stretches of bottomland. It was up to their town or village to keep track of activity there.

Then there were the people on the outskirts. These were true hill people. I'm not even sure you could say they were part of the Kurian Order; they were more or less ignored by all concerned. They came down from their remote hollows and scratched up what they couldn't make for themselves by doing odd jobs or selling the liquor they brewed in concealed stills.

Every town had three institutions staffed by the Kurian Order: the New Universal Church meeting house, school, and residence; the firehouse; and the community center.

The community center was usually the largest. In older towns, an entire block of buildings would often be renovated, linking all the old storefronts and apartments into one large warren. Children were given basic-skills training. There would be a room devoted to telecommunications, with phones and screens and sometimes even a computer or two. There were areas for exercise and places for small artistic performances, a little health clinic staffed by a nurse and midwife, a cafeteria, and a government office where one updated identification papers and the numerous licenses that went with existing in the Kurian Order. The wealthier towns usually had a public pool or bathhouse.

In larger towns with more people who worked for the Kurian Order, there was often a mirror version of the community center just for Quislings and their families, similar to the main community center but cleaner and better equipped.

As for residences, the Kurian Order preferred that its population lived in communal buildings. The remaining houses, if they were large enough, supported two or three families by subdividing the space. Only the Quislings had the luxury of living alone, but those at the lower levels often chose not to, preferring the safety of being around others or living above a community center or some other place with around-the-clock security. This was a land of old grudges, and Quislings had a high rate of mortality from suspicious accidents. Those at the top of the pile often had guarded estates, miniature versions of the White Palace with full-time, live-in staff, plus the usual guard dogs and gamekeepers wandering outside their fences.

The church was less comfortable but cleaner than the community centers. Unlike the community center, the church was open to overnight travellers who would otherwise be stuck; they might always check in to the local NUC building and be given a cot, sometimes with a privacy screen, a sliver of soap, and a clean towel.

Everything in a church center folded for easy storage, including the staff. Once, when sheltering at an NUC center during a strong thunderstorm, I opened a closet and found a human female cleric in full habit, snoozing on her back with her legs sticking up the closet wall.

The Church serves a surprising mix of propaganda into everyday business. Of course, on Sundays there are the homilies, announcements of births (never deaths), and requests for volunteer labor on tasks that make the community a little more livable, from shoveling snow to urban "repurposing"—teardowns of old houses, in other words, after the Church has cleared the dwelling of identifiable family ephemera.

In larger cities, there are screens in every room running "human improvement" programming. About all you improve is your knowledge of various tragedies in human history and the miraculous arrival of the Kurians the moment before mankind would flutter, dim, and die like a guttering candle. Every half hour they would break for weather and rose-tinted biographical segments about local Quislings. Beyond the constant droning of the screens in every room—including the church proper, unless services were in session—every piece of paper passed out by the Church, every plate full of food or mug of coffee, bore some phrase or piece of iconography expressing the value of the Kurian/Human "symbiosis."

The closest thing these little towns of the Coal Country had to a newspaper were their local church bulletins, put out—with no small amount of pride—by the senior class of schoolchildren under the supervision of Youth Vanguard leaders going on in their education and senior clergy. They sold advertising space, selected and placed a few photos, and wrote about local events. Usually it was small sports teams and leagues and announcements about events at the community center or outings (there are trips to Washington DC and the Carolina Coast mentioned in an issue I saved and brought out with me). I suspect the hard-to-find paper mostly ended up serving as sanitary tissue or for wiping up spilled grease, though the editorial page of every issue, which reprinted statements from the Archon's office, always had a helpfully blank reverse side, so letter writers were often forced to send NUC propaganda along with their family news.

Serving three worlds: Earth, Kur, and the Next.

The young of any community spend a great deal of time at the church. In the larger towns, there are multiple day-care centers alongside the school (church education stops at twelve years old for most who are bent on a trade or further technical training; a few intended for higher education stay on until age fourteen or fifteen before being shipped off to boarding school—one of the requirements in most Kurian Zones is that anyone intended for higher education is severed from his family.

The third institution every town has is the firemen in its station. I've never encountered the like in any of the other Kurian Zones, where firemen served in much the same fashion as they had pre-2022 or today.

In the Coal Country, the "firemen" served as the first line of defense of the Kurian Order. They put out fires, yes, but they would also speed off in their trucks to resolve barricade situations, set up roadblocks, or turn their hoses on gypsy encampments of day laborers passing through the mountains. A regime needs a body numerous of strong-arm men to swing the clubs that break the heads of its enemies, and in the Coal Country, if you were young, strong, and followed orders well, you could almost always find a berth in the firehouse. After a year of service where you apprenticed on a provisional for your food and bed, any signs of talent for the job were rewarded with a permanent posting. Unlike almost any other Quisling role, you did not have to be familiar with the current New Universal Church opinions and decrees; you just had to follow orders well and stay reasonably healthy by avoiding tobacco, drugs, and alcohol. The pay was twice what you would make on the railroads and three times what you could earn in a coal mine, so it was an attractive prospect for any young man. I suspect that was the lingering influence of the elder Maynes, who first organized the firemen—he was a notorious teetotaler and tobacco hater. The firemen did their drinking and what smoking they could afford out of uniform and out of the public eye.

Like firemen elsewhere, they were called to scenes of fire and accident. Unlike other firemen, rather than take the victims to a hospital, they usually shuttled them off to the Reapers. The Coal Country Kurian's Reapers would oftentimes spend the daylight hours sheltering in the fire stations somewhere out of the way, waiting for an accident victim to be brought in.

This aided the regime in that there was less pounding on people's doors in the middle of the night and taking away of one of the elder members of a household deemed past his usefulness. Everyone could understand someone dying in a railway accident or being crushed during logging—it made death more palatable. They would sometimes drum up business for themselves, by travelling pell-mell along the roads in the rain or gloom in the hope of hitting a cyclist or frightening the horse of a rider, causing her to be thrown and injured.

So, bullies, hooligans, and people who enjoyed inflicting violence on others put on the vulcanized black-and-yellow uniform of a fireman.

The firemen enforced a kind of xenophobia on their town. Locals were encouraged to phone the fire department if they saw a stranger without obvious purpose. Vagrants passing through fell into the hands of the firemen more often than not. Smugglers moving goods between Kentucky and the coast knew which highways were farthest from the fire stations, and where they had to travel overland on unmarked paths.

They had only one summer of police-action training, out of state in the wilderness of the old Marine Corps base at Parris Island (complete with one three-day weekend at Folly Island near Charleston with a generous enlistment bonus to spend, of which tales were told in the firehouse years after), but that was enough for the sort of bruising work they were expected to handle.

In my whole time accompanying Maynes around the Coal Country, I did only one service I am truly proud of.

It was a moment of opportunity, not part of the routine. While on the highway heading west toward Big Stone Gap, we saw a disabled Maynes Lumber truck blocking the road ahead, and another vehicle's operator—a local milk van driver—waving his arms frantically.

The lumber truck had blown a set of tires, and while the driver was surveying the damage, his load had come loose and come close to crushing him to death. He was trapped from the midthigh down by pine trunks thirty feet long and easily a foot across.

The trapped driver was screaming that his legs were broken.

"Should we just put a bullet in his head and put him out of his misery?" Maynes asked Home.

Luckily, they were clean fractures; there was no visible bleeding, and nothing had rearranged his joints.

Using bits of bracing chain and wooden supporting wedges from the lumber truck's load, plus no small amount of muscular energy, I opened a large-enough gap in the logs. The milk van driver said he'd have thought it would take a loader to move the logs.

"Leverage, that's what Hickory does best," Home said.

"You'll be driving in no time, Lucky," MacTierney said.

"My name's not Lucky," the driver said. "It's Escandero."

"It is from now on," Home put in. "If you'd been slower by a foot, your pelvis would be in three pieces." (I have substituted pelvis for what he actually said, because crushing wouldn't break up the principal feature of male sexual anatomy in that manner.)

We wrapped "Lucky" Escandero in blankets after MacTierney and Home did a professional job of bracing his legs on a hardboard; then we put him in the stretcher brackets in the van, using the rear emergency door.

"You yell out if you're going to puke from the pain, or anything," Maynes said. "I don't want the carpet to smell like puke for the next year."

"I gave him a shot," MacTierney said.

It was taking effect. The driver was mumbling something about not wanting to be on the R & R list, that he was a quick healer, could drive using just his arms and a cane, and so forth.

MacTierney, as usual, thought to radio in the disabled vehicle's information so the local troopers could clear the road and see about reloading the lumber.

As we dropped him off at the nearest NUC hospital, I tugged on Maynes's shoulder. "Lucky heal all proper?"

"All proper," MacTierney said. Turning to the admitting doctor in the clerical collar, he said, "Mr. Maynes wants the best of care for him. Rehabilitation, everything. He'll be checking up in a week or so on Escandero's progress. He's a good driver; we want him back."

Maynes had said nothing of the sort, but MacTierney was a decent man.

The Headhunters

May is one of the sweetest months in the Coal Country. With the warmer weather, more like summer than late spring, Maynes stepped up his travel schedule. He wasn't always truck-hood adjudicating or hearing appeals. He'd also stop in for surprise inspections of Maynes Conglomerate holdings, or just spend a day in a rail yard chatting with the workers about diesel fuel supply and signal problems. We were on the road almost every day and frequently didn't see the palace again for three or four days at a time.

The Appalachians turned a green so bright that a painter depicting it would use a palette full of yellow, too. But driving at this time of year on the chancy, badly maintained mountain roads took skill. There might be a rockslide or downed tree around every bend, and potholes filled with water could be deceptively—and wheel-wreckingly—deep.

Sadly, there were also vast scars in the landscape. Mining coal doesn't always mean digging tunnels; you can also tear down the side of a mountain to get at the veins. There were dozens of these suppurating wounds on the landscape filled with men and machinery and dust. For every one working, there were two abandoned, or still half used by the locals to scrape a little extra coal for their own use or trade. The abandoned surface mines were only partially reforested; in many places the scars were too deep and there was no soil to support the exploitative early trees and brambles. Black bears and raccoons and bats would move into the caves created or exposed, so the scarring of the landscape was of benefit to a few afterward.

Maynes, after his initial suspicion about me, began to treat me as part of the team. Not an important part, I was rather like a big, friendly dog to him. He would reach up and scratch the hair on my cheek or forehead when he greeted me in the morning. I don't care to be touched, especially not about the snout and ears, and I had to suppress the instinct to return his hand minus a few fingers.

It didn't stop me from imagining the cartilaginous crunch or the salty, hot surprise of fresh blood.

He learned that I had a taste for nuts and took to tossing me a big brown paper bag of walnuts if he thought we were to be long on the road before reaching our destination. I made a point of carefully collecting the empty shells and returning them to him in the brown bag, as though they were ammunition casings that could be reloaded.

I enjoyed this time, especially when we left the towns behind and negotiated the mountain roads. The hills and trees drew sound and absorbed it like a sponge, so that it seemed I could hardly hear the throaty blat of the exhaust. Home drove, alert and both hands holding the wheel in firm fingers, MacTierney with his lap-folder full of notated maps and communication printouts. I sat in the back, holding either a shotgun clamped to one side of my improvised seat or a battle rifle on the other, ready to grab up either at a threat or a flash of game. Maynes liked to bring home his dinner freshly bled.

Other than some mischievous boys in Logan who startled us by throwing a handful of lighted firecrackers in our wake, the days passed without any danger worse than negotiating a road washout or a flood-damaged bridge.

As one draws closer to the borders of the Coal Country, particularly those parts joining Kentucky or the Southern Appalachians, less so the Virginia border, the country becomes wilder and sparsely settled. The roads degenerate into jeep trails, then paths. Only a single maintained highway links the Northwest Ordnance to the Coal Country, and another extends up toward Maryland and Pennsylvania, largely used for maintenance on power lines and the railroads.

Most of the Kurians like a strip of wilderness that takes a day or two to cross dividing their zones. Escape becomes more hazardous, as the Nomansland between is stalked by bandits and bounty hunters. If you are lucky, the former will only strip you of your possessions and subject you to sexual pawing and penetration. The latter will usually do the same, then haul you and your family to whichever nearby Kurian Zone pays the best for still-breathing humans. Of course, this sort of brigandage has its hazards, for a bigger band will swallow, absorb, and sell off a smaller one. Now and then Kurian Zone Special Forces engage in training in the wilds of the borderlands and are happy to use live targets for their live ammunition. These bandits have been overly romanticized in the past few years; only a very few did anything more than passively resist the Kurian Order. Most aided it by feeding the captive and the kidnapped into the regime's Molochian maw.

Late one May afternoon, we drove into a border post on the Coal Country side of the border with the Northwest Ordnance, along that lone highway heading over the Ohio River a few dozen miles away. A little roadside town existed there for the benefit of the truckers who would drop a trailer at the border and pick up one to be returned into their zone (at this time, east of the Mississippi there were very few cross-zone drivers; west of the Mississippi convoys under escort could pass through).

The town had a small trooper station representing the Coal Country Order, a little repair facility, and a clapped-together mass of cypress planking that served as a combination hotel, bar, and grill for the benefit of those waiting for a load to show up called the "NbW Roadhouse."

It was a pleasantly warm day. An overnight rain had dropped a heavy shower left over from April, but it had blown north by the time we finished breakfast, and the day turned nice. The long-promised summer had arrived at last. The roads had more than the usual pedestrians, bicyclists, and bus riders out enjoying the filtered sun, hot enough to be felt upon bare skin.

Someone had inserted the word "whore" into the NbW Roadhouse sign, with an arrow to clear up any doubt as to where the substitution belonged.

"What's the NbW stand for?" Home asked.

"North by west," MacTierney said.

Home looked at the other side of the sign as we passed it, perhaps hoping for a coda. "I was hoping for 'naked beautiful women.'"

"Hope away. It's a sunny afternoon. Maybe some skin will be out hanging her wash in the raw."

After checking fuel and fluids courtesy of the trooper station, with only two duty troopers supporting a single vehicle patrolling the highway from the Ordnance border to the nearest crossroads, we idled outside the Maynes Trekker. I pretended to go to sleep with my back against the warm radiator. Home and MacTierney engaged in their usual conversational nothings, with MacTierney giving answers that showed he was only half paying attention to Home's chatter; yet Home pressed on with the conversation nonetheless.

"Wonder if there are any quality girls in the roadhouse," Home said.

"Wouldn't know."

"Not, like, pros," Home said. "They'd starve out here, doing a couple truckers a week. Just girls working the bar. A pair of tits always makes me feel like staying around for another round."

"Don't say. Do you ever talk about anything but pussy, Home?"

Home ignored him. "Still, bad country for a woman. Nowhere to shop, nothing to do that isn't a two-hour trip on a bike. In good weather."

MacTierney looked at the sky. "Now that the storm's blown out. Don't know that it'll stay good. I bet we get another before long."

"Suppose if there is any gash open for business, Mr. Maynes will smell it out. He could find pussy on a drifting iceberg."

The sound of distant motorcycles echoed off the NbW. I stopped pretending to sleep and rose.

"Trouble, Boss?" I asked.

"Could be," MacTierney said. He was the only one who spoke to me in tone and terms other than those you might employ on a dog. "King, stay here. Don't let anyone into the Trekker, and if they try to block it in, swing around in front of the roadhouse and pick us up. . . . Home, best if we get to Maynes."

They hurried across the road. The engine noises were identifiable now, a few motorcycles. I could see a mass of headlights moving south toward us.

Just to stay on the safe side, I slipped into the driver's seat and pulled the Trekker around to the NbW. I saw one flash of concern from MacTierney and Home—perhaps they thought I was panicking and running south—but when I backed up again, neatly parking on the "wrong" side of the road, still facing south in case we needed to escape, they hurried in to get Mr. Maynes.

The new arrivals were a convoy of large vehicles and a few bikes. They slowed as they pulled into town, and at a signal from a diesel horn perhaps stripped from a train, they pulled over on the shoulder opposite the NbW Roadhouse. All the vehicles bore the red-and-white nine-square checkerboard of licensed bounty hunters, though a few had added tic-tac-toe, obscene crosswords, or chess endgame layouts with black markers or some such.

Painted on the side of the bus were white block letters: ZIHU'S ASSURED.

MacTierney and Home reemerged from the roadhouse. It had gone quiet inside and faces were populating the windows.

I opened the door of the Trekker to speak to the humans. "Boss come?" I asked.

MacTierney shrugged and Home let out a low "hoooooo!" "He paused to refresh himself. He's getting dressed. But we're not leaving; he's greeting the newcomers on behalf of the family and the Coal Country."

"It's Zihu's mob," MacTierney said to Home.

"What ass-red?" I asked, pointing to the sign.

"Assureds," Home said. "As in assured of not being klinked up as Reaper fodder."

They parked with a precision unmatched by any military convoy I witnessed in my career. On the edges, motorcycles light and heavy pulled up, their riders waiting for orders to switch off and dismount. Stripped-down pickups with high-clearance suspensions and crew-served light cannon, .20 mm drum-guns, and the best Italian-made barrels with Japanese optics, had leather harnesses for the comfort of the gunners. The bikes and pickups had tow cables, chain saws, and other accoutrements for moving obstacles out of the way. A bus and an armored van carried the payload—captives and valuables scavenged from their trips into the wilderness. A small tanker truck idled at the heart of the formation.

Maynes joined the other two on the porch/sidewalk in front of the roadhouse. He was still closing buttons. "We're not the only visitors to this one-holer, I see," he said.

"Fresh out of Kentucky," Home said. "See the piles of legworm skins tied on the pickup roof?"

"Wonder if they've picked anyone up?" MacTierney asked no one in particular.

"They might just be running bodyguard for a brass ring, even a Kurian and his Reapers," Maynes said. "The transports might not even have any rabbits.*"

These days, I often hear a misperception about headhunting bands that deserves correction. They did not simply sweep the countryside, raking up warm bodies for the Reapers. While that justified

---

* Eastern slang for runaways. Those who purposely dwell in the Nomansland that isn't freehold or Kurian Zone are sometimes called "hares."

their existence in the Kurian Order and gave them a welcome in different Kurian principalities, the bands would also gather labor for large projects, return runaways to their home counties, and even act as an escort to skilled technical personnel who wished, for whatever reason, to switch from one Kurian Zone to another.

Those fleeing a Kurian Zone weren't the wretched barefoot lumpen prole figures depicted in popular culture. A moment's exercise of reason will illustrate: who is most likely to foment an escape? A person with the imagination to envision a better life, the intelligence to pick a course of action that gets him over the border, and the drive to carry out the plan. Generally the individuals and families who would "rabbit" were superior specimens just to make it out of their township and across a divide.

For those who point to the photographs of those emerged from the brush looking like a lice-infested feral tribe of reverted humans, I can only commend them to traveling almost path-free border country for a few hundred miles, moving out of sight by day, and holing up at night in deep ditches or barn stalls in an effort to hide the aural signature the Reapers read—then pose for a photograph.

The caravan therefore had both a comfortable bus for dignitaries and paying customers and an armored car for captives to cover any eventualities. They had the rude welds and checkerboard paint job over primer that identified the owners as licensed bounty hunters and prisoner transports. The bus would carry those who might be valuable as more than just fodder, while the armored car would usually make its first stop at a Kurian tower or a basement door of a New Universal Church fortified cathedral.

"Let's be hospitable," Maynes said. "Home, with me. MacTierney, radio in a report to the palace and the troopers, just in case our boys across the street are asleep at the switch. King, out of the Trekker. I want you walking tall at my heel, please."

Maynes must have enjoyed his "refreshment"—he was a little drunk and being polite in a baronial way.

Crossing the street, we passed close to one of the gun-mounted pickups. "So this is what stupid smells like," the gunner remarked to the driver. His voice crackled with fatigue.

"It's civilization. After a fashion," the driver replied. "Be grateful for it and don't go giving us a bad name in a zone."

The bounty hunters hung an advertisement for personnel on a wire clipboard bound to the grille, where it could be read by the vehicle's lights, if needed. It was printed on the blank side of some church bulletin—a frequent source of paper for those who had a hard time finding inexpensive stationery. Someone, perhaps a bored rider on the bus or in one of the trucks, had handwritten each one with a marker.

I saved a copy and reproduce it below:

GOOD MONEY, BARTER, and GRATUITIES!
INDEPENDENT WORK!
DRIVING AND SECURITY EXPERIENCE!

Interested in the risks and rewards of travel? Want a valuable, protected job? Our caravan is looking for a few motivated, tough-minded individuals seeking the experience of a lifetime. We bounty hunt, personal transport between the Ohio and the Greensboro-Asheville corridor. Fifteen years of valued service and extensive interzone travel. Good training, experience, money, and bonuses, all travel supported. No bravos or cruelty jukes, we want smart, careful individuals who can play on a team.

The bounty hunters surveyed us. We looked official, but since we had just sidearms and the civilian-looking Trekker, they were probably wondering if we were the local honcho or travellers like themselves.

Maynes introduced himself to the driver, offering to shake hands. They held a brief conversation—Maynes was friendly and didn't brandish his name as either stick or carrot. The driver pointed to the SUV with a heavy-duty off-loading suspension, light-bar, and several radio aerials.

I stayed at Maynes's heel. He sauntered over to the black monster; it reminded me of the big doctor's vehicle we'd crammed into on our escape from Xanadu. I smelled sweat and musky perfume like incense on Maynes as he passed. I'd long since come to the conclusion that my employer could find time for an assignation in the middle of a knife fight.

A little black-haired man in a red leather coat hopped out and greeted Maynes. He reminded me a little of a portrait I'd seen of a young Napoleon Bonaparte; he had the same cherubic features and serene, fixed-on-his-star eyes, though Bonaparte was Mediterranean and this fellow was Asian. I wondered how he came to command such a mob; usually they were led by the biggest, toughest thug in the group. I checked his hands as they shook—the stranger had had a manicure recently.

He introduced himself as only "Zihu." When Maynes gave his name, Zihu grew suddenly wary and took a step back from us.

"Well, Mr. Zihu," Maynes said. "You mind showing me what you're importing to the Coal Country?"

"Not an import, Mr. Maynes, just transit," Zihu said. He formed his words slowly and carefully and had the flatter tones of the Midwest, sounding to me like a man of Kansas, Nebraska, or Iowa. Perhaps he was some scion of one of the brass ring estates in Iowa, making a name for himself. "We're on our way to Baltimore."

"Ever been in the Coal Country before?"

"I did my trade in the Ordnance, but they've been cracking down of late, more permits and checks on visitors and border security. I don't mind crossing a palm or two with silver, but paperwork gives me a headache. I'm trying the eastern seaboard, assuming I can find a route through these darned mountains not blocked by a slide. I thought you people were good with shovels."

Maynes shrugged. "You must take that up with the Kentuckians, Mr. Zihu. Don't believe what they tell you about the Coal Country. We're richer than we look."

A thin, rat-faced man with a big courier case fell in behind Zihu. "Everyone's accounted for. Scouts want to know if they can bed down."

"If the locals don't object . . . ," Zihu said, raising an eyebrow at Maynes.

"We're a little suspicious of strangers, but that doesn't mean we're inhospitable," Maynes said, waving a hand toward the trooper post. "You'll just want to check in with the troopers, is all. They might want to take a quick look at everyone's faces, unless you want to post a travel bond."

Zihu turned and muttered something to the rat-faced man, who walked over to the troopers.

"If that's an example of your muscle, I can see how your mines are so productive," Zihu said, looking up at me. "Can I acquire another like him here?"

"He's one of a kind," Maynes said. "Let's see what you're taking across the Coal Country."

Zihu lost gracefully. "Of course," he said, showing a small smile. He led Maynes over to the armored car. "I've one paying customer in the bus, a trade delegate heading for a ship in Baltimore's outer harbor. Brass ring. We've also fifteen benighted souls netted on the run."

Home crowded up, eager for a view of the captives.

The rat-faced man returned. "They're fine with the standard New Universal Church bond," he told Zihu. "You'll have to sign off."

"Rota, open the bin, please," Zihu said. "Our hosts might be interested."

Home used his flashlight to pass over the faces of the poor captives huddled within.

A sickly, pale girl of about fourteen years was chained to the armored car bench, keeping to the lee of an older, heavier, dark-skinned female. Her hair was still a childlike white, but her body showed that she'd started the transition to adulthood.

"You can turn that one over to me," Maynes said, pointing. The girl-woman tried to burrow into the fleshy breast of her protector.

"How much are—"

"I'm not buying," Maynes said. "I just want use of her for an hour or so."

"Oh, I hope she has puffy little nips," Home said. "I love the puffy little nips."

"Just remember, droits and all that," Maynes said. "Wait your turn."

"Let's talk inside, shall we?" Zihu asked. "I hate discussing business in the wind."

The NbW was filling up with drivers, mechanics, scouts, scavengers, and other assorted personnel of Zihu's Assured. The woman in charge of the rooms was issuing orders for cots, soap, and laundry tubs for the men fresh from the Kentucky woods. Her scruffy staff moved quickly; they seemed to know how to convert the bar and upstairs rooms into a hotel in short order. A heavyset man with wary eyes was negotiating the exact price in labeled Kentucky bourbon of bullets, pharmaceuticals, and other light and easily negotiated items.

I'd long since grown accustomed to stares from strangers, so I ignored the curious eyes on me from the newcomers.

"Damn, there'd better be a bed available," Maynes said. "I'd hate to have us welcome that girl to the Coal Country on a firewood bin." Maynes, like many such deviants, believed that all men shared his sexual tastes—even if they wouldn't admit it. In Home he had a man who enthusiastically shared them.

Maynes showed the good grace to buy his visitor a drink.

"Mr. Maynes," Zihu said in his flatland drawl, "I feed my captives. If they're hurt, I bandage them up. I have nothing to reproach myself about their treatment." He let his voice rise to a level that could be heard throughout the barroom, and his men quieted. "What happens once I get rid of them is not my concern. I don't let my men touch them. If you want to take her off my hands, we can talk price; otherwise we will seek another route to Baltimore."

"Or," Maynes said, "we could impound all your vehicles and confiscate your weapons while we call in the churchmen to verify your bond status. In fact—"

Zihu zipped up the red leather jacket.

The little rat of a man lashed out. Metal glinted on his knuckles, and Maynes caught it across the teeth. I reached out to block the blow but wasn't fast enough. Though I couldn't connect, I could still get my fingers around his throat.

A pair of hands attached to powerful arms grabbed my arm as I reached and thrust it down to the tabletop in an iron grip, like a man pinning a rattler before cutting off its head.

It never ceases to amaze me how matters among humans can turn so sour so fast. Even a dogfight is signaled by a few seconds of raised hackles and growls. Among humans, a mild disagreement can often escalate to violence, leaping by intermediate steps. I wonder if emotions were more under control when men fought duels and had an established protocol of offense, challenge, and answer.

"King, shut that door!" Maynes shouted through his split lip. The bloody ribbon of flesh wagged like a second tongue. Home had drawn a gun but hadn't fired it yet, keeping a group of Zihu's men away from Maynes's other flank.

I needed my hands free to close the door. I dispensed with the biker in my hands by lofting him up. The wood in the high ceiling must have been a fair ways rotted, because he punched through, leaving a hole and a shower of dust behind.

They tell me he was in fact retrieved from the third-floor attic, having also penetrated the second-floor ceiling, but tall tales go with tall mountains.

I needed to block the door. The heaviest timber available was the bar, but I couldn't bring myself to destroy such fine finishing to the wood grain—the bar had carved-in grape vines and no fewer than three beautiful figures at the corners. Instead, I pried up one of the booth tables. The support came away with some nasty-looking four-inch wooden screws in the base, so I held that end toward those outside and stepped to the door. The glass would have gone eventually in a fight like this, so I didn't overly regret wrecking it as I thrust the support through.

The biker rushing the door gave a squawk as one of the twisted wooden screws bit.

Two bullets made it through the wood before others yelled at the fools to stop firing—"Zihu's still in there!"

Home had a bottle thrown at him and flinched, giving one of the throng a chance to knock the gun from his hand with a collapsible club. Maynes was doing well but swinging wildly. Still, his windmill blows had felled one man and backed Zihu up to the bar. Zihu circled and made for the back door. Maynes fell on his leg as he passed and bit down like a savage dog.

It occurred to me, braced there with my shoulder hard against the doorjamb, that in the movies my David and I would sometimes enjoy, the fights between leaders of the respective heroes and villains of a story were always the most spectacular. Zihu and Maynes were pawing at each other on the floor like a pair of teenagers fumbling through their first bout of lovemaking.

The brief oncoming roar of a motorcycle sounded, thunderously echoing off buildings outside; then the window and wall next to the door split with a crash. A black motorcycle with a massive shield at the front, reared up on its oversized hind wheel like a fighting stallion, crushed floor and furniture before it settled on its side, shedding two men and knocking over Home and his remaining opponent and staving out a panel in that glorious bar. The riders, wearing a mix of leather and chain mail, tumbled off the bike, goggles askew from the crash, and each drew a heavy automatic pistol.

I did my best to follow orders. If I couldn't hold the door, I could try to throw them out as fast as they came in. Taking a position a little back from the door and the hole in the wall, I picked up one of Zihu's mob and sent him spinning like a bowling ball at some others rushing in from outside. I achieved what's known in bowling as a "cocked hat" split, leaving two to one side and one to the other.

I used the leverage from a thick post to kick out at another, who dodged under it. My fist connected with the head of a man in a heavy Kevlar vest coming through the door behind a shotgun barrel. He and his gun hit the floor with a satisfying clatter.

Matters behind me had gone from bad to worse. Both packs had instinctively rushed to the defense of their dominant wolf; the Zihu pack was just larger. Maynes had been pinned against the bar, with the diminutive Zihu poking a knife up into his throat from one side and a nickel-plated revolver pressed against his temple from the other. Both Home and MacTierney were on the ground and Zihu's men were efficiently hog-tying them with cordage and cuffs designed for the purpose.

A deafening shotgun blast made all of us duck. Fortunately, my ears had been flattened against my head, offering me some protection from the noise.

"Fellas, you kill a Maynes, you have his blood after you'rn," the bartender shouted, sounding to my outraged ears as though he were underwater. "It's not bullshit. He's the grandson of old King Coal. He's Coal Country royalty, with friends all up and down the East right into the Control."

I took three quick steps toward Maynes. Some of Zihu's bully boys closed around the bar, but I shouldered through without undue difficulty by dislocating their shoulders.

Zihu lowered the knife. "Admit you're beat."

Maynes thrashed. "Road trash can't whip me." Blood splattered from his split lip and Zihu winced in disgust.

"We're beat!" MacTierney shouted. "Admit it, Mr. Maynes. Please!"

Maynes thought it over. He laughed. "Yeah, we're beat. But you fellas threw the first punch. The blood's on you. In more ways than one."

Zihu nodded and released Maynes's jacket.

"I think Three-King Jake's got a broke neck," one of Zihu's men reported from the Kevlar-wearing gunner I'd struck.

"We'll let the Church sort it out," Zihu said. "Maybe we can just be bygones over this?" He extended his hand to shake.

Maynes brought up his knee and caught Zihu in the crux. It was just the sort of move I had come to expect from this specimen of mankind.

"No!" Zihu gasped, but a gathering throng pressed toward us. I pulled Maynes over the bar and followed him. The heavy oak would buy us a few moments of protection—

"stop this nonsense!" A voice like a broken steam pipe cut through the gloomy, freshly aerated bar.

Those of you who live in these happier days have probably only seen waxworks or leftovers of the Reapers, though I know some lurk in the more remote jungles and deserts of the world. I will spare you the dangers of the journey and meeting.

They are of average Golden One height, which is to say about two heads above most male humans. Pale, fleshless, and stretched-looking, with a mouth full of black fangs, they're just human-enough in expression to give sane humans a case of the horrors. To me, they look like a mad and depressed painter's portrait of a human corpse. Their muscles are like steel cables, tied directly to long, grasping fingers I've seen push through viscera and muscle as easily as you might thrust your hand through a layer cake. It could throw me through the wall as easily as I'd lofted that unfortunate biker. Only a Bear with his blood fully up has a chance hand-to-hand with one.

One of the Coal Country troopers stood behind it. The trooper pointed at Zihu and whispered something.

This Reaper was the most scarred I'd ever seen. Its face bore white lines running every which way, like a pad of paper that had been reused for tic-tac-toe. Its upper lip was missing, giving it a rather maniacal grin. The usual black fangs had been plated over with stainless steel and reinforced with wires near the root like some kind of disastrous experiment in orthodontia. The label "Frankenstinian" is often used in describing the Reapers, though the lurching image evoked mischaracterized their lethal precision of movement— but on this specimen its use would be more apt than most.

Home and MacTierney averted their eyes. I believe MacTierney muttered a prayer, but the bar and one of Zihu's men absorbed any distinct words.

"What are you doing here, Screech?" Maynes said, breaking the intimidating silence. I'd never heard a Reaper called by a proper name.

"collecting an excise," Screech said. It stepped forward, and the Zihu men gave it at least twice its reach in space. It occurred to me that a mathematically minded person could come up with a neat little algorithm to describe the velocity of humans and how it varied with proximity to a Reaper.

"That's all I tried to do," Maynes said.

"we did not elevate the Maynes family just to satisfy your need for sorry little cumboxes."

The Coal Country Kurian operating the Screech-Reaper must have picked up an odd vocabulary in his time.

"i will take over the negotiations with mr. zihu. you may retrieve your men and take your vehicle to the next brothel on your list."

Screech took Zihu over to a corner of the bar and began to speak to him. Zihu put on a brave face, but his body language read as "cringe."

The bartender gave Maynes an iced towel to press to his lip, and I helped MacTierney and Home out of their bonds. Unfortunately for Zihu's bounty hunters, I ruined the restraints in the process.

"What happened to Bronson?" one of the bikers asked.

All eyes rose to the hole made in the ceiling by the biker I'd tossed. It looked like a splintery stick figure.

Another whistled. "Never seen anything like that outside a cartoon."

"I see the name Maynes everywhere in the Coal Country," said a dirt-encrusted scout who looked as if he'd lived for a year on top of a motorcycle. "What did he do?"

"Created the craziest family between here and Salt Lake," the bartender said quietly.

"But they run everything here, right? The Kurians put them in charge?"

"Ya-huh," the bartender said. "The family was important before the big breakdown. The grandfather had money and land and owned some radio, TV, netfoss, all that. Meant he had senators and judges lining up to kiss his hairy ring. After it all went to shit, he somehow kept his radio station running. The flying umbrellas dealt with him, made him the conduit for food, vaccines against the ravies virus; you wanted lights back on or fuel oil, you talked to one of the Old Man's people. The Kurians liked how he ran things around here, so they gave him every coal mine worth having hereabouts.

"That's the real power, the coal. The Northeast needs it to keep from freezing to death in the winter, and the Georgia Control needs it to power its factories in the Carolinas. Take a word of advice and make a copy for your boss: tread a little lightly in these mountains. There's more power here than you think."

Maynes knew the country better than any of his closest family. Sometimes he had to give tours to visitors from other Kurian Zones. His usual detail of MacTierney, Home, and me came along. Maynes and Home put on suits and neckcloths that were the local workingman's variant on a tie.

Maynes, who made a convincing bon vivant with the average Coal Country functionary, treated a tour like an unpleasant rash. He itched for it to end when he wasn't medicating with bourbon. His drinking wasn't so much an attempt to get through the night as to ensure that his charge would call an early night.

The first visitor I saw Maynes escort was up from Georgia, studying coal production. He was involved in turpentine farms and had come to see how the Maynes Conglomerate treated its miners.

He was an ugly little fellow who looked like he'd exchanged blows from an early age. He had a blotchy, mottled face, a crooked nose, a heavy, callous brow, and two missing teeth. I silently thanked the Fates that I'd ended up with Maynes instead of with an unpleasant-looking man like him. Most of his conversation was complaints about the weather, the lack of light on the valley roads, and the state of the highways and bridges.

After a couple of drinks, Maynes roundly damned his family for sticking him with "jumped up pickers." A picker, to Maynes, was a person fit only for the roughest manual labor in the coal mines. I noticed that he rarely used the epithet on some of his citizenry who probably came from "picker" stock—it was usually reserved for Quislings and churchmen.

Whenever we ran out of liquor, we went to the Maynes store.

The Maynes Coal Company Store always impressed. Called the Red Hen Pantry and Sundry, it had an appealing painting of a red hen on a nest of wildflowers. After the grim industrial spew of the slag heaps and extraction conveyors, the bright hues were a welcome relief.

It disabused me of the belief that company stores were designed to extract as much of the worker's paycheck as possible and return it to the corporation. The food was plentiful, nicely displayed, and at a price substantially lower than noncompany stores, from what I'd seen of Coal Country barrows and supermarkets.

There was even a more exclusive store within the store that you could visit with the right kind of ID. Church officials, management, labor committee heads, firemen . . . the apparat of the New Order could get luxuries, at luxurious prices, of course: soaps from the south of France, Jamaican rum, Cuban cigars.

"It's Elaine's work, these stores," Maynes always said proudly. "Quite an achievement. The way she explains it, cheap necessities cut down on a host of other problems. Theft and pilfering of company property, black market trading, attitude, even industrial sabotage, can all be prevented by a good supply chain at on-the-square pricing."

It was not long before I met Elaine.

Night Ride to Maryland

On a very few occasions, Maynes left the White Palace with only me accompanying him.

You could be forgiven for thinking that he took only the Grog out on his hunts for teenage girls, but I believe Home went with him on those nights. He and I ventured out alone only when he had a chance of meeting his sister on one of her business trips. She was the one member of the family whose company he sought.

"We have to pick my sister up. She's out east."

Maynes looked unusually good for the early evening.

It was a three-hour drive on the bad roads to Frederick, Maryland. I had no knowledge of the roads, so Maynes sat up beside me, pointing out landmarks—at least those that could be seen on a night with irregular patches of electricity along the roads.

I'd already proven to him that I had a decent memory for things I'd seen before. "You'll have no trouble getting back."

"No sir, no trouble. Long way. Need gas?"

He looked at the gauge. "We're good. They'll probably have some at the conference, though, so we'll get another half tank there, just in case."

We were out of the mountains and into open country of green

hills. It seemed to be patches of farmland mixed in with returned wilderness. As it was night, I saw little of Frederick itself. We parked outside a hotel (a big bird like a crane figured into the hotel's logo, but I don't remember the name) along the highway, glowing like the last bulb in a string, surrounded by darkened, boarded-up structures.

"Thought I'd surprise you," Maynes said as his sister walked out in response to a page. "A little birdie told me you're breaking up early. Any marriage proposals this time?"

I am not the best judge of human physiognomy. I knew she was female and Maynes was male, and they both had the same sort of hair. She was younger, both in age and in the use of her body—Maynes's habits had aged him prematurely. "You don't have to keep tabs on me, Joshua. You know I'm staying at the palace and dying a spinster."

"Nay-nay, you're always welcome here."

"Ah, admirable caution. I'm glad your failure elsewhere has taught you something."

"You know I've never failed at what matters to you."

Elaine Maynes returned a sour smile.

"Ready to leave crab country?"

This was a side of my employer I hadn't seen before—thoughtful, easygoing, making an effort to please.

"I have to say good-bye to a few people from the production working group. The Georgia Control rep invited me to a party, but since it's not on-site, I can decline. If anything, it'll enhance my reputation as someone who stands up to the Control. Or as a lady who doesn't like those sorts of parties."

"You're beautiful when you get political," Maynes said.

I noticed through the rearview mirrors that the lights in back were off.

As we travelled, bumping along the potholed roads and negotiating the odd border-area washout, it occurred to me that this particular transport was vulnerable to anything but someone taking a potshot from the side of the road. Guerillas or gangs of headhunters looking for snatchable aura could seize the three of us easily enough.

Once we made it back to the Coal Country, Maynes stopped at the first all-night diner (located at the edge of a rail yard that rearranged trains day and night) we came across and descended from the van to get a sack of whatever greasy hash the place offered.

He brought me a coffee, loaded almost out of its liquid state with saccharine. "Here you go, old cock."

Hair disheveled, half-drunk, and smelling of drying sweat and sexual musk, he'd clearly been in a tryst with his sister. I wondered how much of a secret this was with the rest of the family, and if it had anything to do with Maynes's being in an unimportant sinecure and his sister's being relegated to production. But again, I had to wonder who was really running the Maynes Conglomerate, since the Maynes family members appeared to spend most of their time throwing elbows, backbiting, and hamstringing their relatives.

The night and the empty road made me nervous. At every moment I expected the blast of a bomb buried in the gravel that filled the potholes between the better-paved sections. Perhaps I'd been too long a guerilla and knew what easy pickings I was.

I relaxed a little as we came into the Maynes county, where the White Palace waited for our return. I was within easy radio distance now, in the event of an emergency.

I came around a wooded bend and suddenly horses surrounded me, their teeth and eye whites bright in the headlights. Only the fact that I was travelling at less than thirty miles an hour saved me from a collision with one or more of them.

A figure astride a horse in the mob flashed by. It was white as moonlight, mouth agape, thin hair streaming. The lathered horse had no saddle, just bloody tooth and claw marks about its neck. Human? The face was human, vaguely. The body was too thin and wasted, a starved corpse like that Gollum character from the pre-Kurian Tolkien movie. But I was tired and needed sleep, and I saw it for only a second while trying to avoid turning a Maynes horse into the next NUC fund-raiser stew.

Now that I look back on it, they were probably horses from the Maynes ranch on the other side of the ridge from the White Palace. As for the rider? I would say it was my imagination, a waking dream, but no other dream has ever made my fur stand on end like that even years later.

By the time we returned to the White Palace, it was well into the morning. The sun would be up in a few hours.

The Beer Garden
on the Cheat River

Elaine Maynes had a soothing effect on my employer. Over the next ten days he issued a great many grants of clemency. The petitioners had to listen to admonitions to do better and warnings that eyes would be watching, but something in Maynes's friendly smiles and handshakes said the slate was wiped clean. We were sometimes cheered when leaving one of the Maynes Conglomerate holdings or while driving out of town. Maynes enjoyed these ducal moments, and he opened one of the armored glass windows just wide enough to wave regally as we motored out of town.

Rather than a grim, glowering pile of muscle, I saw myself turning into more of a mascot for Maynes. Sometimes he'd give away a bottle of bottled-in-bond whiskey for the worker at one of the sites who could guess my weight. He let kids touch my fur, moving from the silkier parts on my limbs to the bristlier fur atop my head, lifting the laughing kids so they could touch. They'd sometimes sit, four or five abreast, across my shoulders and slide down my arms, using my limbs like fire poles.

Old-timers said it was the nicest June in three generations. I had not the experience on this side of the Appalachians for comparison, but it did grow hot enough that I borrowed a clipper from the stables at the White Palace and trimmed my lower leg and forearm hair down to bristle. A veil of thin cloud drawing down from the north made the sun somewhat waxy rather than blazing, but it was still bright enough to make the dewy leaves glitter in the morning. The humidity stayed comfortably low.

I found the drives with Maynes could be contemplated with pleasure. The stops were as distressing as ever, but the drives were something to look forward to, negotiating the difficult, slide-washed roads with quiet green forest chirping with birdsong from the cool shade.

Speaking of the roads, the spring rains had done their damage, with heavy soil and broken trees dumped on the mountainside roads. Sometimes Maynes had to drive back to the nearest town and press-gang a labor contingent to clear a slide. The men enjoyed the work, with either Home or MacTierney using our vehicle to get a lunch and coolers of lemonade and beer for the workmen. Maynes joined in, and he had access to dynamite, so there was good fun when a few sticks were employed to turn a fallen tree into matchwood or blow a boulder into pieces. After the excitement of the explosion, these West Virginians usually let loose with a sort of wailing whoop-hurrah, each trying to outdo the others in making noise, eventually returning to their shovels and draglines reenergized.

Maynes paid very good wages for this sort of day labor, and was usually cheered when the work was done. He accepted it with a regal wave out of his bus window.

We had spent the morning in the eastern part of the Coal Country so Maynes could sign off on some trade agreements—the usual swaps of coal and timber for more finished product from the industrial patches in southern Virginia and the Carolinas. Other members of the Maynes clan had negotiated the terms, but as he was highest on the current bloodline tree, he often had to sign for the Conglomerate. Fifteen minutes of signing papers, a ceremonial toast of recycled water with the Quislings from the Georgia Control, and once back in the Trekker, Maynes insisted that he was done for the day.

Maynes never showed the carousing side of himself at these exchanges. His proclivities were something of an open secret in the Coal Country, but perhaps he was smart enough not to suggest weaknesses that others might exploit. Or he didn't care for the zipped-up, professional Georgia Control men and women.

"An hour and a half with tight asses," he said, on return to the Trekker. "Let's find some food."

We stopped at a little riverside eatery that was nothing much to look at from the roadside—a plain white storefront with a grease-stained rooftop—but out behind was a wooden sort of beer garden and balcony overlooking the filled-to-the-banks waters of the Cheat River rushing toward their joining with the Monongahela below. Home had recommended it: "The food's better than average, and they brew their own beer from one of the Cheat River springs. Good brew. They could probably keg it and sell it, but they don't want the paperwork hassles."

The owners weren't just craft brewers; it looked like they were gardeners as well. Peonies and irises were in bloom in flower boxes and beds. The flower boxes had scrolling of stylized barley and hops—fine work, and I instantly warmed to whoever had designed the boxes. I was glad Maynes was in a mood to forget about his duties, and it wasn't the sort of place where he'd dragoon a woman off to the transport and then let Home take his turn.

We sat outside. They found a metal milk-crate for me and put a small pillow on top—from the stains, it looked as though several generations of dogs had given birth on it—and I was able to sit at eye level with my companions in reasonable comfort. Home was right, as he usually was on matters of food and drink. The owners took as much care with their food and barleywine as they did with their blooms.

Some teamsters with horse wagons, drivers with gum-and-rust diesels parked out front, a quiet middle-aged couple playing dominoes, a group of young mothers whose kids were at the rail tossing buds into the river, and a pair of troopers were all enjoying the weather, beer, and food.

Maynes liked the food so much, he'd ordered a potpie, and while we waited for that, we enjoyed the beer. I'd just finished a large draft of lemonade—the cheapest beverage on the menu; Maynes was happy to buy us all a single beer, but we were on duty—when my ears pricked up and tracked in on the sound of singing.

The sound came out of the Monongahela Forest and the low ridge of mountains beyond the river to the east.

There were about fifteen youths, plus two young adults and an older man in a dungaree version of the simple New Universal Church clean-lined jacket-and-collar.

The youths, despite their layers of flaking sunburn and bug bites, glistened like polished apples. White, straight teeth, even the incipient beards on the young men seemed to be growing according to plan. They wore survival vests, bellows pockets crammed with tools in a vivid combination of blaze orange and optic yellow. They were led by two older young adults, in khaki versions of New Universal Church day wear. The males wore red bandannas and the females white.

Maynes, with his healing, stitched lip, drew a few surreptitious glances from the outing as they fell into a more orderly line outside the garden gate. They stared more openly at me, as though I were a trained bear wearing a conical hat at a child's birthday party.

"Before lunch break, we'll have a song," the female Youth Vanguard leader declared.

The horse teamsters stood to leave, but the female Youth Vanguard leader stepped in front of the gate. "Everyone will be so disappointed if they can't perform for you, friend."

"Music, too," Home said.

"Hope we're not in for a hootenanny," Maynes said. "Church sing-alongs sour my beer."

"You nailed it, Boss," Home said.

"Badges say Cooper's Point," MacTierney said. "That's over the Virginia line. Wonder why they're poking around up here?"

From what I understand, Kurian Zones frequently probe and test their neighbors. While the histories make much of the coups and consolidations and so on, they were rare. The Kurians would much rather keep their populations content with stories about how bad it was on the other side of this or that border, or blame a shortage of fresh food on the incompetence of the neighboring principality.

"Martins, say the pledge while the others get out their instruments," the male Vanguard leader said. Though a bit undersized, he had the alert, energetic appearance of a pointer waiting to be released into a field despite what looked like the dirt of the morning's exertions.

The shortest child at the end straightened and extended his neck like a curious turtle. "We the growing future, in order to form a more perfect Human, commit Justice and ensure Sustainability, provide for equality and promote the superior to secure the Blessings of Symbiotry to our guides and our posterity."

The youths opened up satchels and extracted a couple of instruments—some bongos, a harmonica, and a small flute joined the guitars and banjo. They broke into a camp song, something about helping hands and feet making light a friend's burden:

"Friend, helpful hands never pass or flake,
They beckon for a brother's weight."

I recognized the music, but not the words. Like many of the more popular Youth Vanguard songs, the sprightly jingle had been reworded in the Free Territory into a tune about eating corn biscuits and peanut butter ("jammers") on the march:

Corp, pass them jammers down this way
It's all we're gonna get today.

"How fit are you, friends?" the female leader asked those relaxing with their meals and beer.

A few of the drinkers and diners gave nervous gulps. Maynes snorted.

The male gave a single, resounding clap. "Give them an example. Remember, we've been doing hiking and field craft exercises all morning. And just think of what the soldiers in Mississippi have to overcome!"

It is easy to forget the terror the Youth Vanguard wielded. When relating such scenes, I, Ahn-Kha, witnessed, I am called an exaggerator, a fabulist, even a straight-out liar. There is more evidence than my testimony, my reader, if you can stomach the experience of viewing the photographs and remaining video footage. But that is outside this account. Suffice to say, that at a denouncement from a member of the Youth Vanguard, you could easily have your career wrecked. I have even heard, from those who have seen it, that the Vanguard carried out summary executions—a rarity in the Kurian Zones, where blood and vital aura are conserved for the Reapers and their animating Kurians. But each of the Youth Vanguard leaders carried a black nylon holster along with the rest of his gear, a symbol of trust and authority.

They put their charges through a series of exercises. Maynes ignored it, cracking peanuts and either tossing them into his mouth, or down toward the riverbank, where some local squirrels would race for them.

"You Coal Country people have a reputation of being tough as nails. Let's see you try," the woman suggested, smiling broadly.

MacTierney rose to his feet with the others, but Maynes threw a peanut at his ear. As it bounced off, drawing a glance from the target, Maynes shook his head.

The diners formed themselves into a line opposite the youth troop and performed, slowly and cumbersomely, the exercises. One of the drovers broke wind as he bent, drawing some giggles from the children.

"That's not funny," a male leader said. "A demerit each."

The simple calisthenics grew more laborsome. The exercisers panted and sagged.

"What's the over/under on heart attacks?" Home asked.

The elderly couple stopped. Smiling, they held up their hands as though in surrender. The Youth Vanguard leaders turned solicitous, also smiling, and offered to help them back to their seats.

"You show a remarkable tolerance for idleness," the male said to our table. "Also, smell. When did that Grog last bathe?"

"That's just my aftershave, kid," Maynes said. "From my grandfather's estate. Eau de Senate Cloakroom. Don't you like it?"

"Strange that such a healthy and important young man is idling in a beer garden," the Virginian said.

The wife of the middle-aged man suddenly fell to her knees and vomited up her lunch.

As though given permission by the others stopping, the rest of the exercisers broke off.

"No one told you to stop," the female Vanguard leader shouted, slapping a hand on her pistol holster. She stepped over to the woman who'd vomited.

"Your system's better off without all that beer in it. Clean up that disgusting mess. Now!"

She looked around helplessly, and her husband knelt and helped her scoop up the vomitus with their bare hands.

MacTierney, looking a little pale, excused himself from the table. Odd how the bodily functions of another species do not provoke the same visceral reactions. My head spun and I fainted at the birth of my own children, but I once carefully helped replace a pair of popped-out eyeballs that had resulted from the concussion of the bombardment of Big Rock Hill on a man.

"I think you gentlemen should take their places," the Youth Vanguard leader said.

"Who's going to—," Home started to say.

Maynes tossed another peanut into his mouth. "Hey, King, you weigh as much as all of us put together. Go join in. Hippity-hop, now. Let's see if our Youth Vanguard leaders can do as many push-ups as you."

"By my authority to protect . . . ," the male leader began, drawing his pistol from the holster at his waist. It was a mass-produced re-volver, probably a .38, hardly a military-grade threat or the sort of weapon a professional assassin sent to kill Maynes might employ, but it was clean and oiled and deadly nonetheless.

I dislike displays of authority above the barrel of a gun. I have never seen anything good come of them. In fact, useless bloodshed is often the result of such exhibitions. I reached out, engulfed the van-guard leader's hand, and rendered the revolver less dangerous, at least to anyone but its user, by bending the barrel into a pinch-point. The bones in the Vanguard leader's hands broke rather more easily.

"Why don't you get your little parade back across the Virginia line," MacTierney said, sheltering in the doorway with a shotgun aimed. "Take off those scarves, first. We've got some people with puke all over their hands who need some rags to clean up."

MacTierney had shown flashes of empathy before, but this was the first time I'd seen him seriously jeopardize himself for others.

It would have been easier for him to sit and enjoy his barleywine. The chances of any of the beer garden people taking such a chance over him would require high math to express.

In the confusion, most of the clientele slipped away by river path, road, or footbridge across the Cheat.

"The family wonders why I have need of bodyguards," Maynes said.

The White Palace was well named. It served not only as the practical seat of governmental power for the Coal Country; it was also the social center for the wealthier Appalachian Quislings.

Maynes avoided most of the social events at the White Palace, and for the few he did attend, he had no need of me. For those occasions, I worked outside during the arrivals and departures, helping attendees and guests of the palace with their luggage. Because of the duration and difficulty of even short trips thanks to the roads, checkpoints, and so on, for most events about half the attendees remained a day or two. For my work, I sometimes received a tip in the local coin currency used for small exchanges—usually about enough to buy a cigarette or two, had I been of that habit—or pieces of candy from the more knowledgeable about Gray Ones and their legendary sweet tooth. Sometimes I would be given crayons, I suppose so I could better amuse myself by drawing on the walls of the barn, or slivers of soap, old toothbrushes, and other hygiene odds and ends.

I always went to some effort to keep my skin and fur clean using the shampoos, soaps, brushes, shammies, and other excellent materials available for the riding horses, but I don't think the gifts were a reproach for my personal habits. I could always find use for stiff new bristles on a toothbrush, in any case. Matter always seems to find a home between my longish—compared to a human, that is—toes.

I never saw more than glimpses of what the guests would do for these parties and events. The White Palace had been a hotel of the old world, so it had cooking and laundry facilities to match. They put me to work in the laundry, washing bedding for the guests. I would wrap a pillowcase around my snout to keep out the boric acid and soap flakes used to clean the bedding and work the huge machines that washed and dried fabric.

As I recall, there were four major social events in the Coal Country important enough for Maynes to circulate, sober and circumspect in his sexual drive for a change.

The first one I witnessed was in the spring, at the beginning of May. Heyday, it was called in the Coal Country, but I've heard and seen "May Day" elsewhere. Young women would put flowers in their hair—the older women of distinction simply added them to their hats—and men added them to lapels or wove them together into garlands to wear around their necks. Gifts of flowers from one's apparel were a way of signaling romantic interest. Strawberries were worked into almost everything. The Maynes family even managed to lay its hands on extraordinary rich blocks of European chocolate ready for melting and dipping. Gifts of chocolate-dipped strawberries often symbolized the beginning of a formal courtship.

At the height of summer, there was the Appalachian Horse Show, a Saturday-to-Saturday gathering the first week of July. Many members of Coal Country society raised horses, for their own pleasure and sometimes transport—though they were the one class wealthy enough to have reliable personal transportation in the form of cars and small trucks.

There would be polo matches and drag hunts during the day and barbecues and pig roasts in the afternoon and evening, with Coal

Country society members showing off their horseflesh, apparel, and eligible sons and daughters. Young couples would ride out together. Theatricals, fire-balloons, and concerts filled the night air with cries of excitement, music, and laughter. We Grogs worked with a will handling all the horses.

While informal buying and selling of horses and associated gear would happen throughout the week, celebration would end with a "charity" auction featuring horses and saddles to benefit the New Universal Church and a fund for Injured Miner's Relief and Retirement.

I helped in one of the drag hunts by acting as a search target, a semiserious game of hide-and-seek between me and roughly two dozen young women and men on horseback. Many of them rode with pistols and even rifles in saddle holsters, which caused me a little worry in case one of them became overzealous when closing in for the "kill." As it turned out, my worries were groundless.

I'm afraid I did not make for much sport, as I was exhausted from taking care of horseflesh from the predawn until midnight over the course of the week. They brought me to bay against a limestone wall on a steep hillside, dismounting for the kill. Had it been an actual pursuit, I would have risked the climb, but I settled for holding up my hands and being pelted with fruit taken from the remains of their saddlebag lunches. They led me back, loosely tied behind the hunt captain's horse, to the picnic grounds where I received a round of applause.

By the time it was over and the horses had been packed back into their transports or ridden off the White Palace grounds on a string, the other Grogs and I were so exhausted, we slept for three days.

A second summer party, "Labor Day," was a holiday carried over from pre-Kurian times. Unlike the Appalachian Horse Show, there were events all over the Coal Country celebrating the day, and Maynes barnstormed the country in his bus, visiting as many picnics and market-fairs as he could fit in. One way or another, almost every family in the Coal Country managed to procure beef for barbecuing or burgers—I suspect the Maynes clan made arrangements for a massive import of cattle, either on the hoof or already cut into sides.

We never saw the White Palace events, being busy in the smaller towns, but I learned they put on an opera or a musical play in the natural amphitheater in the hills.

The Winter Carnival is the longest running, a season of gatherings that stretches from the traditional Thanksgiving time of late November to the New Year. Typically, the White Palace swirled with activity throughout the season with many small parties, culminating in the biggest celebration of the year to welcome the new calendar.

The New Year's party, unlike the others, was an occasion for the regular workers and small businessmen to attend and even stay as guests of the Maynes family. Maynes showed the most animation at the New Year's party. He enjoyed mixing with "his people" as he styled them.

The staff, even the Grogs, joined in the celebration. Even the poor cooks had the night off, the celebrants made do with premade soups and wrapped sandwiches and pickled offerings to go with their winter beers, vintage wines, bourbons, and other spirits.

Why this digression? I wished to give an idea of the lifestyle and pursuits of the privileged "Quisling" class, if you will, and also show that society in this part of the Kurian Order was not so sharply divided. Again, there is a natural impulse for diarists of their own life under the Kurians to make the Quislings more evil than most actually were and their own histories free of any taint of collaboration beyond the minimum required for survival. In the Coal Country, the Quislings had, for the most part, good relations with those under them, even admitting them to their most exclusive streets and homes at times.

Now we shall turn to the opening of the great rift that would bring down the Kurian Order in these rugged hills.

About a quarter of Maynes's "appointments" never happened. Before his final interview and adjudication of their case, they disappeared into the hills—though on one occasion while I was with him there was a suicide reported.

Maynes reacted nonchalantly to the evidence that information about his schedule was leaking out of the White Palace. "Just as well; didn't want to talk to that son of a bitch anyway"; "They'll run him to ground and he'll be sorry"; or even, "This is a small patch of ground, taller than it is wide. Everybody knows somebody and word gets around."

From a man who drove around in an armored bus that rattled like a hailstorm when birdshot bounced off it or flaked on the inside where it had absorbed a bullet from a deer rifle, such an attitude showed courage, or perhaps fatalism. The Coal Country was a long, long way away from any organized freehold. The Green Mountain boys were closest and had the best path in, but they were busy in New England and on the Great Lakes. Southern Command was the next closest, but that would have meant a long and difficult trek across Kentucky or Tennessee.

I remember only one time when Maynes seemed to have doubts about the Kurian Order. The town constables caught a man at the hospital incinerator in Charleston.

No one could say where the Kurian who ran the Coal Country resided. There was no obvious Kurian tower, and there were not many Reapers, perhaps because the mineral-rich mountains interfered with the link between the Kurian and his avatars. I have no idea of the actual number, but it must have been low. If the Coal Country was not the Kurian Zone with the highest human-to-Reaper ratio, I would like to know which zone was. I only saw one, the same one several times, thanks to a distinctive injury to its lip. But back to the incident in Charleston.

They'd caught a man named Hollis, who'd climbed a wall in an effort to get at the incinerator. In the Coal Country, bodies were disposed of by cremation. The New Universal Church mortuary would place those unfortunates consumed by the Reapers in special body bags that could not be opened again without breaking a very obvious seal and releasing a dye, a method similar to that used to thwart bank robbers, I understand. The Kurians did not care for photos of Reaper-punctured victims to be distributed, at least not in the areas organized by the Georgia Control.

Hollis sat in the hospital security cells. I never think of a hospital as needing cells, but this one had six, all painted a shade of green so light it could be mistaken for white. MacTierney said he was a woodworker. He looked like one, or perhaps a toymaker out of a children's book—he had the same kindly eyes and tiny spectacles worn at the end of his nose that you'd expect to see on someone who constructed Pinocchio. He had no weapons, no camera or other recording devices. It was a mystery.

"What kind of game were you playing?"

"No game. I was looking for my daughter. Nine years old," he said by way of clarifying.

"You thought she'd climbed over a twelve-foot wall?"

"No, she was taken away by you all," Hollis said. "God will damn you for it. I believe there's justice, you see."

"Why was she taken?"

"Genetic deficient, they said. She had the Down syn-der-roam."

"And she made it to nine? You hid her, I suppose?"

"Yes. Until that bastard Dwight David Metcalf found out his fool son had been arrested for stealing from the Maynes motor pool. He thought turning her in would save his worthless heap of oily haired dirt."

"Law's the law," Home said. "You and your wife could have saved yourselves a heap of heartache by letting the hospital take care of it when she was born."

"Why take lives like that?" Hollis asked. "She gave nothing but love."

Maynes intervened. "Children with that syndrome—they absorb too much schooling and medical attention. The state can't afford children like that."

Hollis jumped up so suddenly, his glasses flew off. "The state didn't spend a dollar on her. We taught her ourselves. We kept her in our home. Of course, I never dared bring her to a hospital, so what medical care did she receive? Who did she ever trouble, that she had to die for it?" Somewhere in that speech his glasses landed with a clatter.

Maynes looked as though he'd been struck across the bridge of the nose.

"We can't have mouths that eat or hands that don't produce," he said, sounding as though he were reading off a card someone had handed him at the last second.

"That's a churchman's reply," Hollis said. "Strange to hear it from someone like Bone Maynes. You and the New Church never got on." Locals in the Coal Country always dropped the "Universal" part of the New Universal Church.

Maynes remained silent for a moment. Home patted his holstered pistol as if trying to draw Hollis's attention to the symbol of authority.

Maynes finally bent, picked up the spectacles, and handed them to Hollis.

"Give him a couple of handfuls of ashes and let him go."

"What about the police—," MacTierney said.

"Have them send the paperwork to my office. Hollis, I'll give you a ride home. I expect you'll never say anything about what you saw here."

Hollis shrugged. "I didn't see much except a few pitiful figures sealed up like tinned WHAM! If you all think it's a big secret what's going on in here . . . well, it ain't."

"By rights he should be the next one into the incinerator," Home said. "All this does is free up a slot for someone else. What's the point of all this if we're just going to let guilty men go free? No justice in it for anyone."

"Let's hope not, Home," MacTierney said.

"Let's hope not what?"

"That there's justice. I have a feeling we might not like the taste. Speaking of taste, let's get out of this ash heap before I breathe any more people."

"Hollis, I'm truly sorry about your daughter," Maynes said as we left. Hollis had his hand in his pocket with the little bag of ash he'd been given. I wondered how often that splinter-bitten hand had held his daughter's.

"Then you're working for the wrong people, Mr. Maynes. The wrong people."

Maynes was sullen until we returned to the White Palace. He had one large drink of bourbon and, much to Home's dismay, didn't scrounge around for a girl before turning the Trekker home.

THE BECKLEY BLOOD

The Coal Country Revolt is only sometimes mentioned, and rarely described in the histories of the Kurian Order. Those that do describe it all have the beginning wrong. They place the start of hostilities with the mine revolts.

I saw the genesis with my own eyes. This witness insists that the revolt started over cookware.

You might say the long slide for the Kurians east of the Mississippi began because someone miscommunicated, or loaded the wrong boxes in the wrong railcars, or mislaid a piece of paperwork or attached the wrong boxcar to an outbound train. An unknown depot clerk on some siding ended up with a shipment of Pennsylvania iron and enamel cookware, which they no doubt quietly sold off as soon as the pickup could be arranged. For my own curiosity, I would like to know where the error occurred, but I fear the information is forever lost (though if a reader of this account knows anything about the issue, I would welcome a letter).

It began on June 17, 2073, a few days before the anniversary of the arrival of the Kurians. In the town of Beckley, there stands a big semicircular market with a sort of triangular crown atop it. It was known as the Beckley Marketplace and was open to the public.

Mostly, it sold locally made wares and it had a flea market a good deal more colorful than the bland "company stores" that all carried the same mass-produced shelf-stable foods and necessities. The Beckley Marketplace had advertised a large selection of big enamelware pots, large enough to be used as a Dutch oven or a stewpot for a family full of hungry mouths. Because of endless scrap drives, good iron cookware was hard to find, especially in larger sizes, and these were imports from a well-known Ordnance ironworks near Pittsburgh.

The locals were long accustomed to procedures for handling scarcities. Grandmothers and aunts would stand in line, often all night, waiting for the doors to be unlocked on the day the stock went on sale (frequently, it didn't show up until near closing time, leading to more waiting). The oversized enamelware pots were to go on sale June 16, but by closing time at the Beckley Marketplace they still hadn't arrived, and hundreds of people had been waiting close to fully around the clock without result. Inquiries with the staff were met shiftily.

I suppose families took turns standing in line, but it presented difficulty, and whatever calluses had been formed by the eternal line-waiting of the Kurian Order had been stripped off and skin rubbed raw by the second day of being in line.

The next morning, the stock finally appeared. There had been a serious mistake, and the items on sale were tiny little saucepans suitable for melting a small amount of butter (or chocolate, on the rare publicly approved holidays it was made available).

Knowledge passed, as it tended to in crowds, that the mistake had been known the day before and they'd kept everyone in line in a hopeless attempt to rectify it. So even those who were used to error and fault felt betrayed by the lack of information that would have allowed the wait in the line to be ended rather than extended unnecessarily.

The crowd, having passed the knowledge from frustrated buyer to buyer, acted with the same collective alacrity. Did they move as a flock of sheep, or a pack of wolves?

According to two survivors I later talked to during the on-again, off-again "troubles" in the Coal Country, there was talk in the crowd of going to the Beckley city hall to complain. The idea of a mass demonstration may strike most of those who knew something of life under the Kurian Order as more than a little curious, but as this account has tried to show, the Coal Country was an almost unique instance of the Kurian Order in practice.

They left the Beckley Marketplace and headed east to the old bank at the corner of Main and Old State Route 210, where the private Gateway Store now harbored a few luxuries for the use of the Quisling families with a special needs pass. While the crowd had been right about the problem being known by the Marketplace since the day before, they were wrong in surmising that the Gateway Store had received a shipment of the correct cookware.

They found it locked and barred. The staff had working telephones; in all likelihood they had heard about the trouble at the Marketplace and locked up as soon as the mob was reported marching in their direction.

Had the local authorities talked to the frustrated shoppers, admitted and apologized for the foul-up and promised an answer within a day or two posted at the Marketplace, everyone would probably have gone home to await the official notice of when they might expect to be able to buy their pots. Instead, the local authorities panicked and retreated to the city hall or fire station, which was already blasting the emergency call-up siren.

Maynes, who had been just a half hour away from Beckley by road, arrived right after they set fire to the Gateway Store (it had been broken open in the search for the cookware). The workers ran out the back door, unmolested by anything but shouted insults.

Sirens were blaring from two tall buildings in the few square blocks of downtown Beckley as we picked up speed on the better-maintained town roads. I was driving the Trekker and Maynes directed me to pull up behind the city hall.

A mass of youths in green school uniforms and black combat harness vests, unzipped and in a few cases inside out, hurried up the street in a double file toward the stolid toast-colored administration building with its prairie-school clock tower. It was obviously a pre-2022 build, and someone had made an effort to make it look attractive rather than just utilitarian concrete laid square. The vertical architectural lines could be called either reassuring or solemn, depending on mood. There were holes where old letters had been pried off the top. I could still make out a weathered halo around the word "judicial." Tables with guns were being laid out by some hurrying state troopers, and plastic bins filled with boxes of ammunition waited next to the tables.

"Crapaheenie, they've called out the Youth Vanguard," Maynes said as he directed me to stop.

"Somebody panicked," MacTierney said.

Home unlocked the gun rack. "Ya think?"

In the older part of Beckley, a former college served as a campus for the Youth Vanguard. The students are often the children of Quisling technocrats, scholarship winners for Youth Vanguard activities, or those who have managed to impress the regime through the standard tests that all children are put through upon entering school and then every four years thereafter. They are the seed corn of the Kurian Order and most receive a basic military education as part of their studies.

These were students at a small technical college inside the city limits. Those attending hoped to become midlevel management in one Kurian Zone or another, supervising power plants or transport facilities. Thanks to its "backwater" location in the Coal Country, the college was also cheap to attend, a consideration for the less-better-off Quislings who wanted their sons and daughters to improve their standing.

Having seen them used as a first-response force in Beckley and as a last-ditch defense line (in an action years later in Northern Missouri), I have come to the conclusion that their employment as such shows both the basic depravity and weakness of the Kurian Order. Ordering schoolchildren into combat guarantees a tragedy of one sort or another.

In the case of Beckley—well, I shall describe it as accurately as I can and allow you, my reader, to form your own conclusions.

Maynes had MacTierney wait with the Trekker while he took Home and me into the administration building. He learned that something called the "Crisis Committee" was meeting, or whatever elements of it were available that day in downtown Beckley. He left us waiting in an upstairs hall while he went into the meeting.

Home and I watched a couple of trooper patrol cars pull in, and the now-armed Youth Vanguard file off to the east. I counted seventy-four grouped into three platoons, each with a magazine-fed carbine.

Maynes stormed out of the meeting room, and we hurried downstairs to the sound of unanswered phones buzzing from all the offices.

"Half of the county management's run; the other half has grabbed its guns and headed to the riot."

By the time we arrived, the Youth Vanguard Armed Auxiliary had blocked the streets leading to the city downtown with police and fire vehicles. Two off-road trucks and a motorcycle, all with just-fitted light machine guns in the permanent mounts that stood empty save for drills, were covering a road running west. The firemen had rigged their hoses to push the crowd back with water, but the curly-haired seventeen-year-old and the veteran retired sergeant commanding the Auxiliary ignored the firefighters.

Maynes tried to find someone in command. A senior trooper had his few uniformed men behind their nose-to-nose patrol cars, but he couldn't speak for the firemen. The Youth Vanguard had a veteran "military trainer" but was under the command of a curly-haired seventeen-year-old with a buttercream complexion; his eyes were shining with excitement and his combat vest was stuffed with magazines for his carbine. The boy looked to his trainer for guidance in placing his forces, and the trainer was clearly trying to win favor with the boy. The firemen had both guns and water cannon. All three groups were ignoring one another, though they'd coordinated enough to block the street with their fire trucks, squad cars, and a school bus.

Smoke rose from the burning store and the sound of windows being broken was audible off to the east.

"Anyone think to send a couple uniformed officers off to calm everyone down?" Maynes asked the fire chief.

"You want us on the firing line, too?" Home asked. "There's a good view down the sidewalk."

"God no," Maynes said.

The firemen ignored him, as did the deploying Youth Vanguard. "You've no military authority in this situation," the curly-haired youth said from within his two-sizes-too-big uniform, prompted by his grizzled old training sergeant walking with the aid of a cane. He had a set of captain's bars that looked as though they'd been taken out of their jeweler's case that morning.

"Your funeral, kid," Maynes said. "Sarge, you sure you want the Virgin Hairy here? Doesn't seem the right man to run this show."

"He's got the rank at the college," the sergeant said. "He's a big rail baron's kid. I'm just here to amplify and clarify."

One of the firemen, sitting in the cab of his vehicle, stuck his head out the window. "Crisis Committee says that if they head downtown, they have to be dispersed."

"Dispersed how?" Maynes asked him.

"They didn't say."

"No one wants responsibility," Maynes said.

"I do," the Youth Vanguard leader said.

The entire line of armed figures behind the cars on the street nearest to us stiffened. I drew myself up to my full height and looked down the street.

A motley collection of old women, mothers with kids in tow, and a smattering of teenagers who probably should have been in the church schoolrooms was proceeding down the street in two distinct throngs clustered to each sidewalk. The younger were nearer to us and the Youth Vanguard, the older ones facing the troopers. Some were banging the tiny saucepans together like miniature cymbals—at the time, none of us knew that a missing cookware delivery was at the heart of the disturbance. No one on the Crisis Committee, or anywhere else at the Administration Center, knew anything beyond the mob attacking and looting the flea market before moving on to the biggest store in town.

The Youth Vanguard, now sighting down their carbines, exchanged comments up and down the line. Beckley was not a big city; no doubt the students recognized a face or two.

"The Crisis Committee is in session. You are all subject to the military discipline under the Riot Protocol," the curly-haired teen with his honorary captain's bars called through the megaphone.

"The Crisis Committee," Maynes said. "That's a word to strike fear in the heart of the desperate."

The protest march-cum-riot stopped. They were close enough so that even those with below-average eyesight (common with humans past the flush of youth) could see the guns arrayed against them.

I did not hear everything the crowd shouted back, but some of the teenagers sporting sledgehammers and crowbars knew him. It seemed curly hair had a local reputation for filching women's undergarments off the drying line and using them for sexual relief purposes.

He didn't give them time to do much more than process the implied threat. "Fire!"

Who can say why he gave the order? My own guess is that he wanted to make a name for himself as a decisive leader with the Vanguard, his college, or perhaps his family. A quick, harsh lesson that ends with a few bodies in the street appeals to some of the Kurians who think their brethren and Quislings go too easy on the human herd.

To their credit, about half of the Auxiliary members pointed their guns high enough so that the bullets would land a thousand yards behind the crowd. But enough rifle fire still swept the crowd to make wounds blossom on humble clothing.

The troopers blasted away with their shotguns.

The machine-gun fire from the heavy vehicles was the worst of all. The firemen, each man chosen for his instinct for brutality, handled their weapons well. Whole groups of women tumbled down as though their feet had been rigged with trip wires.

Screams of fear—and aged rage, as it seemed even the old women of the Coal Country were ready to finish a fight once it started—broke out from the crowd.

I expected the crowd to run, especially those in the back, but instead they threw themselves down en masse. Were they instinctively following the example of the falling bodies?

"Shoot above their heads, you fucking idiots!" MacTierney yelled. No one heeded his voice. Home was content to hoist himself up by the rearview mirror on the bus for a better view. Maynes made a couple of notes in the little notebook he kept in his breast pocket. He checked his watch for reference.

I was tempted to take the driver's seat and floor the Trekker into the big fire truck with the two machine guns and unused fire hoses. The insanity of having such equipment available and ready without using it was incredible. Wouldn't it have been better for the regime to have water running in the streets instead of blood?

"Someone's going to catch hell over this," Maynes muttered.

"Better not be us," Home said. "Think we should get gone?"

"The family is going to infarc face-first into the soup course tonight when someone mentions it at dinner. That I was around for it, too. They hate it when the family name gets associated with real rough stuff."

"Me help fight? Me help fight? Mehelpfight?" I asked, tugging at Maynes's sleeve until he had to shift his feet to keep from falling over.

MacTierney handed me a first aid kit. "Go drag one of those kids out of the street."

I tossed an ammo belt up into the eyes of the gunner. He had the sense to let go of the gun as he fell sideways; otherwise he might have sprayed the barricade with machine-gun fire.

A few bottles and rocks clattered off the parked emergency vehicles or crashed behind us. Foolish, but understandable. Another wave of gunfire from the Quisling forces ripped across the street in answer. I kept my ears tightly closed against the noise—both the rifle reports and the screams from the injured and dying.

"You'll go through your whole wad, shooting like that," the old sergeant told the Vanguard Auxiliary blasting away. For all the emotion in his voice, they might have been kneeling on a rifle range, instead of shooting into a public street cluttered with bodies and two tipped-sideways strollers. A baby still cried in one.

"Wicked good shooting, everyone," the young captain called. "Law and order will be upheld."

Whose law? What order? I wished to ask. I counted more than twenty still bodies in the street and a few wounded, wide-eyed in disbelief at the damage a few grams of lead could wreak in mere flesh.

A song written a decade after the events in the Coal Country had a line saying Beckley's streets ran with blood. That might be a bit too poetic—blood tends to pool when exposed to air, and the poor-quality asphalt soaked up the dreadful liquid. I wish I could claim, as the song does, that the blood flowed like an accusing finger toward the parked fire trucks, but it didn't.

So, what does this bloody, unfortunate incident have to do with a major uprising a year later?

This began a period of troubles in the Coal Country. The blood on the streets of Beckley wasn't poetic, but its effect cannot be underestimated. Grievances aren't forgotten in these thickly wooded mountains. These slopes are the scene of America's most famous feuds and the largest armed uprising between the 1861 Civil War and the advent of the Kurians. The people of this country, once they start a feud, see it through.

After the Beckley Blood, the Kurian Order saw the first of its difficulties in getting coal out of the country, and heads gathered for the Kurians. Oddly enough, the locals had not opposed the order in any major fashion, other than failing to meet plan after plan for the increase in coal production. The Kurian Order had laid down rules, explained by the New Universal Church, and as long as it did its selecting and gathering and head-hunting in an orderly fashion with a minimal amount of corruption, they hunkered down and took it.

Who knows what was being planned and gathered for years, waiting for the moment weapons could be dug up and passwords exchanged at lonely fords.

The Beckley Blood meant train derailments and transformer-station fires. It meant police cars with engines fouled by sodium silicate and run until the pistons melted and fused. It even meant house-burnings for higher-ranking Quislings.

Even the White Palace wasn't inviolate. The Maynes clan, although running a relatively gentle version of the Kurian Order, had the blood of Beckley on its hands and became, perhaps for the first time, synonymous with the rest of the Kurian Order. Before Beckley, I overheard plenty of conversations—humans think we're intelligent dogs, understanding our names and a few commands—where any complaint about the regime was qualified with a statement such as "Of course, those poor bastards in the Ordnance have it worse." I'm not about to rock the boat. Some noted that even the Maynes family wasn't immune to Kurian reprisals, citing several from the generation of my employer's parents who disappeared, never to be heard from again. After the massacre, it was as though we'd be better off if we thrashed the whole bunch off east, not stopping till we were neck-deep in the Atlantic.

News of the massacre spread quickly, and just as quickly, the Coal Country began to bite back. The reaction was so fast and so widespread, it could not have been ordered and organized by a formal movement, let alone other freeholds, which some have suggested.

Three days after Beckley, I swept caltrops out of the roadway approaching it and helped replace and patch tire after tire. Maynes could no longer park any of his cars and leave it unattended without a headlight being smashed or a tire punctured. Some of the pranks were disgustingly juvenile—food and drink brought to the White Palace had to be checked for pubic hairs and dog feces. Maynes family dogs and horses were poisoned.

Even Maynes began to take his security detail more seriously. Sometimes a second vehicle loaded with police led or followed our own, especially if we were going into the mountains.

The first train derailing happened within the week. Diesel engines had their air filters removed, coolant drained, and water—or perhaps urine—poured into their fuel tanks, requiring a major overhaul on the precious engines. Switches were rewired. Diesel oil stocks were sabotaged. Bridges were a special target: rails were loosened so that coal trains would derail on the bridge itself, terrifying the crew and causing damage to the bridges.

Man-hours that would have been better used elsewhere had to be put into making repairs and guarding vital rail installations. Trains had to travel through the Coal Country at a crawl so that sabotage might more easily be detected before an accident.

The Kurian Order might ignore the odd dead dog and flat tire, but derailed trains filled with coal bound for the Georgia Control woke the sleeping ogre. It did not take long for the first scapegoat to be bled.

Within a scarce few months, Beckley went from a regrettable incident to something the Kurian Order considered a minor disaster. The Coal Country refused to quiet down. The Kurian Order came down "soft"—issuing new rules about travel, curfews, changing identity card format so forgeries would be more difficult. It increased the protein, fat, and sugar rations for families with one or more members doing manual labor and did a purge of middle management, often a popular move. The disturbances continued.

Then the Kurian Order came down hard. Church-trained informants and agitators were inserted into some of the mines and rail installations—I overheard Maynes and MacTierney discussing the chances of the saboteurs being discovered—and a few arrests came about through their information.

It backfired, and badly. Popular opinion said that the informers simply hurled accusations to prove they were doing their jobs.

As it turned out, there was a sacrifice in the Maynes family: Joshua "Bone" Maynes's beloved sister, Elaine.

The next morning, as I slowly scraped food into my mouth from my tray in the staff cafeteria, I let my ears play this way and that. The White Palace was buzzing like a beehive opened by a bear.

While I slept, two churchmen, a matron, and four troopers had called on the White Palace with a summons for Elaine Maynes. She was ordered to appear for an examination into corruption and malfeasance somewhere outside the Coal Country. I was unable to find out what authority, exactly, ordered the removal, but it must have been either the Church or one of the security organs of the Georgia Control.

Needless to say, she was never seen in the cool halls of the White Palace again. A nephew of hers moved up and took over her job in distribution, and the Maynes Conglomerate moved on.

Maynes didn't travel that day, or the next. On the seventh day after her removal, Home brought me up to his room. It smelled like a ferret cage, and liquor bottles in various states of emptiness lined the dresser, floor, and tables, precisely spaced as though about to be toppled in a chain like dominoes.

We succeeded in dragging him into the shower. MacTierney scrubbed while I held him, with Home trying between shouts to force a little instant liquid breakfast into his mouth. I wanted to suggest using a funnel at one end or the other—I've been told that the sigmoid colon is capable of rudimentary digestion—but I held my tongue. Not for the last time.

With the loss of his sister, Maynes lost all interest in doing his duties. He affirmed—and increased—the punishments handed out, and word spread quickly that they no longer wished to appeal to the Bone.

When Maynes started prowling the roads as the vocational schools let out, surveying the girls heading home or to their paying jobs, MacTierney quit on him and asked for reassignment.

"I didn't sign up to chauffeur a pussy patrol," MacTierney told Home.

I became the official driver. Maynes, of course, would still ride in back, and Home would get out, show his security identification, gun, and the Maynes business card, and offer a ride home to whatever girl Maynes chose.

Word seemed to spread in that mysterious fashion of Coal Country, and within ten days or so, virtually no school-aged girls could be found walking along the roads. They took longer, less obvious routes or hitched rides hidden in delivery vehicles or other sanctioned transport. Maynes took to plunging into the larger towns where women selling themselves could be found, always hunting for the freshest-looking specimens he could find.

I sometimes found it difficult to maintain my composure as an indifferent nonhuman, and at night I would lie on my bedding—they still hadn't managed to find me a bed that fit—and argue with myself over just how much responsibility I bore for Maynes's depravities. The girls were physically mature enough, biologically speaking, and the live-in physician and nurse the Maynes family employed ensured he wasn't passing around diseases, but there is more to life than the physical being. The body heals much more easily than the mind and spirit.

I consoled myself that the locals were growing used to seeing me behind the wheel of a Maynes vehicle. At first, they pointed and nudged and gaped. Eventually this turned into shrugs from some and casual waves from others. This would make my escape easier, once the Coal Country folk grew accustomed to seeing me squeezed behind the wheel of one of the Maynes family transports. Soon, I'd be able to pass without remark.

If anything, Maynes's habits would help my escape. The locals no longer sought to flag him down as he drove through the towns, or to offer him a slice of Mrs. Whoever's famous rhubarb pie, seeking the powerful man's intercession on some family or business difficulty. Even the city constables and rural troopers, who formerly wanted Maynes to know their names and their faces, didn't want to approach close enough to catch a glimpse of what might be going on in the back of the bus.

At the White Palace, a new generation was eager to take charge and grew increasingly contemptuous of Maynes. We would pull around the house, and the family lot attendant and doorman did not exactly jump to attend to the Trekker and team Maynes. The vehicle was washed far less frequently as well. Sometimes I'd find profanities drawn into the dirt on the windows.

Before, there'd been talk of Maynes taking on a trip to Kentucky to visit one of the legworm clans friendlier to the Kurian Order and to set up a more-regular trade arrangement (I understood that the mine owners were clamoring for cheap, plentiful legworm flesh to feed their laborers, and legworm hides made durable and breathable work wear). Home and MacTierney had been talking about the challenges and opportunities of the trip, but all the talk had vanished along with Maynes's sister.

My thought was that they hoped some outraged father would get hold of a firearm or a vehicle big enough to cause a fatal collision with Bone's bus.

We'd leave well after everyone was up and working in the morning, drive to some town where Maynes would sign off on a change of management or a denial of appeal, and then we'd prowl the back streets looking for desperate women. Most had a sad story they wanted to tell someone in the Maynes clan, but Home would cut the talk off with some combination of threat or nasty joke: "Meat's supposed to be going into your mouth, not words coming out, sweetie."

They did pay. Sometimes Maynes even threw in bonus rations or appliance coupons that were supposed to be saved for the most productive workers in the Maynes Conglomerate. I expect word did get out now and then that the bonus washing machine that some shift foreman had sweated all year to earn ended up shoved into the bra of a prostitute.

So at night we'd return to the White Palace. Maynes and Home were often in the back, rattling around with the empties, drunk and swapping miseries or discussing the highlights of their latest sexual conquest like athletes relaxing in the locker room post-match. I'd never been so grateful that I was expected to stay up front and watch the road.

"Bet that old whore could have taken Hickory," Home said.

Maynes sucked down the backwash of a beer and dropped the empty. "Wouldn't mind seeing that. Her eyes popped just a little at every stroke. Bet they'd bug out with him."

"Never seems interested in human women," Home said. "I heard in Chicago they got a Grog show. So some of them must know what to do."

"Coal Country girls probably not hairy enough. We should try Jersey."

"That or he's as queer as he is big."

"Maybe he's a eunuch. There was talk of fixing him if he got into fights with the others, but he's been quiet."

When thinking over my anecdotes of my time in the White Palace, few of them are humorous. There has to be a certain amount of re-laxation and camaraderie for humor to take root, and for me, the White Palace held neither. Living in the stables no doubt cut me off from many routines and friendships that might have developed. This was just as well, because I might have had to do some harm in engineering my eventual escape.

Embarrassing moments may be funny, and my most embarrassing one came shortly after the lecture at the Youth Vanguard College. It was shortly after the presentation to the Youth Vanguard that someone on high decided to get a reproductive semen sample from me. So I was returned to the vet with the nervous ticks. This time, he had a young woman assisting him. She had the look of someone who spent a lot of time outdoors.

I have spent enough time around cattle and horses to know as soon as I saw the rack of test tubes and the artificial cow vagina what was expected of me.

"We have to get a semen sample out of him. Orders from on high," the vet said.

"How do we do that?"

"That's why I brought you in. Don't you handle that at the stud farm?"

"With horses, yes. I don't know anything about stoops."

"I'm more of an ear mite and broken-bone man myself. They say he's gentle with women."

"I'm sure he is, right up until when I grab his kickstand. Then he'll toss me through the window. It would help to have a female in estrus, don't you know that?"

"Not to be had with his species. You'll have to serve."

"What?"

"I have it on good authority that Grogs aren't that discriminating. One of the Maynes boys told me about a show in Chicago he saw—"

"I am not about to do a bump and grind for a Grog, if that's what you're getting at."

I felt sorry for her and had sympathy for the vet. Orders had come down. . . .

The vet smeared some kind of clear jelly on his rubber glove and approached me from behind the cart with the loaf-sized artificial vagina. I noticed it had a little tap in it, like a hot-water bottle. I hoped they'd had enough sense to fill it with warm water rather than cold—or worse, hot.

"Don't worry, sport."

"Hick-ree," I said.

"Oh yes, Hickory, that's what they call you, isn't it? Don't worry, Hickory. This won't hurt a bit."

It occurred to me that I could wreck the office as soon as they touched me, but that wouldn't fit in with the helpful and enthusiastic persona I used in my White Palace duties.

"Can't you just send him into a bathroom with some pictures of a bunch of shaved female Grogs?" the woman said.

"While I wouldn't doubt such things exist, I have no idea how to obtain them," the vet said.

I can growl deep in my throat. The sound doesn't carry very far, but if you are close enough to hear it, I understand it sounds menacing to a human.

The vet looked up at me.

"I told you. A woman is needed."

She approached me and gave a becoming smile. "We both could use a couple beers to loosen us up, I think."

I let her touch me, apply the gelatin, and did my best to indicate complacency by yawning.

The woman sighed. "You know, when they said I was needed at the White Palace, I had another kind of day pictured entirely. Maybe something involving a nice lunch?"

At least they had remembered to put warm water in the artificial vagina. She began to work the tube on me in the time-honored fashion.

"You know, he's supposed to thrust into this. Bounce it around too much and we'll lose the test tube," she said. She smiled and blushed a little.

There are women—very few, but they know where to go for it—who enjoy our kind as sexual partners as a kinky thrill. And I have heard of human males copulating with Grog females—I believe it was an initiating rite for the men training to be officers of Grog units at the KZ War College in Jackson. There are men who enjoy seeing women, their own partners, even. It's odd to be a living fetish totem. This woman didn't seem the type; perhaps she was noting details for relating the story to friends when she returned to her horse farm.

I did my best to get the procedure over with as quickly as possible. It was a relief in several ways when she removed the apparatus.

"Okay, we got . . . Shit. We should have used a bigger test tube."

"Just drain the excess out of the AV."

"Hick-ree done now?"

"Yes, all done. Here."

He presented me with a little tray containing some pseudo-chocolate cookies and juice, as if I were a little boy who'd just returned from school.

"I think you have him confused with a blood donor. He probably wants a cig and a Reboot.*"

"He likes sweets. Given the size difference between us, I want to stay on the best possible terms with this particular patient."

I slowly ate the nearly tasteless cookies and drank the juice. The juice, at least, was delicious. The sweetness took the edge off the embarrassment. A little.

---

* A post-coital recovery drink aimed at men.

TINDER

A heat wave struck at the beginning of September that had all of Coal Country angry and sweltering. Perhaps because no one could sleep, resistance to the regime became even more open. Troopers were having their tires punctured in the time it took them to stop for a meal; a New Universal Church cathedral in Charleston had its bell tower dynamited and a good part of the roof blown off. Or perhaps it wasn't solely the heat; the Maynes Mining Holdings suffered a rash of underground breakdowns. It was plenty cool in those deep tunnels, as I was soon to learn.

Maynes had pulled over behind some truck traffic at a rail intersection where a landslide had blocked both track and road to find out from some loitering troopers whether the blockage was sabotage or weather related—extreme heat and cold did enough damage to the rocky cuts that it wasn't necessarily the work of the nascent resistance.

The trucks eventually gave up and turned around to find an alternate route. Maynes stayed. Some of his old supervisory flair returned as he worked the radio to get more labor transported to help clear the slide.

"Good thing we're set up for an overnight," Home said, checking the liquor cabinet.

"It'll be a lonely night with just the two of us," Maynes said. I was rarely counted as one of the party.

"I could walk back to the crossroads," Home offered. "Maybe there's a girl at that checkpoint coffee stand. . . ."

"More likely a former trooper with a bad knee," Maynes said. "Checkpoints are plum jobs for line-of-duty injuries. Won't kill us to be bored one night. Where's that deck of cards?"

"The nekkid one's in the glove compartment. The regular deck's over the sink," Home said.

"Maybe the regular deck."

Twilight came, and they broke out some cheese and nuts and crackers Maynes kept for refreshment. One of the troopers made a run for sandwiches (and incidentally confirmed that the crossroads checkpoint a mile back was run by a one-eyed ex-trooper, male). I stretched out on the roof of the Trekker. The bugs did not bother me very much once I wrapped a repellent-spritzed bandanna around my ears.

I did not rest easy. I had the feeling that we were being watched. I wondered if the Resistance might be sighting on me with a rifle. While an ironic end at the trigger finger of a Coal Country sniper had a certain macabre appeal—I'd shot my share of human Quis-lings from a distance during the siege atop Big Rock Hill and in other encounters—I decided it was in my interest to relocate. I left the roof and managed to squeeze under the high-clearance Trekker. I also took a tire iron to my resting place with me.

"What's the matter, Hickory?" Home asked as I wiggled beneath the bus.

"Cooler down under," I said.

A half-awake part of me registered that Home had stepped out of the Trekker to relieve himself at the roadside. I noted the sounds of picks and shovels in the distance at the slide. More labor must have arrived sometime after I took cover beneath the Trekker.

I heard a quick but heavy step behind him and startled. I saw a curious pair of human boots—they were brown, in the style that was sometimes called the "Thousand Milers," and they resembled a big, heavy, and high oxford shoe. Old Smoke, the frequent companion of David Valentine and me, had once owned a nice pair she'd taken off a dead Quisling. For a moment I thrilled at the thought that it might be her, but the pair was far too large for the petite Cat.

I dared move just enough to get a view and saw a tall figure in a long coat, sort of a cross between a trench coat and a ghillie suit, reach for Home. It picked him up by the ears and spun around.

It was a Reaper. A little light thrown off by the Trekker reflected off its face, giving it the color of bone china.

"call your boss out," it said.

The Reaper pressed the hands holding Home's skull ever more tightly together.

"i would have a word with you, maynes."

"Help!" screamed Home. His face was either bright red or purplish; it was hard to tell in the low light leaking from the van.

"You could have just knocked," Maynes said. "Home is ugly enough without oversized ears; maybe you can let him go."

I had to give Maynes grudging respect. Most men go meek when conversing with a Reaper. He was his old sardonic self.

The Reaper adjusted its grip. It pressed either side of Home's head. Its fingers tapped his eyes, as if to ascertain whether the pressure applied to the skull caused them to bulge.

I tested the point of my tire iron. If I was quick enough, I could come out from under the bus ready to fight. I might even be able to shove the tire iron into something vital around the jaw and crack it off. The claws would still be dangerous, and Reapers were notoriously hard to bleed out, but pain sometimes dampened communication between Reaper and Master Kurian.

"Bubbbbbbb!" Home managed through locked-together jaws.

"I met a salesman once," Maynes said. "On the road. He tried to sell me batteries. A dog kept sniffing around at his shoes. He got tired of it and kicked the dog to drive it away. What he didn't know was it was my dog. I didn't buy any batteries. How about you drop my bodyguard? I might listen a little more carefully to your message if you do so."

"or i could kill him and we could converse over his silenced corpse."

"Let him go," Maynes said. Then, after a moment's thought, he added, "Please."

The Reaper dropped Home. His head was mottled red and sallow yellow, depending on where the Reaper's fingers had pressed.

"Ohhhhhhh," Home moaned. "Ooooooooh, hurts, hurts."

The Reaper silenced him with a kick. I found this odd; from what I'd seen, the Reapers, once settled on letting someone go, gave them no more thought than a cat giving up on a mouse hole. They bore humans no more personal animosity than the axe does the tree.

"just because you happen to bear the name maynes does not grant you immunity from managed selection," the Reaper said.

I'd heard it called many things, but "managed selection" was new to me. It seemed rather clinical for the Coal Country, where just about every human activity and interaction had a localism attached.

Maynes let out a drunken-sounding laugh. "You just take me, if you really think that. The family's already stirred up."

The Reaper stepped forward. From my hiding spot, I could not see Maynes's reaction to the approach, but I didn't hear any movement in the bus above.

"you are to cease your disgusting depredations and leave the girls alone. it's long since time you took a wife and produced a new generation. alley catting is one thing for a twenty-year-old; at forty it is pathetic. a marriage will be arranged."

"Tell 'em I want pearled stephanotis for my bouquet," Maynes said.

"what did your poet say? 'what a piece of work is man.' we gave you an easy assignment. no office routine, no discipline of being on or off the clock. still, you cannot manage even the few decisions a week required of you."

I saw Maynes's feet appear. He had sat down on the entry steps to the bus. "You want to be in charge? You do all the work. I'd like to see you come crawling into the office every day, leaving a little snail-trail for the janitor."

"parasites, all. worse, necrotics, living off the work of your grandfather. there was a time when the maynes clan was thought to be destined to control the east between the pittsburgh mills and pamlico sound. the work of a lifetime, squandered."

"Then you should have made Elaine director-general of Maynes Consolidated rather than Uncle H.B. She was smarter than the rest of us put together."

"perhaps. but we had doubts about her loyalty. she produced no children. she should have put her womb to work rather than her mind. consider this your final warning. there will be a purge. we are warning you because you have shown, in the past, some skill at handling the human population. after the purge, when they have seen the maynes clan cut down to size, we believe things will settle down and this pointless violence will subside. we expect you to dispense with frivolities and put the coal country back together when the unpleasantness is over. if you fail, we will remove the maynes clan in its entirety and turn the coal country over to someone more efficient in its management."

The Reaper stepped on Home's back as it went off down the road away from the sounds of the slide being cleared. I heard two ribs snap.

"You can come out now, Hickory," Maynes said. "The big bad wolf is gone. Help me with Home; then we're off to the Church's hospital in Charleston."

If I have a regret about my first months in the Coal Country, it's that I didn't take the chance and put a tire iron through that Reaper's hardened skull. Home and Maynes might have panicked enough to escape to Kentucky—it was near enough, and no one would deny Maynes the gasoline or checkpoint transits he would have needed to make a daylight run across the mountains and into the rough and semi-independent lands of the legworm ranchers.

PURGE AT THE WHITE PALACE

I never learned if Maynes warned the rest of his family what was coming. I overheard that one or two fled, but they may have sensed what was about to happen or received the information from another source.

They came at night, in a long line of cars and vans with their headlights turned off. I watched them approach, their vehicles moving along the carefully landscaped lane to the White Palace at the speed of a trotting dog. It was a humid night, so moist the moon and many of the security lights had visible halos.

I considered it a provident time to attempt an escape. I'd prepared myself ever since the encounter with the messenger-Reaper. I wouldn't be the only one fleeing the White Palace, but perhaps I would be the only one physically and mentally prepared for an escape and a few days of rough living, with equipment to extend survival if I needed to.

Of course, a picturesque notch between the two great old national forests was a poor place to set off from, if I intended to go west. The entirety of the Coal Country would have to be crossed before I approached Kentucky and the western slopes of the Appalachians.

I rested my pack on the doorjamb to the barn basement and looked out at the well-tended grounds of the White Palace.

I looked back on the elegant white mass, all its floors of rooms, some with lights still burning, with its murmur of activity even in the earliest predawn hours—this was no pit of evil. There were many good men and women just trying to keep their poor little corner of the world intact and out of more grasping hands.

A party started to cut across the lawn, heading for some parked electric carts. There were firemen, a couple of men in the navy blue of the Maynes family security service, and two Reapers, one at the very front, one bringing up the rear.

"I said mistake," a woman said, kicking at her escort. "Talk to my brothers. There must be a way—"

One of the firemen chuckled. "Don't worry, honey. You'll be buried in the family cemetery just under your pa."

"We own this whole goddamn valley. You can't do this!"

"Guess you were too young to remember your folks being taken away. You remember the night your aunt Sinthee was taken away? You bet it can happen to you."

"The Old Man's mad about how things went down in Beckley."

"Then get the fire chief in handcuffs. I've got nothing to do with security."

"Your production and disposition people screwed up on the cookware. That was what started the riot."

The Kurians were taking a gamble with this purge. The Maynes clan had weapons, command of its own security forces, a communications network; if, somehow, the revolt could spread with its assistance, the world might be astonished at what this flinty patch of earth might mean to the future.

The Kurians were being careful in their culling, however. Had they removed the Maynes clan in its entirety, the plan might have worked. But the Kurians wanted the management network that was represented by the White Palace. In my opinion they thought they would be crushing two snakes with one heel—they would cull so heavily from the Maynes family that the rump portion left would be shocked into meek obedience, and the Coal Country population would see their aristocracy pay heavily for the bloodshed that started at Beckley.

Now they were bringing lines of people, handcuffed or tied together in a sort of daisy chain, and marching them into the hills. I wondered if I should follow. It would be an escape route few would choose, and perhaps the world would need a witness someday to what went on up there.

I saw my employer stagger out of one of the back entrances of the White Palace, wearing pajama bottoms and a sport coat thrown over his bare torso. He had blood splashed on him.

"Aunt Pen escaped you, you numbnuts. Slashed her wrists, soon as she saw the motorcade coming. Poor old Aunt Pen," Maynes said to an officer brandishing a pistol.

"Oh God, oh God, oh God," a woman cried, tied to a teenage girl in front and an elderly man behind. The youngster was clinging closer to her than any knot could achieve.

"'For days of auld lang syne, my dears,'" Maynes sang. Perhaps he didn't care. He seemed drunk enough.

A man whom I knew only as one of the senior sergeants in the White Palace security office approached me. "You'd better look after your man," he said, pointing at Maynes. "Quick-quick. Take him into his room or the barn—anywhere but the back door—and sit on him for a couple of hours."

I put my heels together and gave a knuckle-to-forehead salute. "Yes, sir."

Maynes had sat down to watch the people being dragged out. The first soldiers were already returning from the ridgeline with empty handcuffs and cordage. I recognized Georgia Control insignia. Evidently the principal customer of the Coal Country's product was behind this purge.

I picked him up. "Pickers. My whole family. Bunch of pickers. You stoops keep family? What happens when you get mad—you eat 'em?"

"No family," I said, able to tell the truth for once.

"Telling me how to run this country. Why the hell should they care, as long as the coal keeps moving and we toss 'em a StR* once in a while? I bet the old man went along with this. I'm on the road all the time. I log more hours than the rest of the family put together."

"We work now?" I asked, seeing a glimmer of a chance. I was ready to risk anything rather than endure the sound of one more family extracted from the White Palace. Why didn't the Order tell them they were being relocated and put them on a bus? Everyone would know it was a lie, but the trappings of normalcy made the transition easier.

Maynes shrugged. "Yeah, why the hell not? See what's on the trouble sheet."

I supported him in a walk through the crunchy late-summer grass and back into the White Palace.

He had an office in what used to be the catering sales center

---

* Surplus to Requirements, i.e., someone culled for consumption by the Kurians.

when the White Palace had been a resort hotel. A few shots showing the history of the resort featuring polished-looking brides and relaxed golfers always seemed like something out of another world. Especially tonight. A single gunshot echoed from a floor or two above.

"That's the ticket," Maynes yelled at the roof. "Don't give 'em the satisfaction!"

Finding anything in Maynes's office at this time could be compared to digging a buckle out of the Augean stables. He had a beautiful desk and hutch combination, bird's-eye maple with burls in the delicate strokes of a Chinese watercolor. Such a pity it lay under a layer of greasy paper plates, empty bottles, and an orgy of copulating binders filled with dog-eared, yellowing paper.

Maynes couldn't locate his clipboard with personnel matters requiring his attention, or he had forgotten why he had returned to his office in the first place. I subtly called attention to it by knocking it on the floor with my elbow.

He was rooting around in the liquor cabinet, sadly.

He extracted a gun, a heavy-framed revolver, and a holster and put them on. After a moment's thought, he also took a box of ammunition.

"That'd be funny if I came to it and forgot the bullets!"

Given my employer's sense of humor, "funny" could mean about anything, but at the back of my mind there was the idea of suicide. At least he didn't attempt to load the gun. A little more alcohol and he might not be able to fit a bullet into the cylinder.

"He's in no condition to—"

My footing slipped and I almost dropped Maynes. As I shifted my grip, my elbow rose, regrettably catching the nighttime security man under the chin. His teeth met with a clack like a window shutter slamming. His eyes rolled over in their sockets and he folded at the knees.

"Whaddya think you're doing, Mr. Maynes?" one of the White Palace security staff said. "Shouldn't you be in bed?"

"He should be out in the quarry with the rest of them," another put in. "Damn pervert."

"I'm working," Maynes slurred. "Working harder than you pickers, anyway."

We made it to the Trekker. There were two men in charge of the lot. One of them spoke on a radio and waved me over to the bus. I was following orders after all, getting Maynes out of the way.

I pulled out of the lot. I passed the lined-up Georgia Control security vehicles pulled half off the approaches to the White Palace, sleeping wolves ready to be roused for pursuit, and took what I hoped would be my last look at the White Palace. It looked dingy in the moonlight. I wondered if the new, reduced Maynes clan would bother to keep the windows and paint trim so bright and fresh.

Maynes fell asleep for a while in the back of the Trekker. I consulted a map and the latest information I could find about the roads over the Appalachians. We gassed up on the Maynes account, and I filled thirty more gallons' worth in extra cans just in case.

I had logged forty-odd miles of westward crawling, the speedometer falling exasperatingly lower and lower as the roads grew narrower and worse. We were approaching the western borders of Coal Country when Maynes awoke. He visited the inboard toilet, then joined me up by the driver's semi-enclosure.

"Hey, Hick, when do we get there?"

"Many hours yet."

Maynes yawned. He took a big swig from a three-quarters empty bottle that had been nearly full in his office. "That's too bad. Where are we going?"

"You told me—go east. Straight for Ken-tuck."

"So I did." Maynes blinked blearily and rubbed his eyes. "Goddamn right. Let's go west, old Grog." He chuckled. "West! West! West! Not fast enough! You're relieved, old cock."

Maynes took the wheel.

"Think again, picker," Maynes yelled at the windshield.

My life seemed to be repeating itself, the first time as tragedy, and this time as a farce. I braced for impact.

Maynes, addled by alcohol, crashed through the checkpoint when all he would have had to do was show his ID on the off chance the troopers wouldn't recognize him at once. But fate had not placed me in the employ of a man who could drink and be rational at the same time.

The reinforced front of the Trekker struck the Trooper car hard enough to spin it one hundred eighty degrees.

It was an appropriate end for Joshua Maynes the Third, I suppose. He looked as though he were trying to perform a sex act on the steering column of the Trekker. He was still alive.

Good Grog that I was, I'd certainly try to go for help, especially since the radio had been destroyed in the accident. Or that was how I made it look, since it wasn't a portable model.

Two miles west something flashed across the road. At first I thought it was a bounding albino deer.

I did not get a good look at the death. My impression was that of a stumbling, pale figure running through the woods. A ragged, ever-shifting arc of men and women armed with various weapons, from revolvers to assault rifles, pausing to fire or reload, then moving again to keep the quarry in sight.

It turned its face only once. It was slight, clearly a youngish Reaper, as these things are reckoned. Its pale face had been wounded at the outer edge of the jaw; naked bone could be seen with black tar clinging around the wound—Reaper blood goes gummy and as black as an old human scab almost instantly. The yellow eyes were wide with fear and I felt empathy for it. It had probably been penned most of its life, fed old dogs and cats or rabbits, emotionally at a four- or five-year-old's level—and that was a four- or five-year-old woefully mistreated by everyone it knew.

I had seen "wild" Reapers in action before—on the other side of the river from Little Rock, during the siege of Big Rock Hill. Our enemies dropped them as a disruptive and sapping force during a larger attack. The death of a Kurian would also, I understand, turn its Reapers loose.

It would break through someone's bedroom window and snatch a child, or slaughter a whole family down to the last bird dog. To see such a menace running around loose and not do anything about it would be a dreadful betrayal of what I believed. The lesser sins I'd committed for my own survival as Maynes's bodyguard I felt I could answer for, but to leave this thing wandering the hills—

I checked the heavy old revolver in its holster and followed.

I lost sight of it frequently, but could still track it with my ears. It made enough noise in its frantic flight—so frantic that it frequently struck trees with a thwack.

The ground rose more steeply and I had to choose my path carefully. The Reaper seemed to be choosing an easier, longer route up the ridgeline. I saw my chance.

Using all fours, I swarmed up the steeper hillside at the fastest pace I could manage, the famous Grog charge-gallop that's so often depicted in paintings of skirmishes in the late Liberation.

Though I evidently beat it to the limestone-scarred, wooded top, I lost sight and sound of it. After a few moments of looking and waiting, I made my best guess of the path it was taking and descended. Though the woods on the slope were dense, there was a fair amount of moonlight, and I should have been able to pick out a light-colored figure.

Had it found a cave or hollow tree to crawl into?

I unholstered the heavy revolver and descended carefully, searching for a hiding spot, eyes following the front sight of the pistol.

I had an answer delivered to my neck and shoulder. It had been hiding in one of the trees—I hadn't looked high enough, I suppose, and Reapers are nothing if not slender—and leaped down upon me like a hunting cat.

The wrestling match was short and furious. I had a painful tearing sensation to my shoulder and felt hot blood upon me. I tried to pin the beast with one hand, but it was like wrestling with a fire escape that had fallen atop me. Feeling a sharp stab at my hairline, I instinctively reached up as you might to swat a biting fly. I found myself with a handful of tongue and yanked, hard.

The Reaper came loose with its tongue, and I swung it against a tree trunk hard enough to make it rain acorns as I felt around for the pistol with my hurting arm. It staggered, stunned. I managed to pick up the gun, found the trigger, and emptied three chambers into it at negligible range.

The impact of the bullets knocked it into the tree three times. I managed to get my fingers locked around its throat, braced its stomach with my leg, and yanked hard enough to haul in one of the Gulf marlins we used to fish for off the well deck of the old *Thunderbolt*. Its neck popped and I shook it, lashing it against rocks and listening to cartilage and bones snapping.

Finally, it lay still.

I had wrecked both the young Reaper and my chances for escape. My shoulder hurt every time I moved my arm, and I had blood running from wounds around my neck. I did my best to stanch the flow, but because of their position, I couldn't get a good look at the wounds to do much about them other than apply pressure with my good arm.

Baying hounds sounded in the distance and I saw the flicker of a flashlight between the trees.

Dogs, and I was dribbling blood. They'd find me eventually.

I let loose with my loudest call. I waved my arms. I capered and kicked up leaves and groundfall, which served to mess up the area and hide where I placed my escape gear and supplies. The commotion drove a pair of bitterns from the fen. The two boomed out their anger as they left.

The dogs looked a good deal happier to see me than the men, identified by the badges and hats as local constabulary. They did a good deal of pointing and pantomime until I convinced them that I wasn't just using words in the manner of a parrot.

I did my best to act cheerfully when they sat me in the back of the van and told me to ride, as if I were a lost dog glad to leap into the family car.

They drove me back to the White Palace. The summer sun striking the brilliant white glared so brightly, it hurt my eyes to look. I tried not to become too relieved; this might be the soothing moment of relief before the shock of a surprise interrogation.

As it turned out, I retraced my original steps through the staff entrance.

The presence of the vet made me nervous. I supposed at the time I might be euthanized like a horse, but I steeled myself to take a few of them with me—sparing the vet, who'd been nothing but kind each time he'd attended to me.

I had a deep puncture from the Reaper's tongue, tooth marks that had to be closed with surgical staples, a separated shoulder, some minor scrapes and contusions. All were taken care of with cleanliness and efficiency by the vet and his assistant. They were both uneasy and snapped at each other as they worked. Changes in the power structure often brought that out from those in the middle of the Kurian/human hierarchy.

The staff director came in and muttered something about the big Grog being back. He scratched at his chin, pulling a phantom goatee. I'd never thought of it until that moment, but all the staff members at the White Palace were clean-shaven. Requirement? Tradition?

"Well, Groggie, your charge won't be needing you anymore." Satisfaction with the assessment poured out of him like syrup.

"Mr. Maynes is dead?"

"Might as well be. His brain isn't up to much except keeping his heart beating and lungs working. Docs say it's a deep coma and he'll deteriorate. They might as well prop him up in the topiary between the palms."

"I see him soon?"

"Fix that broken badminton net with him, for all I care."

"Enough of that," the vet said. "I don't want talk like that getting back to Scrappy. He takes after his great-grandfather a bit much."

"I'd rather worry about it getting back to the Old Man," the staff director said.

"Don't tell me you believe that story about his body not being in the family crypt," the vet said. "Rig on the gardening staff says he's seen it personally."

"Rig's never been inside the crypt. Nor anyone else on the staff, unless you count . . . well, himself."

While this conversation interested me, my helpful Grog persona would concentrate on where his next mug of root beer might be coming from. "Who I work for now?" I asked.

"You're due for some R & R," the staff director said. "I wouldn't put too much trust in Rig. Damn drunk."

"You'd be a drunk too if you found bodies like he does when you're mowing the golf course and raking sand. They aren't too particular about what they do with the bodies after they've been drained."

The nurse hurried out with her tray of bloody gauze.

"Enough of that horror talk. How's the big boy's health? Can he handle hard labor?"

"Send him to the mines. They always need strong backs," the vet said.

"To a point," the staff director said. "He's kind of big. They won't much like feeding all that."

"He can eat the other miners for all I care. I'm tired of smelling wet Grog in the morning."

PART TWO

THE BLACK CURRENCY

THE LAST STOP

I was an oddly sized part passing through the gears of the Maynes Empire. Had I been a man, they probably would have made me a security guard at a warehouse or fuel depot and made me work my way up from a clean slate. After all, my drunken superior had given me orders, and I hadn't been clever enough to figure out a way of not following them.

As I possessed a strong back, the default was to send me to the mines.

Why do I use the word default? I fought alongside an ex-Quisling who taught me the term, as he saw it. His name was Post, and we'd first met on the Louisiana coast when I served with a Grog labor detachment I had infiltrated. At the time, he was a prematurely aging lieutenant and heavy drinker. Much later, after he'd switched sides, he would sometimes talk about surviving in the Kurian Order. While these aren't his exact words—my memory is not good enough to recall those without notes—they are faithful to his view.

"You never wanted the system to 'default' when making a choice about you. It started in childhood. The default was to get almost no education at all, just a few years of primary painting horrible pictures about the pre-Kurian past, terrifying propaganda about the guerillas, and reverence for the system and what it was trying to do for mankind. If you defaulted there, you usually ended up apprenticing at eight or eleven to resource work—farming or logging or fishing if you were male; most females ended up diapering or cleaning.

"So the more default settings you avoid, the better an education you can get. Youth Vanguard helps a lot, of course, but in some KZs, only Quisling kids make it in. Funny how geniture aristocracy grows in any society like a weed.

"Then when you're working, the default is to keep you at whatever job you started, have you get married, and have you be a member of the same church, in the same town, with the same neighbors, until you fear change more than you fear them. Then, once you're older and have had all the children you're likely to have, slowing down a bit and not so much able to put in the fifty-five-hour weeks, the default setting of the Order comes with teeth and yellow eyes.

"The Order's default is always to keep you in whatever little sorting tray where you were first placed, like one of those puzzles kids get where they have to put the moon in the moon slot and the hexagon in the hex slot. It takes a mighty effort to make it out of one of those slots. That's why you find so many of the more driven types on the fringes of the Kurian Order, where there's room to widen the slots so they fit in a lot of different ways."

Will Post was a pretty good man even when he was a drunk. Once he came over to the free territories, he became a better one. Sadly, he was badly injured in an air raid near Dallas, and at the time of this memoir had headquarters desk duty from a wheelchair.

In the Coal Country, the default was ore work in one form or another, either extracting it, transporting it, or keeping the men and machines doing those two other tasks running.

So some men in the White Palace security uniforms explained to me, like a teacher with a problem child, that I'd be living somewhere else for a while and working with train carts and shovels.

"Yes, work hard!"

"Good! Work hard, and you'll get honey doughnuts and chocolate."

The honey doughnuts weren't bad; in fact they were tastier than the service pastries I'd had with Southern Command, but the chocolate they sold in the ordinary stores was crumbly, bitter stuff that tasted like chalk.

They escorted me to a bus shelter and the low man on the roster waited with me until a rather dirty bus wheezed up the hill toward the White Palace. I'd encountered coal dust before; it was hard to spend much time in this Kurian Zone without being acquainted with it here and there, but this was the first time it looked like no effort had been made to rid either the exterior or interior of it.

I risked a quick glance at the sign above the missing entry door.

ALL CONSOLIDATED MINES AND LIVING CAMPUS

"Make sure he gets off at Number Four," my escort said.

"Poor bastard," said the driver. He looked like he should be standing beside the road with his thumb out rather than at the wheel. "No luggage?"

I held up my bag.

"You're a regular genie-us," the driver said. "What you throwing him in the hole for?"

"Not my decision."

"Hey, buddy, do me a favor. Talk to your boss about getting me out of this pickle-chiller and getting me chauffeur work. I've kept this thing out of the potholes, so I should be able to take one of the Maynes family to the golf course and back. Do that and I'll make sure he's properly ear-tagged at Number Four."

My ears flicked involuntarily back.

"You firearm qualified?"

"It's in the works. The vetting's done and my picture's turned in."

My escort smiled and raised his chin, a duke getting ready to grant a favor to a peasant while looking down his nose at the request. "Sure, pal. Write down your name and locator number."

The driver extracted an old envelope and carefully spelled out his name in block capitals and added a nine-digit series of letters and numbers, tongue poking at the side of his mouth in concentration. He handed it over. "Don't forget me now."

"Whether I forget or not depends on the big boy arriving."

The other passengers—spouses of miners by the look of them, a couple carrying babies in baskets—didn't seem to object to the driver taking his time with the security man.

The driver indicated that I should sit all the way at the back of the bus. He opened a box under his seat and took out a length of heavy dog chain. He proceeded to belt me into my seat by throwing a figure eight of chain around my chest, then fastening it with a keyed padlock.

I accepted the chains and made a show of sniffing his hands as he checked the lock.

"Hope you went potty before you got on my bus," he said.

As we pulled away, my escort made a great show of pocketing the envelope with the driver's name. When the White Palace was out of sight, I spent a few moments reading the advertising running above the windows of the bus. There was a shiny new placard exhorting the reader to REPORT SABOTAGE! and featuring some steely, feminine eyes looking out of the darkness. An older paper advertised a new fertility enhancer and aphrodisiac:

Increases desire! Enhances pleasure! Assures result!— three effects in just ONE DOSE!

A disclaimer beneath counseled those interested in becoming pregnant to check with their New Universal Church family coordinator to determine the best time for procreative activity.

The oldest and most dilapidated one was for that staple of budget-cutting cooks and food service pros looking for a cheap dish that, with a bit of English on the verbal cue ball, could be called meat: WHAM!—"PURE, POWER-PACKED PROTEIN."

NOW IN EXTRA BOLD MESQUITE

The new packaging was red, white, and green. Same great price!

Same big bug, I thought to myself. I was told by the legworm ranchers, who usually just ate the fleshier, lobster-like meat running down the millipede-like claws, that everything save the hide from a legworm went into a wood-chipper about the dimensions of a missile silo, and came out the other end as gooey pink foam. I'm thankful I've never seen the process from beginning to end, because over the years I've eaten enough cans of the stuff to fill a trailer.

We bounced over the bottom land roads, stopped at a yawning strip mine that looked as though one of the Coal Country Mountains had been extracted like a dentist pulling a tooth, then puttered through a small redeveloped town called Gardenia. The driver lost all his other passengers there, and it was just the two of us bouncing up a crudely patched road that was an amalgam of asphalt and gravel running beside a set of rail and power lines.

He hadn't lied about his skill in avoiding potholes, but this road defeated him. Every few minutes the bus gave a bang-lurch-curse-from-the-driver combination that felt and sounded as though he'd run over a motorcyclist.

We pulled up in front of some brick buildings that looked as though they might have once been an industrial garage and what had clearly been a motel next to a bridge over a small river. The rail line divided here, with the less-used tracks and the power line running up the mountainside.

"Number Four. This is you, big boy. Thanks for not shitting up my back bench."

I looped a finger in his key lock and gave it a good pull. The padlock gave a brief, musical *ting!* as it fell to pieces and I extracted myself from the chains.

"Thank you for ride," I said.

"Hey, that lock cost me four dollars!"

A trio of men holding their ID cards and travel tickets waited at the bus kiosk. An impressive mound of garbage lay in the ravine between the former garage and motel, waiting for the end of days or the next convict-scooper garbage train, whichever would come first.

Leaving so soon? someone had scrawled in permanent marker on the wall of the shelter. *Lucky bastard,* someone else had added in a different hand of slightly smaller letters.

I noticed that one part of the roof of the hotel had a blue plastic sheet covering a hole, held down by what looked like some old manholes.

"Be a minute, fellas," the driver said. He took me to a little corner office of the garage with coal-dusted windows that looked out at the motel. A flower box with a surprisingly robust set of yellow flowers next to the door added a cheerful note to the general sense of quiet entropy.

"Got a new worker for you, Murphy," the driver said. "A Grog. Taller and hairier than most."

A man the general shape and specific color of a fireplug extracted a cigar plug from his mouth and set it carefully on a stained corner of his aluminum desk. He'd been gripping it dead center in his mouth, like a baby's pacifier.

A fleshy girl with eyeglasses rather creatively laced with wire peeked through the doorway of the office's back room. "Hoo-boys, he'll go through the groceries," she said.

"Fuck me," Murphy said. "How many times do I have to tell 'em, Grogs are more trouble than they're worth."

"This one's smart," the driver said. "He talks. Anyway, he's your problem now. I'm due back northeast."

"Look, you want to get along in your lodgings, helps to grease old uncle Murphy. Cat-piss 'grease,' you ape?"

"Grease. Like for cook?" I asked. It still astonishes me, how little evidence the Coal Country apparatchiks needed to think me a half-wit. Even the Gray Ones are clever within the limits of their own tribal civilization, and frequently fought more numerous and better-equipped professional armies to a standstill. If primitive means not being able to lie to yourself properly about the world you live in, then I suppose I am a primitive.

"It does help me pay the market tab. Grease. Yeah, you give me some of what you make; I give you nice things. Good old American business relationship. Understand?"

"Like nice things, honey-buns."

"He called you 'honey-buns,'" the office help laughed. She had a fruity smell about her that reminded me of some chewing gum I'd had at Xanadu.

"Never heard a stoop talk so good," Murphy said. "'Most good as us."

The workers were housed on a campus of buildings that can best be described as tenement quality. The main building was an old, two-story motel. Everyone ate at the cafeteria, an old family restaurant that now ran twenty-four hours—more or less—to accommodate the shifts at the mine.

I've overnighted in swamps that were cleaner. The infestation of biting bugs and cockroaches had to be experienced; words aren't sufficient. It smelled of clogged toilets and kerosene, and even the ceilings were grimy.

The coal dust was to blame. The miners had showers at Number

Four, but they ran only water, cold straight from the well, so only a few bathed there. The rest waited to get home to clean up. But during the wait for the next availability of hot water in the rickety system, they distributed a good deal of black grit.

So their washrooms were filthy with coal dust. With the washrooms black as sin, no one felt it necessary to keep the kitchen spotless, so grease and dropped food accumulated in the omnipresent black dust, attracting vermin. With the rats and cockroaches roaming the kitchen, what was the point of keeping bed linens fresh?

They put me in a clapboard warren of rooms without even a sink or cooking stove.

"Spacious, this. You'll need it," the "housing facilitator" told me.

They found two metal-framed single beds and pushed them together, then tied them with wire. A mattress of shredded couch cushions sewn into heavy canvas did not quite cover the bed's suspension, which bowed into a hammock shape if I did not sleep with my torso uncomfortably across the bar in the center.

I had to take water from a floor tap designed for a hose just outside my "window"—blessed I am to have such long arms—or thread through the partitions to the other side of the building to use a sink. For bathing we filled five-gallon plastic buckets, the sort of thing you see holding potatoes in restaurants, and washed with a rag, then rinsed with another bucketful. But at least it was warm enough to work up a lather.

It's a minor point of interest to architectural and social historians, but there was really no need for this kind of housing. The chaos of 2022 and the ravies virus depopulated most parts of North America (distance saved a few communities). There were houses ready to be restored and used, waiting behind old and weathered Condemned as Unsafe Property notices. The Kurian Order, given its way, preferred that humans lived in community groups, the larger the better, in fact, so there were more eyes watching and ears listening.

"You start at Number Four in the morning. Just follow the other men out and up the road. It's only a mile and a half to the mine, and you'll have fine weather for your first day's walk, looks like."

It was a bright, still morning promising a hot fall day. The workers all left near dawn for their walk. Some kissed wives and children good-bye; most carried plastic coolers filled with their lunches. Their work clothes were mostly dungaree; helmets, gloves, goggles, and hearing gear dangled from their belts. I thought it was strange that the mine didn't provide protective gear. But then not every man carried each item, so perhaps they were custom bits superior to what the mine offered.

I'd made a bit of a show with the other workers on the way up, asking, "Where me work, where me work?"

"You'll find out soon enough, stoop," an older man at the front of the procession said, before going back to grumbling about losing money at cribbage.

A large man fell into step beside me. In fact, he fell into step so easily, I wondered if he'd had some kind of military training, or if close order drill was simply part of everyone's childhood education.

"I show you, big fella. My name's Olson. You have a name, I suppose?"

"Hickory," I said.

"Ticky, more like," the one who'd called me "stoop" said.

"How you know that?" Olson asked. "You and your mom had a groom through that fur, maybe?"

The man half rounded, then thought better of it.

"Awww, you'd just enjoy it if I beat you up some, Ollie," he grumbled.

"The smaller the man, the bigger the talk," Olson said, to everyone and no one.

The mining site was set into, appropriately enough, the crotch of a mountain pointing like an arrow toward the southernmost corner of the Coal Country. That was where most of the coal went that we produced: due south to the Georgia Control. A great pile of slag spilled down toward a creek, shale-colored pus running from the mountain's wound.

Outside the gaping, semicircular mine entrance with its trolley tracks, electrical cabling, and ventilator stacks stood a humble building, the mine office, a ramshackle set of connected trailers with a single two-story red-painted wooden building glowering through windows like filthy glasses over the litter around it. On the other side of the mine-access road were a dumping ground for heavy equipment, some functional, some not, and a scrap heap of pieces of excavating gear.

I could fill pages describing Number Four, an ugly black mouth in the mountainside like a vast skull eye-socket, with

THEY WHO WORK WELL, EAT WELL

painted in letters in reflective yellow such as you see striping roads on the boulders above the mine entrance.

In tiny little felt-pen letters just inside, someone had scrawled:
Nothing to hope for now.

The stale air, the inadequate lighting, the antiquated machinery that required endless labor with shovels and picks and unpredictable blasting sticks—I could go on for pages describing the noisy activity of a coal mine run on a shoestring budget.

For the purposes of this account, a reader need remember only three things:

First, that the mine stood in a remote location; the single rail line that met it passed over two bridges and innumerable narrow cuts. To drive there, you bumped on railroad ties at the bridges, or took a doubtful jeep trail that challenged even the hardiest four-wheel drive.

Second, that it was sort of a dumping ground for misfits and malcontents, both of the Kurian Order and for Consolidated Mines, where blunder and inefficiency would do less harm. I believe I did not have a reputation for either, but I was put here to find out how I'd adapt to mine work. Perhaps they thought I'd go insane underground and start in on my fellow workers. If it suited me, the Maynes Conglomerate might have moved me to a more important operation, and if it didn't, I'd do minimal damage.

Finally, that Amiable Fise (pronounced so it rhymes with "nice") worked there. I will tell more about her later, but in many ways she was the heart of Number Four.

The Olson fellow was kind enough to take me into the mine office, where I handed over the small amount of documentation the White Palace had given me. They took my picture (they had to do some rearranging of camera, light, and backdrop) and made a plastic identification card. Although it came on a lanyard, the foreman who gave me the tour showed me a little slot on a yellow safety vest where the card would fit. "You don't need that dangling into machinery."

I marveled at the picture briefly. There was no sense overplaying things.

I soon accustomed myself to the work. The ten-hour shifts of mining themselves were not so bad. They were good about issuing breaks regularly, and they kept water and hygiene necessities up near the coal face (as a new hand, I was put in charge of excretion, or the "honey bucket," which went out with the slag); the workers usually spent only about half the day in the noise and dust of the actual coal face, doing the messy work of extracting. The rest was maintaining the rickety old equipment, rigging lighting and ventilation gear, or moving coal from inside to out through the conveyor chutes.

But reaching the coal face required a good deal of "travel"—often more than an hour to reach the spot for the day's work from the mine entrance above, between waits for the elevator and walk-crawls to the face. Some of the tunnels were big enough to fit two cars abreast, but there were a great many mines that weren't all that much bigger than the tunnels dug by convicts in prison-escape movies. For a larger figure such as me, it meant almost crawling on all fours through some of the tunnel branches. Neither I nor any of the miners was paid for travel. Idle time for breakdowns did not count, either, even if we were puffing in the unimaginable dark—a coal mine's dark must be experienced to be believed—while waiting for the electricity to come back on. The foremen who kept track of such things for the management upstairs were generous about "correcting" time cards, though, for especially vexing circumstances.

When your shift finished, you crawled back, exhausted, and in my case praying the whole way that you would not meet some laggard late to the relief shift, which would require one of us backing up to a wide spot where we could squeeze by each other.

To add to the miseries of the travel, there were coal conveyors operating with a deafening clatter. Even with wadded-up bits of New Universal Church bulletins stuffed in your ears, you arrived at the coal face with a headache, or young boys and girls pushing or dragging four-wheeled "barrows" of coal to the nearest working conveyor. The Kurian Order often bragged that it took children off the streets and gave them an education. These children certainly weren't on the streets, but their education wasn't all that different from that given a dog or a lab rat: perform simple tasks repetitively and get your treat.

The work at the face itself was not bad. It was divided into three phases: blasting, breaking, and shoveling, with resets of machinery in between as the coal face advanced and the ceiling was shored up with timber or old scaffolding.

The blasting provided enough excitement for a lifetime, for one time in twenty the blasting cap or wiring failed and one of the demolition men had to crawl forward and reset the mulish explosives. Not a month went by when there wasn't an injury or a death.

You could lose yourself in the monotony of breaking and shoveling. During resets we all worked like mad, for during a reset no coal appeared, and no coal meant no food and reductions in off days when visits to town were arranged.

Work always seemed to speed up at the end of the month in a rush to overfulfill the quota. There was some grumbling, but nothing that led me to believe a revolt, so soon to come, was brewing.

The highlight in most everyone's day was Aym—Amiable Fise, our "canteen girl."

She was the reward given to "Those Who Work." If your shift foreman labeled you as a "Prime Worker," your only benefit was commissary privileges. It meant you had the option of buying your lunch and getting a hot meal made fresh rather than bringing one. The price was quite reasonable, usually twenty dollars or about a half hour's work—for most. I found myself eating sixty-dollar lunches, mostly because Aym's food was better than that available down in the dormitory, so her commissary became half my food consumption (for the rest, I paid a small premium to have the wife of one of the workers take the bus to the market stalls for me and fill my simple list). Aym also sold a few necessities: bottles of aspirin and muscle rub, tobacco, gambling tickets for some of the Georgia Control's attractive-sounding cash-prize lotteries, and of course the inevitable range of Kurian Zone aphrodisiacs and fertility enhancers.

I first met her when a miner named Raymond Jones introduced me. He and I were often teamed together by our foreman. He was a wiry shaved-bald man with a very low boiling point who fulminated against either the incompetence of the mine office or his own foul fate for placing him in a hole to work out his remaining years. "Rage," as he was known, needed my help dragging some oxyacetylene tanks that should have been put on wheels. We passed her largish, engineless lunch truck up on blocks and surrounded by a plain, garden-variety security fence stretching from mine floor to ceiling. It stood just past the elevator and lighted shift office. Coal-dusted lawn furniture, no two pieces matching, made an unattended café just outside the window where workers spoke to her and paid for their orders.

Raymond Jones had a blue poker chip with a casino logo hologram on it. Shoved in his ID pocket, it designated him as one allowed to use the commissary.

"Wait a sec," Jones said. "Hey, Aym, customer."

A petite woman's face lighted by unflattering fluorescents appeared at the window. She wore dark sunglasses with oversized lenses and gilded bows that made me think of movie starlets in the old gossip magazines. A smile nearly as wide as the glasses gleamed under her flour-dusted nose.

In her thirties, she was blind (or nearly so; I never learned if she had any vision), and she was the one sunny spot for us in all that dark. No one would call her a beauty, especially not with fryer grease on her face and her hair hidden under a net cap, but no one seemed to mind looking at her as they killed a break. I thought she had a good jawline and nose. I don't hold with physiognomy revealing character, but something about the set of her mouth and cheek muscles made me think the big smile was a frequent visitor.

"I hear someone big behind you, Rage, but he steps soft," she said. "Something weird about his feet."

"It's the Grog. Heard of him?"

"Someone said there was a big, really furry one here. Even talks. I thought they were talking about Pelloponensis."

"I think he's got a rung on Pellers on the old evolutionary ladder. Cleans his ass more often, anyway. Say hi, Hickory."

I resisted the impulse to say "Hi, Hickory," and growled out a "Good morning."

"Wow. That's some voice box," she said. "I felt that in my back teeth."

"That's what she said," Rage said.

He was the only one who laughed.

"You want a drink or something, Hickory? It's on the Number Four Canteen."

I stepped up to the window. "Milk? Choco-milk? Root beer?"

"Really? I don't have much call for that, but I've got some chocolate syrup, or what passes for it around here. Give me a sec."

She felt around in one of the refrigerators and came up with a big brown squeeze bottle and proceeded to make me a chocolate milk. Her workplace was filled with gear, leaving her a zone for movement about the size of a walk-in freezer. She moved about it elegantly; vision didn't make much of a difference for a person who spent her days in something with the square footage of a dog run.

"Enjoy," she said, handing it out the window. I did.

In my first month working at Number Four, I found that once I was down in the mine, the time passed in a blur. Before I knew it, the fall had grown cold and the farmers were setting up roadside stands. Not that I had much opportunity to visit them, or money, as I was still in the process of buying custom safety equipment from a Maynes subsidiary to fit my frame.

Still, I won my blue casino chip to wear in the ID pocket with six weeks of hard work. My fellow miners presented me with an oversized bottle of shampoo—I had a tough time getting the coal dust out of my fur—at the informal ceremony where the foreman handed me my chit. I began to visit Aym daily, as did many others. A female voice, even a thin-throated human one, was a wonderful contrast to the blast and bustle of the coal face, especially when it came with a smile. I may have fallen a little in love with her. I suspect I was not the only one.

She could be as sweet as the real sugar she put in the coffee—the source was a mystery, but rumor had it she had a highly placed boyfriend in the Maynes organization—or as foul mouthed as a Mississippi bargeman. She had a memory for humor based on reproductive desire and always had a new joke or two at the ready.

"Olson, why's a woman exactly like an investment account with the Church?" she asked my first friend while we stood in line for coffee and a doughnut in the morning.

"Dunno, Aym," Olson said, going red in anticipation. Though he was married with several children, Aym's jokes still embarrassed him.

"Because the depositor loses interest as soon as he withdraws."

"Yeah, that's a good one," Olson said, going even redder.

A cat kept her company in the cubicle. It was cautious of me at first and hid under the prep table she used for sandwiches. The cat's name was Crumb.

"Crumb used to be good with the rats and mice, but he's too old and fat now," Aym explained the first time I saw her outside the van. I had started early that day in order to leave early for my lunch, which

I'd grown to look forward to more and more since earning my commissary privileges. She was changing propane tanks for her grill by touch. It was hard not to be impressed; she performed the action without wasting a step or reach. "I have to lay down traps where I hear chewing. Sometime's he'll eat one of the bodies in the trap—acts like he's doing me a big favor—but he'd rather have sandwich meat or canned tuna. Crumb, you lazy bugger, stiffen up and meet this big whatever-you-are."

"Golden One," I supplied.

She returned to the van and took up a knife, slicing the meat and vegetables for the sandwich I had ordered and carefully brushing her knife across a damp towel that smelled faintly of chlorine. She replaced it on a magnetic strip located from memory.

"Sharp knife dangerous," I said.

"Don't I know it," she agreed.

Her face made strange expressions as she worked, piling the ingredients on the bread. Her face seemed now eager, now shocked. It was a bit unsettling at first, but you grew used to it.

"Here you are, Old Hickory." She handed me the sandwich. I ate it using my pick-rake (I had just been at the face) as an improvised seat, propping the handle's end in the nook and sitting on the metal. It was extraordinary—the sandwich, not the improvised seat.

"Thank you," I said. "So good." I had thought that the Kurian Order did away with the blind in the same manner as they did with the crippled and difficult cognitive defects.

No wonder so many of the men picked up their lunches here.

"How long you in mine?" I asked.

"Six years in this one. Before, I was in another. I worked a phone, taking messages and handling shift schedules. I can read a little if I hold it real close to my eyes. This is better. I'm my own boss. I have the wire between me and the men. Up in the office I always had the feeling my boss was looking down my blouse or up my skirt."

"Yes, boss always watch," I said. "Eyes no good?"

"Eyes no good. Since I was eight. Bus accident."

I wondered if she was an informant of the Kurian Order. David Valentine once told me that the Kurians tended to put informant women in working with large groups of men. Maybe she wasn't as blind as she claimed, just fuzzy-visioned. But what would she have to spy on down here? There weren't enough workers on any one shift to count as a threat, even if they improvised weapons out of their gear, and they certainly didn't have access to sensitive sights deep in the earth.

"My life no good," I said, deciding to probe. "Stuck in dark and dust in hair."

"You're one smart Grog," she said. With an effort, she kept her eyes pointed at the air blowing out of my nostrils. "But that sandwich won't be enough. I had to do a platter for the shift office staff this morning. Want the leftovers to take back?"

"You have gratitude from me," I said. I crooked my pick in the corner of my arm and helped myself to boiled bread, cheese, and dried ersatz fruit.

Number Four deserved its reputation as one of the worst in all of Coal Country. The ore was in thin seams that made it difficult to extract and of an average grade. I thought most of the miners were doing marginally useful make-work, paying for their small wages and third-hand, improvised equipment, electricity, and not much else. In a differently run Kurian Zone, most of these men would have been on a collection van. Whatever else you wanted to say about the Maynes version of the Kurian Order, they weren't particularly bloodthirsty.

Each mine face had one power drill. The rest of the five or so workers (once two were assigned to fire and support the drill) at the face did what they could not to attract the eye of the supervisor.

My fellow workers at Number Four could best be described with the palliative word "oddballs." Their former employers would probably use worse phrases. They'd been transferred from other mines or businesses or camps where they'd been irritants, and Number Four was the Kurian Order's way of coating that irritant into a black pearl.

This, of course, raised the question of whether the locals considered me an oddball as well. But of course they did. To them I was a stranger of a foreign species, and bad luck seemed to follow me. It was strange that they didn't trade me off to another Kurian Zone or sell me to a bounty hunter or something equally painless to the system that found me a piece of grit in its oil. But again, the Maynes filter didn't strain as fine as most.

One shift foreman, the one who gave me my blue chip, Bleecher, disliked the underground's cold and had developed a strange diet in response. He ate beans and spicy sauce at breakfast, lunch, and dinner (he carried his own supply) and claimed that his constant farting served as a gaseous form of climate control, heating his jumpsuit, which he'd waxed into tin cloth. I was of the opinion that all the paraffin in his clothes simply did a better job of trapping body heat, but even in the oily air underground, you knew when you were coming up on a team with Bleecher in it.

He always silenced idle chatter. Even if we were hard at work with shovels, exchanging a few words, he'd slap his yellow leather work gloves across his palm to attract our attention, then issue an emphatic order to work our backs, not our mouths.

It shut most of us up, except for Raymond "Rage" Jones, of course. Rage was a bit of a sea lawyer, as they used to say on the Gulf Coast in the Coastal Marines. He wasn't afraid to speak against the Kurian Order, which made him a rare character. He hated lice and bedbugs and ticks, to the point where he kept himself completely shaved, head to toe. He believed I was riddled with parasitic insects. He gave me a wide path whenever we passed, and he always rubbed himself down with turpentine or kerosene upon leaving a shift. I wished I could have told him the story of Hoffman Price, the man who survived years in the wilderness by supporting as many parasites on his body as possible to camouflage the natural human aura the Reapers read. Better a small bloodsucker on your skin than a big one on your throat.

"Rage" Jones was always letting arguments spill over into physical aggression. Usually he settled for a headlock, but every now and then it escalated into punches and he lost his Prime chit for a month. For all the trouble in the mine he caused, I understand he had an unimpeachable reputation at the dorm. He spent most of his time cleaning his body, his clothes, or his room, never drank, and liked to help out with upkeep projects.

There was Pelloponensis, who never had a kind word to say about anything or anyone. He had a sixth sense, which some men who go underground develop, for when and where a collapse will take place. When Pelloponensis said it was time to shore up a tunnel, everyone dropped what he was doing and ran for light and lumber. New workers learned the job from him.

He liked to tell a story of witnessing a Reaper kill a man. He told it to me while leaning against the conveyor that took the coal to the surface, me and a couple other kids new to the mine put on shoveling.

It happened up at an old quarry on the Maynes estate. He'd snuck in to steal from the extensive Maynes orchards one summer night, got hot, and thought he'd take a dip in the pond that had accumulated at the deep end of the old quarry. He wasn't the only stranger on the Maynes grounds that night; a woman was lurking there. Thin and scruffy she was, with the twitchiness of someone addicted to some artificial stimulant or depressant.

"I was having a swim—warm day, but the water was really cold from the previous night—when I saw a flash of white. Thought it was a ghost for a second. Just out of the corner of my eye. Made me hunker down in the water a bit like a startled turtle diving. I peeked up and I saw her, this girl, all scratched up, walking barefoot through the quarry. She didn't seem harmful, so I came up out of the water. Strange thing, though; once I got out, I saw her feet were really clean. I noticed that right off.

"She looked like death already," Pelloponensis continued. "There I was, stripped down, with my clothes thrown over the pears. She gave kind of a giggle. I didn't have much in the way of body hair then—made up for it since. By the time I hit sixty I'll look like Hickory there."

"'You can't be the old guy,' she said. I think." He shrugged.

"Then I saw it rise up behind her. Yellow eyes, staring at her. Seemed fifteen feet tall compared to her. How didn't she hear it? I backpedaled, tripped, splashed into the water as if I'd cannonballed off the cliff."

He paused the story to judge the effect on me and the other youths.

Pelloponensis smirked. "None of you have ever seen one just ten feet away, I guess. Well, I have, and I'm happy to put off the day it happens again for as long as possible. Worst thing is, it wasn't over quick, like the churchmen say if you get them talking about such things. It dangled her by her frigging hair, batted her about a bit with two fingers of one hand. Just a poke from two fingers sent her swinging at the end of its arm like a, oh, what's them things that hang off the bottom of a grandfather clock. The ticker or whatever. Well, whatever they are, she swung around for a bit like one.

"Then I realized there was something else about that monster's face—he was missing his upper lip.

"I think she fainted from all the screaming. Her head sort of lolled back, and that was when he—when he went into her. It was like he unhinged his jaw and an eel emerged—a black, barbed, slimy eel that hit her right here." He tapped his fingers hard at the notch atop his manubrium between the clavicles. Both the boys touched themselves just below the throat.

"I'd always heard they got all sluggish and sleepy after feeding, but not this one. He took her body—beyond pale now, like a piece of chalk—and hurled it in the air like a ballplayer tossing his cap at the end of the game. She splashed down no farther from me than I am to you.

"One of those doll eyes was staring at me while I waited for that bloodsucker to depart. It danced around a bit.

"I waded through the pond, stepping the whole way on sunken logs. At least I hope they were sunken logs—my imagination was running wild. But dead men float, right?"

The boys nodded dumbly. "She had to die sometime," one of them said.

"Kur's got a plan for us," the other said.

Pelloponensis shrugged. "The farmer's got a plan for his chickens, too. Just because you've got a goal in mind, it don't make wrong right."

Once he was safe at home, it had occurred to him that the Reaper had followed him, and not the woman, into the quarry. The thought made him shudder.

Strangely, it seemed like I was learning more about the Maynes Empire off its property than I ever did on it. I'd heard whispers of a quarry and wondered if that was where the Maynes secrets were buried.

Others I frequently worked beside included Galloway, who had a magnificent voice. You could hear him singing in the tunnels for hundreds of meters as though in a concert hall if the equipment was silent. Sikorsky, the mechanic-electrician who had some sort of nasal condition that made him sound as though he had a permanent cold, did his job with just seven fingers and one thumb. Another was my first friend, the easily embarrassed Olson, the strongest of the group and an enthusiastic wrestler—he pulled me off my feet with a clever move the first time we tested our strength against each other.

As with every other gathering away from the ears of the Order in the Coal Country, the conversation frequently turned to the troubles.

I did not participate in these discussions, of course. They took place at breaks for meals. Sometimes I feigned a nap, or if I had heard repeated opinions, I played helpful Grog and refilled one of the water jugs or took away the old rags and towels everyone used to get the worst of the dust off his lips and hands before eating.

The old-timers said that "bad blood" tended to build up every fifteen or twenty years, leading to some kind of fighting against the regime. A few firehouses burned down; there were some disappearances that might be blamed on either vengeance or a Kurian-directed purge; a stick of dynamite might be thrown under a porch or down a chimney. Eventually, the Coal Country "would settle down again with the screws tightened in some parts, loosened up in others, so the coal machine could start production again."

The old-timers admitted that since the massacre, it was the worst they'd ever seen. "And if it doesn't stop, something or somebody's going to come down hard. Then God help us."

Most of the workers thought that it would die down after a while. "It's already chilling out."

Then firebrands like Jones said that snipped telephone wires and slashed tires and derailed coal cars weren't much more than pranks, enraging in the moment, then quickly forgotten. "If we really wanted to put a hurting on the Kurian Order and show them they can't shoot kids down in the street, all we'd have to do is kill coal production through a general strike and occupation of the mines. What else are they going to burn? Church bulletins?"

"Big talk," an old hand countered. "If the coal quit, they'd just have their pastors give the sermons by candlelight. Reapers don't need electricity to find us. They want us cold and in the dark, believe me. They don't need a technological society; something out of the Dark Age would suit them just fine. One more thing to blame on the Resistance."

"I heard the Resistance is giving up. Ever since they got Texas and that chunk of Oklahoma, they've got food and oil. They're fat and happy now," the old-timer named Sikorsky said.

"The Resistance keeps them from taking us back to sticks and stones," Jones said. "They don't dare let things drop too far or the Resistance will walk right over them."

"You mean the Maynes family doesn't," Sikorsky said. "There aren't enough Reapers for everything. It's the people high up running things for them in the Control and whatnot that we have to hit. Without them, the whole rig collapses like a one-legged scaffolding with the screws pulled out."

"Yeah," Rage said. "I say it's about time we start pulling screws here."

"Forget that noise, kid," Sikorsky said. "I used to be like you. You're young and think you'll live forever. You're sick of the whole Conglomerate and think you can pull it down. That landed me here, and I don't have any more chances coming. Better off hunkering down and doing your job."

I hope that I have showed that while Number Four had the reputation of being a last stop, the men weren't the dejected walking corpses that you met in some Kurian work camps, where those marked for destruction puttered away, or philosophized, or lay as though already a corpse, or engaged in a last frenetic bout of drinking and/or sexual activity of one sort or another.

They still had their human spirit—though I think the linguists should come up with another aphorism for that, because it seems nonexistent in many. Perhaps it was just tougher to beat out of these West Virginians, as rocky and difficult to humble as their mountains.

THE FIRST NOTES
OF THE CRESCENDO

We had made it to the winter doldrums and I was now in my second year in the Coal Country. Looking back, I believe I was in a poor mood most of the time but could lose myself in the mindless physical labor at the coal face. I will say this: the constant physical strain toughened me even as it numbed my mind. I turned into the broad-shouldered Golden One of my youth. He looked at me from the mirror, a little less hair about the face and longer drop-whiskers.

Though I am ashamed to admit it, the mine office was pleased with me. The foreman, Bleecher, found me better-fitting safety equipment. Mr. Prapa, the director himself, a bracelet-favoring man with an out-of-season oily tan and all the appeal of dried chewing gum found sticking on a bus seat, rather gingerly called me into his office to ask me if there was a tribe of me up in the Pennsylvania hills, perhaps, that I could convince to come into the Coal Country to serve as laborers.

While sniffing through a bowl of fruit he offered me—fresh strawberries, in winter!—I glanced at a simple report; it seemed that every time I worked the coal face with the rest of a usual six-man crew, production went up twenty-five percent.[*]

I no longer had to produce money at Aym's trailer.

I'd been playing the "helpful Grog" so long, I became him in a way. Ahn-Kha, who once roamed the Transmississippi as a fighter in a famous regiment, became just another scraping Grog, gently pawing at his masters as he waited for his next drink of flavored corn syrup.

I rarely dreamt of escape anymore, or if I did, I went at the coal face with a pickaxe as though digging a tunnel to freedom. I exhausted my brain into numbness. I fell into bed with grit still dug deep into my hair and awoke without expectation of anything more challenging than wondering if I should eat six eggs or a dozen for breakfast. I didn't drink, gamble, or rent women on the weekends, so my wages, such as they were, mostly went to the little farmer stalls set up twice a week near the Number Four dormitory. While I enjoyed doing my own cooking, I usually gave a few dollars to one of the mine wives—whichever one caught my eye as the most ragged and careworn—to cook up my purchases for me. With the rest, on the advice of Olson, I set up a New Universal Church Community Investment account. That caused some confusion at the Church's office, but we simplified matters by having Olson just set up a second account allowing me to draw on it. I trusted Olson, and it was better that I not have too much of a paper trail with the Church, in any case.

For me, life was simple. Work properly, get paid, keep the food supply fresh, and listen for the mine disaster klaxon.

No one made an effort to force me onto the buses for the weekly

---

[*] Our narrator is being too modest here. He also became renowned as a repairman and fixed an old pressure drill. He also sometimes stayed after the shift to work hardware and put two broken conveyors right.

church services, and when the priests visited, they never spoke to me. My sheets and other laundry were mysteriously washed while I was at the mine.

Word passed among the miners—at each retelling it gained a different source—that a purge was coming, and soon. The Coal Country had quieted after the Maynes bloodletting, but not enough. Now the neighboring Kurian Zones were demanding payments in blood to make up the coal shortfalls.

"It never hits the mines too bad," Sikorsky said one morning while we waited for Aym to finish with the customers ahead of us. Sikorsky had a Thermos waiting to be filled. He was talking to Olson just behind, who had a flashlight that he kept inserting "new" batteries into, in an effort to find a functional set. I stood just behind Olson. "But for anyone with gray hair, it's a tense time."

Sikorsky stepped up and handed his Thermos to Aym. She'd heard what he and Olson were talking about. Probably everyone in line that morning had had the same subject on his mind.

"Every time we go through this, I think I'm going to be the first one scratched. I can't sleep. People tell me I look like hell." Aym shrugged. "Then we go through it, and someone like Sikorsky disappears. Good or bad at the job, who cares; something about the selection rubbed the headcount team the wrong way.

"My first one as a postpubescent, I think they were ready to take me away, but my dad volunteered to go in my place. I never knew he liked me that much, my mom was the one who worked with me and found some Braille books, God knows how.

"Do you know anything about it? A church guy tried to tell me once that they hypnotize you like a snake with a bird, so you don't even know what's happening, then you go to eternal life as part of the greater Kurian Consciousness, but he was more interested in fingering me in the confession room than explaining how it works.

"Then Ray Jones said the complete opposite. He told me that they torment you for a little bit before killing you. Said it was like a chef cooking a meal; it added flavor to whatever energy they need from people. You know, our souls or auras or whatever. Of course, all his talk is a little wild. He tried to finger me, too, but I was better at defending myself by then. I'm not walking around with a tattoo that reads 'Finger me' on my forehead, am I?" She picked up Crumb and stroked him. The purring was almost loud enough to drown out the distant echoes from the coal face.

"Maybe it's written in invisible ink. I don't see it."

I Make a Friend

I had been trying to make up my mind about Aym for weeks. She was clearly intelligent and skilled at drawing men out. A Kurian agent would have those skills. But then again, so would a popular barkeep.

I needed a friend. I'd been more than a year now in the Kurian Zone without anyone I could trust. I don't expect most readers to understand—only those who've lived it will. I needed to talk to someone so badly, I was willing to chance death for it.

I'd thought about it a couple of times with MacTierney and almost drove over the centerline, but I always steered back again to the safety of the shoulder.

Many times in my life I've been praised for fearlessly going across Nomansland and into the Kurian Zones. This praise has usually been from speakers who have never spent a night in one. Fearless? Hardly. To survive the Kurian Zone, you become old friends with fear. You get to know fear so well, it tells you its secrets, whispering them in the long nights when probing flashlights and a firm shake of the shoulder come to escort you away. I let fear lead me through dark paths and nights out in the open, where every snapped branch might be an approaching Reaper.

I decided to trust her.

I often took my lunch break at odd hours so others could enjoy a more normal time. I liked the quiet of the coal face when the others were gone. I could break or move coal or tinker with the machinery as I liked, not having to worry about striking someone with a wide swing.

Then when I did eat, I had the commissary trailer and the ramshackle lawn furniture to myself. Someone had added some Astroturf and plastic flowers recently, to make the eating area a bit more outdoorsy. The naked bulbs of the lighting spoiled the effect, though. Not for the first time, I found the human tendency to go halfway and call it good enough vexing.

Aym made me the two sandwiches I ordered. I examined the mine office and elevator shaft, as well as the shadows between, before speaking.

"You are a wonderful cook," I said. "Your food is the high point of my day."

"That's quite a speech, Hickory," Aym said. "Did you have help?"

"I find it convenient to play at being the sort of Grog these men are used to. My kind are more advanced."

"I wish I could say the same about us," Aym said. "I knew there was something funny about you. You scared they'll open you up to take a peek inside and see what makes you different?"

"Something like that," I said.

"I'm good at keeping secrets. Rumor has it you're some kind of plant. They say you've got a device surgically implanted that records everything. I won't tell you the person who claimed that and gave me a name to back it up. That's how discreet I am."

"No. I have no recent, unexplained scars. I remember each wound on my body."

"I didn't believe it anyway. The men at Number Four have big egos—you know that word?—they think they're bigger troublemakers than they are. About the worst that can be said for them is that they're bad apples. Seeing a few scribbled dirty words in church Bibles or hearing talk about going on strike doesn't worry the Maynes clan."

"There's not much left of it."

"They'll make a comeback; you just see. They'll set up some marriages, bring in some new blood; the White Palace will be full again in no time. We're still waiting for our purge."

"You think it will be soon?" I asked.

"Yes. Everyone is tense. I've been sending up coffee and sandwiches to the mine office past midnight every night since your fight. They must think that blind people don't need shut-eye. I wonder if Prapa has to hide something."

"I'm surprised a man like that is a director."

"Number Four is remote. If you want to live with other people, it means a long drive. When I worked in the office, he told me he spent two hours a day driving, in good weather. There are dozens of ways he could be skimming—ghost workers, selling coal oil on the black market, misuse of transport for running white lighting—I wouldn't be surprised if he was doing all of them. It's not that hard to bribe the auditors, and the Conglomerate knows that the chance of a little corruption is better than layers of auditors and then auditors who audit the auditors. Bureaucratic fiefdoms become kingdoms in no time."

"And they have a person like you making sandwiches."

"It's the one spot at Number Four where I can be my own boss. I just pay a concession to the mine. It's a worry, with a purge coming on. The mine would work just fine with my trailer broken down and hauled out of here.

"That scares me. Who knows what they could dream up for someone like me? I'm nervous enough in unfamiliar places."

I respected her enough to tell the truth as I saw it, without any more shading than that required by mannered conversation. "I would not think they would do that—it adds time and uncertainty to the extraction process. Anything could happen in the process Jones described. Though I could see them reserving it for special enemies."

"You think so?"

"They won't take you. You're the best thing about Number Four."

"It's bound to happen sooner or later. We all die. It's just a bit more rational and organized in the Kurian Zone."

"Organized, yes. Rational? Only if you accept that Kurians deserve to live forever at the cost of other lives. I'm told the longer they go on, the more vital aura they need. It must end in holocaust, worlds as stripped of life as I am told Kur is, if that's the truth. I can think of nothing more irrational."

That night, I replayed every word of our conversation in my head. Being able to engage another intelligent, sensitive mind—all I can compare it to is a prisoner long held in a dungeon brought up into the sunlight for an afternoon.

Looking back on it, both of us were taking a risk. Most Kurian Zones had a strong unspoken rule, at least among the more professional classes, against discussing the mechanics of death in the Kurian Order. To do so risked social ostracism at the very least. Among men such as the miners, there were earthy jokes, just as there were earthy jokes about all of life's functions from excreting to procreating.

New Arrivals

We lost two miners in a cave-in. It was for a stupid reason—they were assigned to remove shoring materials in a disused tunnel with a played-out seam and there was a major cave-in. We opened an old disused tunnel that had once reached that seam and dug from the new Number Four as well.

Everyone agreed it was a stupid risk. Even the rawest new miner was worth more than shoring materials, and these men were both experienced.

We pulled them out, mottled and unconscious, and they were unceremoniously loaded onto a fire department ambulance for their trip to "hospital." We never saw either of them again.

Prapa raged about the lost production in the effort to find the men, and very foolishly declared that future rescues had to be approved. Inspired by Rage, everyone started calling the new policy the "Dead Man's Stamp"—meaning that by the time Prapa and the rest of the Kurian Order decided to dig someone out and put their stamp of approval on the rescue, the person would have long since ceased caring about earthly endeavors.

One of the young bucks who joined our shift was named Longliner. He did not look cut out for mine work. He was reedy with a sharp beak of a nose under wary eyes, but as it turned out, he had some strength in those flimsy-looking limbs. He was a friendly young man. I liked him, mostly because I was no longer the new miner. Someone else would be in charge of carrying the shit-bucket away from the coal face every afternoon.

He was self-possessed, for all his youth, and tried to make friends with everyone. I find human charm either amusing or annoying—frankly, I'd rather watch a dog roll over and expose its belly for scratches.

My time in the mines had one amusing diversion. I had a very short-lived career as a prizefighter representing Number Four.

It started on a warm spring day. I'd been at the mine more than six months. The sun blazed, almost unfiltered by lingering upper-atmosphere swirls. You could hear rocks cracking in the mountains when the machinery was quiet.

Prapa, the director of Number Four, was picking through the slag heap, seeing how much coal was being accidentally thrown out with the other mining waste with a couple of men in engineer boots and the jeans-tie-and-corduroy-jacket ensemble under their white hard hats that seemed to be favored by technical professionals in the Coal Country.

I was doing Aym a favor by bringing her empty propane tanks up to the office after my shift, and the visitors stood up when they saw me.

"What is that, a Grog or a white Squatch?" one of the white helmet group said.

"Thunder, look at the size of him!" another technician said.

"According to the White Palace, he took on twenty bounty men in a bar," Prapa said. "He was part of Bone's security detail, right up until he drove into that tree." He inflated his lungs. "Hey, Hickory, come over here. These men have never seen your kind before."

It has often struck me that stories that would be laughably outrageous if told about a man are given credence when one of the Xenos is the subject, even if the one in question is a slightly (if not ripely, at this writing) aged Golden One.

I put down the empty propane tanks and stepped over to the slag heap. The men descended, carefully. One of them tossed a fist-sized chunk of coal he'd found.

"You like to fight, Hickory?" Prapa asked.

I lowered my face and stuck out my hands, palms up. "No, me no fight. No cause trouble. No. Never."

"Never heard of a stoop who could talk that good," one of the engineers said. "You'd think he was human."

"I'd never mistake that for human," the other corduroy jacket said.

Prapa ignored the byplay. "No, no—you're misunderstanding. Fight when it's your job."

One of the men stroked the fur on my upper arm—a bit too sensually for my taste. "He could go all the way, representing your mine."

"What's mine is yours and what's yours is mine," the other engineer said. I didn't understand the reference. Was the mine under some sort of pressure to produce more?

I didn't care to become a fighter, even a part-time one. Were I to succeed, I might attract the interest of another Kurian Zone, the Ordnance, for example. And who knows what rules set up these fights, or how they were arranged to make the contests even? Or what might happen to me in the pursuit of seeing me lose—or win, I guess. The Kurians are supposed to have some combat drugs that make you unbeatable right up to the moment when a blood vessel bursts in your brain. I might be injured or crippled.

"We'll give him a try," Prapa said. His tanned face smiled widely enough that I thought of an orange being squeezed until it spits sweet juice. "Don't worry, Hickory, just a game. Not like your job before. Contest. Boom-boom-boom," he said, pantomiming punches.

Saturdays and Sundays the Number Four ran only one shift each day, and it was a short-handed shift at that. There was coal piling up all over the Coal Country because of transport "accidents" as they were now being openly called.

Prapa and the mine's senior foreman, Castaway, came to collect me at the dorm. Castaway said it was time for my "contest." If I won, I'd have three days off with all I could eat. If I lost, I'd still get two days off to recover.

"Hope you're hungry," Prapa said. The gold bracelets on his wrist jangled as he continually tapped his knee.

We piled into a charter bus from the Coal Country transport line. It smelled like unwashed humans and the scented sawdust used in bars to clean up vomit. A contingent of our own miners came along, paying Prapa a small fee for the ride and admission.

Prapa, drinking the whole ride, announced that he'd bet heavily on me. It seemed as though the whole mine had bet on me. According to Rage, who loved watching punches being thrown almost as much as he loved throwing them himself, even Aym had placed one hundred dollars on me, which made me feel like a traitor to the rest. I did not feel guilty for the other miners. I am aware that a fool will lose his money one way or another. At least losing a bet doesn't poison the liver in the manner of the cheap liquor a won bet would have otherwise gone to purchase. But Aym had put up that cash out of regard.

We pulled up in front of a ruin of an old beige-colored hotel near Charleston. It had a vast atrium running six or seven floors—it was hard to tell with temporary lighting—and it smelled of damp ruin. A low roar of voices inside—men struggling to be heard without outright shouting—sounded like surf on a ship's hull all around.

They'd set up portable lights run by a noisy generator, illuminating the sanded tile floor of the atrium into a glow that hurt the eyes. The atrium was square, and on the balconies running up into the darkness, spectators hung over the rail like idling sailors on a ship.

They hustled me off to the stripped kitchen, where I changed into a red knit scarf that I wrapped around myself as a sort of loincloth. Prapa painted the number 4 on my back in red barn paint, as though I were some kind of advertisement, clearly not giving a whit how sticky it would become as it dried. This steeled my resolve, and I hoped Prapa hadn't been engaging in his usual bragging about how much money he'd bet.

I never learned the names of my "trainers." One was bald and short; the other muscular, save for an enormous, drum-tight belly. The trainers didn't really know what to do with me. I got the impression they didn't do much training; their equipment looked limited to stitching pugilists back together after a bout.

The boxing ring had no ropes or corners, just a circle about thirty feet across. I was told being pushed out of the circle was an automatic defeat, but it appears they changed this rule at the last minute when they saw me.

There appeared to be an argument about my competing. The fight rules for the Coal Country bouts were in a small three-page pamphlet, and I saw Prapa arguing with the referee and some of the other mine directors and fight officials (the officials wore little red-white-and-blue boutonnieres of the Sports and Recreation Club, one of the few times I've seen the colors of the old American flag combined in the Kurian Zone).

There was a good deal of muttering about my size and reach. I looked up, but the figures on the balconies were all shadow and outline, like crows lining a wire on a gloomy night.

The referee wore a black version of hospital scrubs, save that the shirt hung down to his midthigh, with a red sash wound about his waist. He had scarred skin as dark as the coal we dug. Despite his gray hair, he looked as fit as any of the waiting fighters. No one told me directly at the time, but the red sash was for when he would oversee a duel. He would unwrap the sash and tie the duelists' left arms together (or right arms, if the left arms were dominant).

My opponent was small, even for a man, and as he warmed up, he did an elaborate back-and-forth with his bare feet that reminded me of a dance move.

My trainers made "fighting" gestures with their fists, a comical pantomime of "Put your dukes up, for God's sake." I flattened my ears and raised my fists.

The other fighter didn't like the look of them. He came inside my reach and gave an experimental duck-and-punch to my stomach. I let out a whoof! and covered up, backing away.

"No, no, stay in the ring! Fight!" I heard Prapa scream.

My opponent, after a moment dancing away from the counter-blow that never came, stood flat-footed, perhaps not believing his luck.

"Yellow as his fur."

"Wasn't he a bodyguard for Maynes?"

"Winner!" the referee shouted.

Director Prapa looked like a man on his way to his execution the whole ride back. Or perhaps all the alcohol had rendered him somnambular.

When I told Aym the story during our second real conversation, she tilted her head back and laughed. "Weird thing is, the man's so sure of himself. He takes himself more seriously than anyone else takes him, director title and all. It's never occurred to him that there's a reason he's at Number Four, too."

I had been longing to learn more about the Coal Country and how the arrangement with the Maynes clan got started, and I finally had my chance, but I was even more curious about the firemen. They had been on my mind since the massacre at Beckley. Most Kurian Zones had low-level toughs to keep order, close enough to the locals to know who the troublemakers were, but not so well armed and trained that they could cause trouble if they turned their weapons against their masters. The firemen of the Coal Country seemed an imprudent mix of heavily armed and badly trained. As far as I knew, the fire department arrangement here was unique in the Kurian Order.

"How did the firemen get started?" I asked.

"First fire marshal, it was. Bear Torril. He believed himself the perfect revolutionary. Pure intellect and all that. No emotion, no conscience, no regrets. He hated rich people like you couldn't believe. Until you saw the bodies.

"He rode around here after the collapse, the ravies—there were little groups of survivors here and there. He'd be very helpful, offer a ride, ask them about their lives before. When he found someone who he decided had too much money, or too nice a house, he'd find some excuse to stop and get everyone out and kill the ones he'd chosen.

"Of course, most of what they owned was only on paper, so they'd lost it in the collapse.

"That brought him to the attention of the Kurians. They didn't like him killing people, but they admired his efforts to remake the world in a different image.

"Imagine that. You survive everything. Civilization's gone, the ravies kills and scatters everyone you know, and along comes a college dropout who decides you used to have too much and he sticks a knife in your back.

"The Kurians put him to work rounding up people he thinks might give them problems. He starts working out of a fire station because you can live there twenty-four hours easily enough, maintain your vehicles.

"So a riot starts. One of his guys actually had been a fireman. He showed the others how to use the hoses. Next thing you know, they're serving as a real fire brigade.

"The Kurians had him make other 'fire teams.' The ironic thing is he'd started out as this would-be revolutionary or anarchist or whatever you'd call him, killing rich men, or formerly rich ones, and just a few years later he's using water hoses on desperate people.

"Turned into a real mean old bastard right up until the end. Still convinced he was changing the world? Who knows? He had no problem killing 'em, poor as well as rich.

"In the end, they just want power. That's what it's always been about.

"Funny thing is, he knew what it was like pre-2022. My old man said everything they say about that time's a lie."

Director Prapa paced the mine like a caged wolf for the next few days, finding fault everywhere. We spent three days tearing apart drilling gear for cleaning and maintenance ordered by Prapa; then the foremen came down and reported that the director was furious with the drop in production.

With the purge looming, everyone felt that he was certainly on Prapa's list. Word of my loss in the ring spread and I began to get speculative looks. They were probably wondering if I was large enough to feed two Reapers.

"He's really mad about the loss of his four-wheeler," Sikorsky said. He had the best connections in the mine office. "He had to sell it to pay gambling debts. And his boat. And the tow rig. Now he either gets to drive a mine pickup or his wife's natural gas wagon."

Rage chuckled. "I heard that was just some bait in the water to let the sharks know the real meal is coming. Wonder where he'll get the rest of the money? Can't borrow. Nobody in Coal Country's rich, except the Maynes family."

Perhaps as a threat, Prapa took to wearing his militia uniform to work, with his old Youth Vanguard decorations in a neat little row under the lighter patch that used to hold his name tag. It seemed he felt that, for him as director, having to wear his name would fall in the area of lèse-majesté.

Some men look like a sex crime waiting to happen no matter what uniform they put on, and Prapa was one of those. He tried standing with feet out and arms clasped behind; he tried carrying a walking stick; he tried sporting a shoulder holster with bullets slipped into the bandolier's loops. The men still snickered when he passed. Whoever he was trying to impress, it wasn't the miners. Were there other eyes watching Number Four? If so, why would they be impressed by his strutting?

Smelling faintly like mothballs and the witch hazel his wife used to mask the mothball odor didn't help, either. Men of substance didn't smell as if they'd been sleeping in a basement footlocker.

When the lift dropped to the mine level during my shift four days after the fight, the witch hazel odor told me Prapa had ventured into the dark face of Number Four. I had a premonition of trouble. I've only had a handful of such feelings in my life that I can recall, but each time they have proved correct.

I'd been five hours at the coal face and had an appetite that wouldn't reject raw dog or cooked rat. I'd smelled stew cooking in Aym's commissary cage as I'd passed it while travelling to the face, and I'd finally found time to sample it. She'd given me a double portion and fresh cider in my canteen.

"Cider's going to be running short until the fall again. This is the last of the overwinter supply," she said, filling my stainless reservoir up. "Sorry if it's a bit vinegary."

"Sweet. Sour. Both good," I said.

"Wish I could have a radio down here," she said. "Help pass the day. Sikorsky promised to rig something, but he can't find parts."

"I could read to you," I said.

"It might look odd, or blow your big smart Grog act."

The lift began to whine. "Those pulleys need oiling again," I said.

"Tell me about it. Drives Crumb nuts. He hides whenever it's in use."

"Prapa," I said as the lift banged down to the tunnel.

I sat down with my back against the bench outside (I was too big for the rather narrow bench itself, but the wood was better than cold rock), and I went to work on the stew. It wasn't bad, though I suspected it had been made from horse meat.

"Our yellow Grog's stuffing groceries, I see. No fear of a sandwich in that one."

Prapa looked down. Crumb was nuzzling his ankles and purring.

He stomped on the cat, or kicked it, hard. I didn't see the actual blow. I heard something snap, and the cat clawed away from Prapa, one rear leg bloody with exposed bone scraping awfully against the ground as it moved.

"Crumb!" Aym shouted. "What?—"

Prapa, sick of the yowling, pulled his revolver. Aym recognized the sound of a hammer being clicked back and threw herself toward him. He stiff-armed her, knocking her into her kitchen cart.

The loud report snapped painfully off the tunnel walls, making the gun seem three times as loud.

Crumb lay limp with the terrible stillness of a corpse. Aym crawled, feeling around for her pet.

"Fuck *me*!" Prapa shouted, looking down at his foot. His work boot had a hole in the arch and a fragment of bullet. "That burns. Look what your damn cat did, you tin cunt."

"All he wanted was a tickle," Aym said, her broken voice sounding as though it had a tough fight in exiting her body.

To this day, I wonder what would have happened had I relieved Prapa of his revolver and left him lying on the floor as still as the dead cat. With the five remaining shots I could have easily procured transport and left Number Four. Would I have made it halfway to Kentucky before the dogs were upon me? The excitement of an escape (and probably the return of one big furred corpse) would have short-circuited the anger brewing at Number Four. It might have saved many lives.

It was a decision point that passed before I had time to think. Prapa moved on to the shift office down the tunnel, and I helped Aym put her cat in a tinfoil tray. She decided to bury Crumb outside, as there was nowhere to bury him in the tunnel near her trailer.

Prapa's foul mood was not dispelled by killing the cat. He put everyone on overtime (without wages, the only compensation was food and drink and wash water brought down by wheelbarrow).

The purge would begin on Friday of that week, though it was officially called a "review." It would be conducted by a triumvirate of the New Universal Church, a Maynes representative, and one of the shift foremen, randomly selected by a name draw.

"Review," in the parlance of the mines, was an inspection of the mine, a health examination of the workers, and sometimes interviews. But everyone knew what would happen to men deemed surplus to requirements. There was nowhere to go after Number Four.

Word passed unofficially even before the notices went up in the shaft lift. The miners didn't need to worry about physical fitness— the vigor of their jobs kept their muscles like suspension cable—but some of them broke out their New Universal Church Guidons and familiarized themselves with old maxims and the latest offerings from the Church.

"Think as a species; work as an individual. You are your contribution to the future," one miner mumbled over and over. I felt for him. Much of the language in a Guidon could be shuffled around without losing much meaning, for it had little to start. "Work as a species; think for the future." "Your individual contribution is you" is in the same spirit as "Contribute as an individual; work for the future; you are your species." They're all much of a muchness, as your writer Carroll said.

Others, some of whom couldn't read beyond simple everyday signs that they recognized the same way a reader today would see a creation mark, were refreshing their memory of what had been discussed in services.

"What was in church Sunday?"

"The homily was about pre–Kurian Organized Deprivation. You know, starving the world so a few could live fat."

"They might shut the whole mine down. We're goners then."

"Nah, they'd just send us around the other mines."

They worked the next shifts so hard, half of the miners were ready to be thrown into a collection van just so they could sleep for a couple of hours before the last dance with the Reaper. As bad as the exhaustion was, the dirt was worse. I began to feel I would never get the grit out of my fur, and I began to itch as though infested with hellpit mites.

"Yeah, every couple of years we go through this," an old hand named Barnesworth told me. He usually worked a different shift, but he had put in for overtime this week just to show that he could still produce at a double-shift rate. He had an extraordinary physique for a man who had just turned sixty; if he was wearing a hat and you saw him from behind, you would take an oath that he was a man in his midtwenties.

I paced myself as best as I could, but I soon came up hard against my limits. I had taken over for two others, and I let them sleep while I extracted coal. As long as our shift's quota was met, who cares how we managed it (too often by shoveling more slag into the conveyor, but mistakes will be made when you drive men in this manner).

They started calling me John Henry, who, I understand, is a folk hero. I was happy to earn their respect, but it is easier for a "Grog" to apply strength in such a stooped-over fashion.

My own examination was simple enough. The doctor, after startling at my entrance, said, "I don't know enough about this kind of Grog to even tell how old he is. He looks fit enough."

He had me kneel. He looked into my eyes, ears, and at my tongue. If you ever want to look as though you know a good deal about Golden Ones, my reader, examine their knuckles. A sick one of my kind will spend more time going about on all fours, which will be indicated if there are fresh calluses and a rubbed-raw look.

And as we age, we go white above the eyes, a washed-out, almost clear white very different from that on the face or belly.

My file for my mine work consisted of two sheets of paper and a big blue tag—which I suppose referenced my work as Maynes's bodyguard.

"He hasn't been here long, but he's a strong worker. Never causes trouble. Stubborn, though." He looked up at me. "You stubborn?"

"Stub-burn?" I asked. "Not know stub-burn."

"Stiff-necked," the doc said, pointing to his neck.

"I don't think pantomime is needed with this one. Says he's un-usually smart, almost as smart as a man."

"I work hard. I dig coal. I get along. No laziness," I said. "No laziness, no never."

"That's quite a speech."

"He drives, too."

"There's nothing like him around here."

"The vet at the White Mansion says they live out in Omaha. Very independent. They've caused some trouble to the rail lines, I suppose."

"No touch railroad," I said. "No trouble."

On my way to the half day of work Saturday, the group of men walking up the road to the mine discussed who had been taken away on

Friday night. We'd lost Grimm, a handyman who did odd jobs around the dormitory. The mine office staff had two of theirs go, but one of them was promoted out of Number Four to replace a petty thief at another mine.

"No one from the dark crew?" Rage asked.

"Not that I've heard," Sikorsky said.

Foreman Bleecher met us at the elevator exit in the central run. He usually scowled, but today the lug nuts at either edge of his mouth were screwed down even more tightly.

"We only lost one, boys," Bleecher said. "Aym."

I tried not to show emotion, but my knees wobbled on me and I went down on all fours. No one in the shocked shift noticed. According to my reading, humans go through five stages of grief: Denial, Anger, Bargaining, Depression, and Acceptance. I believe I faltered at the gap between Anger and Bargaining. I felt my blood pound, the fur atop my head rise, and my ears go hot and flat against my head.

I'd already privately resolved to take Aym out with me, when eventually I escaped. She'd helped to bring me out of the funk that steady, exhausting work had allowed me to sink into, like a swamp, where thrashing seemed only to make more tendrils of futility cling to my fur. I would have led her across the Appalachians, carrying her on my back if nothing else. Strange, for I hardly knew her. I wondered at the agony of some of my human friends who'd had loved ones just disappear.

With those thoughts running through my head, I turned my attention back to the rest of the shift.

"Aym?" several miners said in angry tones. I could smell the anger on them.* "Why?"

"She practically lived in her cage," Rage said. "There's not one of us here who wouldn't have gone in her place."

"That so, Raymond," Foreman Bleecher said. "Well, they only took her at midnight. Go on up and volunteer to go in her stead."

"Could we do something about it?" Olsen asked. "Sign a petition or something? Bring it to the Church? Nobody at the mine would claim that she's a useless mouth."

"Petition? What did they put in your breakfast kibble this morning?" Pelloponensis asked.

"Want Aym back," I put in. "We need our food."

"Hey, even the stoop's pissed," Rage said. "We got a united front here."

"A united front and three bucks will get you a ride into town," Sikorsky said.

"We could ask to see the paperwork, I suppose," Bleecher said. "Maybe there's a cock-up between the three reviewers."

"What's done is done; let it go," another miner put in.

"Just be glad there weren't more."

"We'll just see about that!" Rage said. "C'mon, Sikorsky, Pelloponensis."

"What's up? You going to volunteer to take her place?" Olsen asked.

"Hey, Hickory, you come, too?" Rage asked me.

---

* Our narrator may be using a metaphor here, but the Xeno Department of Miskatonic-Copenhagen has done tests on "Gray Ones" that have shown that an isolated specimen able only to smell the air of another group imitates the emotional state of the group it can neither see nor hear.

"Time for work," I said. I wanted to think. I'd learned only a little about the victims of the Kurian Order and where they went after pickup even during my time with Maynes.

"The firemen are on their way!"

"Jesus, Rage, what have you done?"

"They won't do shit. Not while we have the mine. Prapa, too."

"There's more coal where that came from, numbnuts. We're not even ten percent of production. All they have to do is add another shift at Fourteen and it'll more than make up for us."

"They called the firemen? On us?"

"We should send a messenger. Offer."

"Yeah, and get shot in the leg for it."

"I know," Pelloponensis said. "We could tie a message around the Grog's neck and send him out. Not like one of us getting shot." He didn't bother to lower his voice or speak as an aside, as an older sibling might when proposing a trick on his uncomprehending younger sibling.

They had the fire trucks parked blocking the road down to the housing.

I counted fifteen rifles pointed at me. If something went wrong, I'd be dead before I heard the sound of the shots.

"Me messenger," I said.

"Bring it. Slowly."

I took robotic steps forward, pausing every time a foot touched or left the ground.

A fireman with captain's bars read the note. "They have Prapa. They want one of their workers back. Taken last night."

The firemen were no more afraid to talk in front of me than the miners inside. The thought flashed across my mind that dogs understand a lot more than they let on; they just think it's politic not to react.

Number Four mine is on strike. We protest the removal of our break attendant, Aym Swanson.

We have Director Prapa and Foreman Bleecher under guard. No harm will come to them for the duration of the strike. We retain them only to prevent a seizure of the mine by force.

The mine, equipment, and supporting buildings have been wired with explosives. Any attempt to remove us by force will result in the destruction of the mine, machinery, buildings, and, of course, ourselves.

Our only demand is the return of Aym Swanson to her duties.

The next day it rained, hard, turning most of the open ground at Number Four to mud.

"Ahh. Listen, you. I'm . . . coming. Coming in to talk over your demands."

It was Murphy's voice, cracking and hesitant, over the bullhorn.

Murphy was shaking all over and greasy with sweat. Something was wrong beyond the exertion of crossing Number Four's front yard.

A figure in one of the standard firemen's black-and-yellow raincoats stepped carefully across the mud.

"That's Fatty, all right."

"I'll go out and check him," Barnesworth said. "I know him better than any of you."

"Bleecher, go out and cover him."

"I can do it just fine from in here," Bleecher said from his rifle sight. "Something about this stinks. Murphy would make us come to him in this piss."

By fully extending my ears and concentrating, I could just hear Murphy. "Barnesworth, you have to help me," Murphy said. "Everyone's got to come out of the mine. Today, within the hour."

Barnesworth said something in return, but it was lost in the drizzle. He was facing the other way.

"He's wired! Explosives!"

"No, let—," Murphy began.

Barnesworth made it two steps before disappearing in a boiling mist of fire and fleshy debris. The concussion shattered windows already pierced and spiderwebbed by bullets.

A messy trail of pieces of Barnesworth lay on a path to the mine.

"We should send Prapa out," Longliner said.

"Are you nuts?"

"Prapa?"

"You were the one who wanted to take him hostage in the first place."

"No, the kid's got a point," Bleecher said, eye still aligned on his sight. "It's the mine that's important. Prapa's just a functionary. He'll sound every gong in hell to get us working again. It's his position on the line, too."

Jones stood behind Prapa with hands on the ropes around his wrists. "Okay, Mr. Director Prapa, we have two demands. First, back to the understanding that nobody who works in the mine gets repurposed. We understand accident and injury and all that, but working in the dark and the dust ought to earn us some privileges. Second, we want Aym back if she's still alive. Everything goes back to normal."

"How about no more Grogs doing mine work?" Pelloponensis said.

"Best thing to do is walk out behind me quietly," Prapa said. "That's your only chance of resolving this and getting things back to normal. Right now, it's a Coal Country matter. I bet no one outside the White Palace knows about it. But if word of this strike spreads out of Number Four . . . your lives won't be worth spit. No repurposing—they'll just come in and kill you."

"This is Boss Murphy, guys. Let's stop this nonsense now. Prapa is a jackoff—you know it; I know it; the folks at the White Palace know it. He's done."

"We're dead men," Sikorsky said. "Sure as shit."

"Old thumbs there is right," Pelloponensis said.

"Let's not give them the satisfaction. Let's blow this mine to hell and all of us with it," Sikorsky said.

"Just how will you do that, wiseass?" Pelloponensis said.

"Easy. Mess a little with the ventilators and kick up enough coal dust to fill Broadway. Touch it off with naked flame or some blasting caps."

"Let's not go crazy here. Like the man said, this is still fixable," Longliner said.

"Says the man who said we need fast, direct action."

"He was taking hemorrhoid cures, I bet," Pelloponensis said.

"Anyone going to ask the stoop's opinion?"

"No fight. Work hard," I said.

"Anyone who trusts these jackholes, feel free to walk out behind Prapa," Sikorsky said. "I'm not going to be around when the music stops. Let the Hoods yank some pieces off you. I'm staying put."

"Hey, guys, it's me," Galloway said through the megaphone. "Prapa—he's . . . he's gone. Yeah, they took care of him permanently. A—a representative from on high is here, and he's saying that he's done with these games. The mine needs to go back up, right now. All we have to do is say that it was a big misunderstanding, that we weren't on strike or anything, that it was a broken shaft elevator and power loss. We say that on the radio and everything's good. No more Prapa, either."

Nobody moved, but they still listened intently.

"They're treating us right," Galloway continued. "I just had a big steak dinner. With sauce and steak fries. Still sputtering when they brought it to me on the plate. The . . . representative says that nobody else is going to die, provided we go back to work. I'm not reading a prepared statement or anything, just telling you like it is. Hope you come on out. Air must be getting pretty bad down there if Bleecher is eating nothing but beans and WHAM!"

I found this exchange humorous enough to record verbatim, but I do not remember the speakers: "We can't just skulk in the mine like bats. If I'm going to die, I don't want it to be in Number Four."

"You know why it's called Number Four, right?"

"No, I don't."

"Two number twos."

"You need weapons? I get weapons," I said, picking up an old tarp used by the mechanics to stay off the wet ground when working on the mine machinery.

I took a short, flat shovel I'd been sharpening at the edges and climbed up into the attic of the mine office to a chorus of creaking framing. I had to negotiate a weeping willow of phone and power wiring, none of it tacked down, just running from the roof peak down to the offices and so on. What a fire trap, but typical for the Kurian Order.

I found a ventilator, removed it, and climbed up onto the roof. From there it was a fairly easy jump onto the hillside. I climbed with the tarp over one arm and the short-handled shovel in the other.

If I was having trouble with Number Four, I'd post some people on the ridgeline above, just to make sure we had the place surrounded.

The footing on the hillside was bad, with many loose leaves and dirt. I found a solitary tree and, climbing it so that it was between me and the fire trucks blocking the road, I surveyed the hillside carefully.

Yes, there it was. They'd even bothered with sandbags.

It was a small gun emplacement, with a machine gun aimed so it was covering the area between the mine office and the underground entrance, plus the scattered vehicles parked on the flat. The soldiers wore trooper camouflage; they were probably mobilized off their regular patrol routes and put into battle dress until the crisis passed.

The gun itself had another two-man team covering it from the gunner's blind side.

I descended the tree and unrolled the oily tarp. I covered it with some loose bits of bracken and grasses, then wormed under it. I inched my way up the hillside, crawling using my elbows, with legs limp.

It was exhausting work and I had to take frequent rests. The insects were noisy that night and covered the steady crunching—deafeningly loud even to my flat ears—of my crawl.

Grogs and humans have similar night vision in that we're both more sensitive to motion when the light level is low. At last, I judged myself close enough for a rush. I surveyed the four-man detail one more time. The gun crew was still concentrating on the mine entrance and vehicle park below. The gunner must have seen something, because he was looking down the sights of the weapon, ready to tracer-snipe. As for the flank guards, they were sharing a tin of tobacco and talking, too softly for me to pick up anything but the watermelon-watermelon-watermelon of background stage dialogue.

Behind a patch of bramble within a few meters of the troopers, I ever so slowly gathered myself into a ball, set my feet—

I rose up out of the grass and sent the tarp sailing at the flank guards. Ideally, a nervous trigger would fire at that rather than my own form rushing at them with sharpened shovel raised.

My appearance, rising from nowhere as though I'd been magically transported by a djinni, froze them both for the three seconds it took me to cover the distance. They reacted too late. I stuck one with the shovel just as he was raising his rifle to his shoulder and swept the other up in my arm like a long-lost friend.

Shovel-wound had a look of dull amazement in his eyes with his skull almost cut in two, the unicorn horn of the shovel handle sticking out and forward.

The one I'd swept up I raised over my head. I hurled him at the machine-gun crew.

I retrieved my shovel from the trooper's head and waded into the trio, swinging.

One managed to draw a pistol and fire. The light and the noise of the shot startled me for a moment before I finished the three men.

Sloppy. I must be slowing in my age. Once I would have taken all four of these third-rate draftees before any could get a shot off.

I didn't feel the bite of lead, but sometimes you don't know you've been shot until you see the blood or after the fight.

I retrieved the tarp, spread it out, and tossed their guns and spare ammunition magazines on it. I listened uphill for sounds of investigation and heard nothing. With the extra moment allowed, I took the crew-served weapon off its tripod and laid it on the tarp, folded the tripod, and added the belt they'd loaded and extra ammunition cases. Now we would have a surprise for the besiegers if they tried to storm the mine in a rush.

I rolled the tarp up and carried it as carefully as the bearer who carried the rug-wrapped Cleopatra into Caesar's Roman Alexandrian headquarters. I shouldered it and moved downhill.

A shout and a shot pursued me. I sped up, dropping the shovel in my haste.

Like a Father Christmas wearing a coat of blood and brains, I bounded down the hill by threes, with the weapons collected in the tarp bouncing on my shoulder.

A shot passed close enough for me to feel the air pressure change as it passed through my fur. It is a unique experience, the brief touch of a bullet's path. I wrapped my legs around my burden and started to roll down the hill.

I fetched up against the mine office. The troopers were popping up and down like a line of prairie dogs, getting off shots. I retrieved one of the carbines from the roll, checked to see that it was loaded, adjusted the sights, and returned fire. Ineffectually, I might add, but I was shooting uphill with a rifle I'd never used before.

Had the troopers been a little more aggressive, they might have taken the office by a quick assault, if they'd been able to get by me. But things were still at a standoff and no one was eager to overstep their orders.

They were still plinking away, and I hugged the hill so they could no longer see me from their position. I picked up the machine gun—it had a convenient handle on the barrel and a pistol grip—and rose up to give them a real taste of fire, but they'd either gone to ground or backed off. Perhaps the bodies of their fellow troopers had given them something to think about. Were they up there, wondering what would have happened had their lieutenant selected them to man the gun?

Time and Chance happeneth to them all.

The mine buildings now had a "grazing line" of dirt and debris showing where the machine guns of the firemen could cover. We scuttled from room to room like crabs, keeping heads below the bullet holes. Where there were no buildings or parked heavy equipment, we'd dug trenches so we could crawl from point to point in safety.

It seemed as though there were fewer vehicles surrounding Number Four after that first week. Rumors flew, that other mines had joined in our "strike" (if all-out battle could still be called a strike) or that the regime was trying to hide the fact that fighting was even going on by only keeping small contingents around to starve us into surrender.

I suspect it was just the Kurian Order being economical. They knew we would wear down eventually (they didn't know the callused toughness of miners) and surrender.

They tried dropping mortar shells on us, but it was too easy to escape back underground.

Unbelievably, we were smuggled fresh food, firearms, ammunition (but not enough). The runs were carried out by boys who snuck up the mountainside. They usually came at dawn or twilight, wiggling through the underbrush.

Explosives—those we had plenty of. We rigged bombs and flung them into the parked armored cars and fire trucks of the firemen and troopers through a simple counterweighted arm that turned a collection of hammered-together bracing wood and plastic conduit into a trebuchet fired up and out of a ventilator that had the fans removed. Once we fired it a few times, we were amazingly accurate with it.

Rage, dirty fighter that he was, had the idea of rigging one of the bombs to look like the detonator had fallen off. A pair of firemen went to retrieve it, perhaps to launch it back at us. The real detonator was activated by radio signal. It turned one of the firemen into scraps of dog meat and struck the other hard enough that he had to be taken away in an ambulance.

We started off with about seventy men and women. By the first week we were cut in half. Some of those were casualties; these weren't trained soldiers and we lost many to surprisingly accurate sniper fire. There must have been at least one among the troopers or firemen who was an expert shot. The rest simply slipped away from their posts and either surrendered or tried to get away into the wilderness.

We were all on edge. At least we could sleep by going deep into the mine where the lights and noise couldn't penetrate, though there were persistent threats from the Conglomerate that they'd helicopter in something called a fuel-air bomb powerful enough to blow the mine up entirely.

BLEECHER'S TRY AT A RESOLUTION

We ended up with two prisoners. A trooper patrol on the slope west of the mine stumbled across a fireman machine gun position, which panicked and opened fire on their allies. The two trooper survivors ran blindly right into a couple of our miners who were creeping forward to throw explosives at the machine gun and were taken underground.

Rage suggested using them as decoys against snipers during relief of the men guarding the motor pool and ruins of the mine office.

Bleecher saw it as an opportunity to try to negotiate a settlement.

"I hope that means you're volunteering to sit down at a table across from a damn Hood," Pelloponensis said.

"Just because I was foreman doesn't mean I don't side just as strong as you about the demands," Bleecher said.

After a little more bickering at an informal council of war (I missed the bickering because I was at the mine entrance with the machine gun), Bleecher walked out, waving a white flag and escorting the prisoners.

"A cease-fire is in effect," a loudspeaker atop one of the fire trucks boomed. "A cease-fire is in effect."

We watched Bleecher stand with a couple of firemen, tiredly

talking and pointing. He turned over the prisoners and the discussion continued. Bleecher seemed to be begging at one point. Finally, two firemen grabbed him and a third emptied a ten-gallon jerry can of what was obviously gasoline on him.

Then the group of firemen released him and began poking at him with those little butane torches used for lighting fires in kindling and fireplaces and so on, the ones that produce a flame at the end of a six-inch tube. Bleecher frantically backpedaled toward the mine entrance until one of them tired of the game and set him alight at the waist. To our horror, he was soon engulfed in flame.

"A cease-fire is in effect," the fire truck boomed.

I fired a burst with my machine gun into the man who'd set Bleecher alight. The others raced for their trenches.

Bleecher staggered toward us, a living pillar of fire. I fired a second burst into the kindly supervisor who'd bought me countless root beers at the end of an overtime shift, and he fell. So much for all his attention to duty as foreman.

"A cease-fire is in effect," the fire truck yowled again, a little more shrilly. We allowed a couple of medical armbands with a stretcher out to get the fireman I'd shot.

"Jeez, what a way to treat a thirty-year man," Sikorsky said.

"Only thing big about him was his belly. He was even small in his corruptions."

"I'd say they're done negotiating with us," Pelloponensis said. "They'll just keep at us until we're all dead."

"There's movement behind the fire trucks," Rage shouted from his vantage in the mine offices. "They're backing and filling. Can't make up their minds."

"I'm tired of this. Let's give up. I don't care if they kill us, as long as I can get some sleep."

"Here they come again!"

If they gained control of the mine entrance and the ventilators, we would only last a few hours, if that. They could pump in old-fashioned poisoned gas (the Georgia Control was known to use it in its brushes with the amphibians of the Florida Everglades). So to control the mine entrance, we had to control the above-ground office, the junkyard with its array of heavy equipment, and the giant beetle and daddy longlegs conveyor rigs for loading coal onto the railroad cars and sorted and dumped slag. Then, of course, we somehow had to control some of the mountainside above, or they could just shoot down on both. With our handful, it would be an impossible task once they mustered enough forces to overrun us.

It is my belief that the Coal Country was trying to handle the problem at Number Four quietly. The troopers, firemen, and other reliable armed groups were stretched very thin trying to prevent sabotage of the rail lines, and the Maynes family and its mystery Kurian must have feared that if word of further disorder leaked out, there would be an intervention and takeover, probably by either the Ordnance or Georgia Control.

The Kurian Order always had a hard time finding troops who could be trusted with firearms. I heard innumerable stories of men who passed through all their training, scored excellently on all the political reliability and psychological exams, and then, within a few months of being issued arms and ammunition, gunned down a major or colonel and his staff at a checkpoint to avenge a beloved grandparent or aunt who had been taken away.

Word was getting out, at least to others in the Coal Country, through bus-stop and back-fence networks. Though we did not know it at the time, the Coal Country was already arming itself and intervening on our behalf. Some inventive garage mechanic was producing tire-destroying strips that could be rolled and unrolled on the roads. I got a look at one of these during the fighting—it was regular chain-link fencing with nails and machine screws bent into barbed fishhooks. Tires were another weak point in the Kurian Order; there were always rubber shortages and most tires on transport vehicles were "recycles" made out of shredded rubber and nylon cable. The strips created by this unnamed genius shredded such tires into walnut-sized chunks, leaving cargo idling until replacement tires could be found. For transports on the more lonely roads, their cargoes were salvaged and distributed as quickly as army ants could strip the bones of a fallen horse.

"A cease-fire is in effect," that speaker wailed again. For a moment I thought I was dreaming about the death of Bleecher.

Murphy from the dormitory was walking out, holding a white handkerchief in one hand and a manila envelope in the other.

"There's an offer of a deal in here," Murphy shouted. "Nobody shoot."

The loudspeaker continued its message about a cease-fire.

"Fellas, they gave me a message for you. No weird moves now; they got a gun on me," Murphy said. "C'mon out. I can't get any closer to the mine or they'll shoot."

The men at the bullet-riddled, half-collapsed mine office and junkyard shrugged and made "all clear" signals.

I volunteered to go out and talk to him. Pelloponensis disliked Murphy; I think he went just to finally tell him what he really thought. Sikorsky and a kid named Queever rounded out the group.

"Why do you always step up for this crap, Sikorsky?" Pelloponensis asked as we walked out.

"My grandfather came from Poland," he said. "I remember the last time we saw him. He told me: 'We Poles, sometimes the only weapon we have is courage.' I think he joined the resistance a little while after that, or at least that was what he told my father."

"Where's Poland? By New York?" Pelloponensis asked.

We approached the dorm supervisor. He was standing in the hunched-over manner of a man who'd recently been punched in the gut. Perhaps he feared a bullet in the back.

"They told me to give you this envelope," Murphy said, handing over the manila envelope while the loudspeaker continued to call out the cease-fire message. I promised myself that someday I'd find the fireman in charge of the siege at Number Four and stuff him through the bell of the loudspeaker. "You're supposed to read it and send me back with the answer. They say you have exactly two minutes to read it and decide."

I noticed that the end Murphy had been holding was wet with perspiration.

Murphy was sweating . . . melting, rather, so much water seemed to be running out of him. Greasy sweat, too; it glistened like the leavings of a frying pan that had been used to cook bacon.

Oddly, I thought, his chest and armpits were dry. I've seen men sweat from the Caribbean to the Dakotas, and they always sweat most profusely from the armpits, followed by the back, brow, and chest. Why would his brow be covered in beady, greasy sweat but not his armpits? Was something thick blocking it?

"Run!" I told my compatriots.

Thanks to my reach, I knocked them back and away from Murphy. Just as we were going down, a strong wave seemed to strike, a remorseless hand shoving us to the earth and a wall of noise and heat licking over us and leaving us dazed with a foggy, underwater sensation. I dragged my companions back toward the mine, feeling blood run from my nostrils.

The sniper got Queever, the young miner who had proven himself an excellent self-taught shot though he'd never held a weapon until the previous week, but the rest of us made it back to safety.

In talking it over later, we decided Murphy had been forced to wear what he probably thought was a heavy bulletproof vest, but it had turned out to be filled with explosives and a few pieces of tin designed to act as fléchettes. Murphy probably had not realized he was a walking bomb—the sweat was simply from his being in physical danger for the first time in his life. I'm sure some part of him suspected he was a pawn that could be sacrificed.

Pelloponensis had inadvertently escaped with the manila envelope. After testing the closed version for a trap, we decided it either contained nothing but air or a single sheet of thin paper.

You're fucked, it read, with the seal of the Coal Country Firemen beneath.

I was the only one wounded. I had a few pieces of shrapnel in me. Sikorsky extracted them with a pair of tweezers and stitched me up with fishing line from the office. One sliver was too deep for him to reach. I've since seen it on X-rays; it appears to be minding its own business, probably encased in some sort of protective cyst my body formed around it. I tell the doctors it is my "decoration" for the fighting at Number Four.

Sadly, it's the only one ever issued, at least to my knowledge. I am hoping this memoir might change that.

THE SECOND RIOT CONTROL—

"No. The hostages go right by the entrance."

I had little use for Prapa or Murphy.

All the equipment was handy. The trick, as Sikorsky said, was not being around when it went off. It was entirely possible that as soon as the fans began to move the finely ground dust, friction between particles or heat from the motor could set off the explosion, killing all of us.

Luckily the water mains were all in the mine buildings. Otherwise the fire trucks might have been able to put enough water on us to make shooting back impossible while they stormed Number Four.

Over the next three days we lost three more. David Valentine, a student of the Civil War that divided the former United States more than two hundred years ago, once told me that General Lee lamented the loss of some key troops in one action or another. Lee noted that troops he lost were gone for good, whereas the enemy seemed to have limitless replacements. We weren't even doing as well as that other generation of rebels; the last casualties we had inflicted were those in the assault after Bleecher was set on fire.

Just holding out was a form of victory, however. The first evidence that we had that there were repercussions for our "strike" came in the form of a limousine. I had seen one or two in Ohio during our search for Gail Post two years ago. This was the first one I'd seen in the Coal Country. It was not an elongated one, but rather a simple, overlarge sedan with blacked-out windows and shining grillwork.

"What the hell's that?" an office strongpoint observer asked, looking through a hole in the wall with binoculars. He woke Pelloponensis (we had an informal arrangement that one of us guarding the strongpoint could sleep while the other two kept watch on the approaches and each other) who stared blearily through the glasses as he strapped on his hard hat.

"White stripe across the roof. Church, most likely," Pelloponensis said.

Again, the fire engine loudspeaker announced that a cease-fire was in effect.

We took advantage of the cease-fire to hurry back to the cave mouth, bringing the accumulation from the rainwater catchers. We'd run out of lives at this rate before the soap ran out, but water for bathing was running short.

A black-suited figure strode out across the gap between trooper and firemen vehicles and the scrap-heap protection in between them and our own shot-up lines. White showed at his collars and cuffs, and he wore a red silk tie. He strode purposefully, as serenely as if he were walking up his home church aisle in a ceremony.

"That's the Guidon," one of the regular churchgoers said. "He's right below the Archon in Baltimore. He's out here a couple of times a year for graduations of Youth Vanguard and investments of new clergy."

"I have an offer," the churchman called. "Let's put a stop to this foolishness, my children."

"That's what's always pissed me off about the damn Church," Sikorsky said. "We're always children. I'm a fuckin' grown-up. I can figure out whether to wash before I go to bed or when I get up, I don't need a church bulletin telling me which saves more soap and water in the long run."

"I like your nonbathing solution," Pelloponensis put in. "Saves everything all around."

"Who wants to go get a face full of this message?"

He looked like a senior churchman. He was heavy, with a red nose that had nothing to do with cold.

"I go," I said.

"I wonder if he'll be wired."

"Hey, Hick, go out and check him for bombs," Pelloponensis said.

"Watch out for gasoline cans."

The churchman smiled. "Don't worry, friend; I'm not covered in explosives."

"I no afraid," I said.

"Do you always speak like that? I've met several of your kind. They were all brighter than the average human. With such a big head and flexible nasophyrangal cavities, you should be able to speak much more clearly than that."

"Are we supposed to trust you just because you're clergy?" Sikorsky asked.

"No, you're supposed to trust me because I'm powerful," he intoned.

"Let reward be punishment and punishment be reward."

"It was just a blind woman. Are you willing to kill yourself and all your comrades in a war over some girl? She wasn't even pretty."

"Pretty means little in a mine and less to a Grog. She was kind to me."

"Kind. You're willing to let death loose in this valley again over that?"

"Perhaps if we proved willing to start a war over a single girl, they would give up trying to take them."

"Would it change matters if you knew she volunteered to go? She chose to sacrifice herself so none of you would be taken. Now the Order is willing to accept you back into the fold, but you'll have to select one of your number to pay for your crimes. There have been too many deaths for no price to be paid. The troopers and firemen wouldn't stand for it.

"In the Church, we're always looking for those who can face the arithmetic. The arithmetic becomes too much for some. Even churchmen with years of schooling and the discipline of constant positive reinforcement. Sometimes their bodies sicken; then their minds go. But perhaps five percent of humans have the necessary steel in their constitution to look at the world and not flinch. I think you aren't the type to flinch."

"I've never met any of my kind in the uniform of the Church."

"Oh, you'd have your choice of clothing. Even the Maynes household wouldn't be able to offer you what we could.

"You've no doubt interacted with many of mankind. How many are in any way remarkable? How many are missed by anyone beyond a small circle when they die, whether from natural causes or a more methodical end?"

"Murder with sophistic flourishes," I said.

"Don't give me easy answers. You're clearly intelligent. Why end up as another body on the pile?

"Just as monkeys and lab rats and tissue cultures must die so that we can have healthier bodies, we also need to eliminate the human waste to have a healthier society. You could think of yourself as a powerful white blood cell, searching for the unhealthy and necrotic. What would you like? Food? Females? I can assure you, you'd get the best of everything. We'd like to see you produce others similar to yourself. We find that you nonnatives have a more clinical attitude toward humanity."

I remember little else of the encounter. I started laughing; I know that. They still thought I must be a strong back with a weak mind, caught up in events beyond my control and looking for an exit. I was still laughing when I returned to the entrance to Number Four.

"What was that about, King?" Pelleponensis asked.

"The shepherds of the Church wanted me as a sheepdog."

"Hope you peed on his leg, big guy."

Two more days passed. The strain of the hopeless, cutoff position would be hard enough on trained soldiers. These ordinary men were cracking. It was one thing to die fighting in a hot rush of emotion, a desperate, mass suicide; quite another to go on day after day being whittled down in ones and twos, living off trickles of water or even morning dew sponged off rocks. With food running out, they wouldn't even have the strength to lift a sharpened shovel against another attack before long.

Everyone knew it was over. The only question was whether the denouement would be another assault, or a mass surrender that would probably end with all of our bodies in a ditch, waiting for a bulldozer to cover us with slag.

I was determined to chance an escape into open air while I still had strength.

"There is no point in hiding the truth any longer," I announced on the morning of the third day.

"Hey, Big Yellow's gone all verbose," Pelloponensis said. "What are they doing now, talking to us through him?"

"I admire how suspicious you are, but I assure you that's not the case. I am a Kurian agent out of the Northwest Ordnance," I said.

"An agent?"

"I can't tell you my mission. This wasn't part of it, but it may end up helping after all. Should any of you wish to switch to a new region, just give the password 'lost: sourball' to any churchman or captain or above in the Ordnance. Don't forget the 'lost' part. 'Lost: sourball'—they'll set you up."

If any of them ever reached the Ordnance, the password wouldn't do them any good at all, but they'd probably receive good treatment on the chance that they'd aided an agent from the Ordnance.

What really mattered was that they believed me; they believed me enough so that even if they were brought before some high official of the Church with Fates-only-know-what powers and abilities, they would be able to have their conscience read as clean.

"I believe I will be able to cause enough chaos out there for you to either escape or surrender as you see fit. I have certain—abilities—that should allow me to slip away after. I will do my best for you for the next twenty-four hours; then I must continue with my mission."

When night fell, I took six bombs and, crawling carefully through the wrecks of the junkyard, wired them together to blow. One charge I put under a pair of gasoline cans for some additional flame; another I buried in a mass of taconite pellets inside a piece of concrete sewage line to make sort of an oversized poor-man's claymore. I rigged everything to a switch I could reach by crawling into a little hollow I scooped out under a defunct crane.

I covered myself with an old tarp and crept out beyond the junkyard. The first observation post of the enemy was a good hundred yards away over ground covered in bits of slag and brush. I didn't want to get too far beyond the junkyard; I needed to retreat to it as soon as I started my "commotion."

I don't know if my bombs killed even a single Coal Country fireman, but with a couple of squads pursuing me into the junkyard, I at least scared them enough so they backed out. Mortar shells and illumination rounds began to rain all over the scrap heap.

Their flash was just what I wanted—the light would affect the eyes in the hills no doubt looking down into the cauldron of Number Four.

I'd marked my escape route early, a muddy notch in the hillside running up the south-side ridge. There were several spots on the hillside providing a good view of the seasonal watercourse, and there would surely be a sentry at at least one. But thanks to the water that came and went with season and rainfall, there was a lot of brush and young tree life flanking it as well.

I watched them strip the miners naked and load them into a van. There was not much doubt about what would happen to them. Other firemen were laying charges; they would blow all the mine shafts of Number Four, even the abandoned ones.

All through the fighting at Number Four, perhaps from the moment they'd taken Aym away, a resolve had been building within me. This slipshod Kurian Zone known as the Coal Country was as rotten as a termite-riddled house with sawdust falling at the slightest rap on the planking. It wouldn't take much for it to come crashing down. Aym, and thousands like her over the years, couldn't be retrieved, but they could be avenged.

Few knew better than I the state of the roads in the Coal Country; I'd picked my way across them often enough. The truck carrying the naked, captive miners wouldn't make very good time, and there was only one road out of Number Four to take. I picked up my weapons, including my sharpened shovel, and set off quickly, keeping just below the ridgeline.

I found what I was looking for: a boulder above a notch in the road and a downed tree I could use as a lever. It took some small effort to properly position the tree and pile up a few stones against a larger rock outcropping to use as a fulcrum.

The kidney-shaped boulder, about the size of a children's plastic play-pool, careened down the hillside in a satisfyingly destructive manner. Unfortunately, while some of the debris that it brought in its wake wound up on the road, the boulder itself bounced off the bank opposite and came to rest in the drainage ditch along the shoulder. I extracted my tree-limb lever and hurried down the slope. My pick-exercised muscles were able to work it back onto the road with just a few minutes' work. I decided I had the time to perfect the positioning, so I moved it to the side of the road where it would come into view at the last possible moment from a driver descending the track from the mine. I didn't put it square in the middle of the road—another vehicle might precede the truck and the drivers might take the initiative to get out and remove the obstacle. Instead, I filled one side, so a careful driver could go around it using the very soft shoulder at a crawl.

Then I concealed myself next to the drainage ditch under a layer of hacked-off redbud and waited.

They must have kept the transport at the mine an extra hour in case anyone else gave himself up before the charges were detonated. A pickup truck with fireman markings was the first vehicle I saw. The driver went around the landslide just as cautiously as I would have had I been behind the wheel, and took no more notice of it than he would the other three or four bad sections of road he'd probably encounter that day.

The collection van waggled into view, rocking on its worn-out suspension. It was a boxy, utilitarian vehicle. I'm told most of them were converted parcel-delivery trucks—they got better gas mileage than armored cars, which had better uses. Kurian Zone mechanics never seemed to get around to working on those accursed vans.

Like the pickup truck, it slowed to negotiate the boulder. Unlike the pickup, when the right-hand wheels spun up and out of the shoulder drainage, it had the Coal Country's sole Golden One clinging to the door and rusty running board.

My sharpened shovel opened the passenger side window before the guard riding next to the driver had time to do much more than throw up his arm against the spiderwebbed safety glass.

I reached in and extracted the passenger. He didn't quite fit out the window, but I made him do so, a little noisily and messily for him. It was an object lesson in always wearing one's restraint harness when driving. I threw the Church's collector into the woods, where he left a provocative red trail for the scavengers to follow.

Inside, the guard was fumbling for his pistol. He was wearing his seat belt, and it was caught over his holster.

"'This day's black fate on more days doth depend; this but begins the woe others must end,'" I said.

The muddy and somewhat bloody apparition speaking to him made him pause long enough in his fumbling for his sidearm that he was probably still processing the quote from *Romeo and Juliet* when the point of my shovel caught him under his chin and the New Universal Church was down one more collection driver.

I took control of the wheel and gearshift and wrapped my toes around the clutch and accelerator. I took the van down the first turn-off trail I could find and pulled it out of sight. There was enough brush displaced to make it obvious to a searcher, but traffic coming down the road not looking for a missing van probably would not notice it.

The nine naked miners flinched when I opened the door.

"You're about fifteen miles from the mine down the access road," I said. "I'm sorry I can't do more for you, but I wish you luck. I think there are some clothes for the Church in those lockers. You can have the shotgun in the mount and the driver's pistol, if you think those will help."

Pelloponensis cleared his throat. "Hey, Hickory, sorry for all—"

The apology wasn't really necessary for either of us. "I have other matters to attend to. I'd keep off the roads if I were you. At night, try to find livestock and bed down as close to them as you can. It'll confuse the Reapers. Perhaps the dogs as well."

"I'm not running like some kid who just saw his first Hood," Pelloponensis said. "They started a fight with the miners. If there's anyone ordinary in the Coal Country who isn't at least cousin to someone working coal, I'll dig a hundredweight holding my pick with my ass cheeks. We're going to finish this fight."

PART THREE

Conquest and Cleansing

On my own, my chances of making it out of the Coal Country and into the western slopes of the Appalachians were better than even. I could cause enough chaos to set things in an uproar that would give the other escaping miners a chance.

Walking away from a land where men I considered friends died in a fight we shared would be dishonorable. It would be understandable—anyone who'd ever fought against the Kurian Order covertly might even say just getting away alive was a kind of victory—but dishonorable nonetheless. If I ran, I would taste the bitterness of the act for the rest of my life.

So my staying was the easier choice. One might even say it was the default, to a Golden One, since the sense of keeping one's honor clean lightened any burden.

What a laughable way to start a war—dirty, tired, and almost unarmed. I needed a serious weapon.

A successful guerilla blends into the local population, living invisibly until he chooses the right moment to strike, like one of the praying mantis species that has developed to look like a dead leaf.

I, however, looked like exactly no one in all of Coal Country. A local would comment less on an oak growing up through the center of a highway intersection than he would on me.

A guerilla also needs knowledge of the land and the disposition of his enemies. My time with Maynes had given me that. A guerilla also needs a feel for the locals. Will they aid him, or turn him over to the authorities? Except for a very few favored by Maynes Consolidated, the locals held a long-simmering grudge against the Order. They were already in revolt, even if it was a slow-motion, dead-of-night sort of resistance.

Third, a guerilla needs motivation. I was sick of this stinking principality, rotten to the core and painful as an infected tooth. But I could not just leave. Once you've witnessed a certain amount of kindness and cruelty, you're bound to a place, and if I fled without trying to make it better, I would regret it for whatever days and years I have left in this life.

I had a pretty good idea of where to get weapons.

I thought the shadows were playing tricks on me, turning the black, blasted form into one of those multilimbed god-statues from across the Pacific.

Had such a god descended on this quarter of the Americas, I could not have been more shocked, once my brain interpreted what had come shambling out of the hills.

It was one of the Reapers, sent into Number Four—or rather a pair of them. One was terribly injured, its torso having been severed in the area of the pelvis and turned into a tarry stump. The other carried it, lashed on its chest with webbing belts. The Reaper still in possession of its legs dragged a third, reduced to a head and most of one shoulder.

The head on the tied-on torso searched. Its eyes shone against the black mask of smoke, soot, and the dried blood both wore. The Reaper with the legs had a terribly disfigured face. One eye was a black mess like a roasted mushroom.

It occurred to me that the Kurian Order must be pressed if it had its members searching the hills around the mine with such a contraption. Whichever Kurian was animating these must have been down to his last Reaper, or very nearly so. A Kurian without his Reapers might not starve to death per se, but without infusions of the vital aura from his victims, he will wither like a drought-afflicted tomato.

I had no sure weapon for killing one of these murderous machines. Bullets would only slow it, unless I was very fortunate in placing the rounds.

Sensing my uncertainty and an advantage with predatory instinct, it stalked me, the head with intact vision clacking its teeth together. Could the piece of brother Reaper have meant something to it? Or did it just want to unnerve me with the unsettling sight of the living puppet?

I removed my belt and wrapped by left hand in it so that the buckle lay across my knuckles, and I snapped a branch off with the other.

I waved the branch, testing its reaction. Both heads followed it, the head on the legless one slightly faster. I stepped to the side; it imitated me.

I could run, perhaps outrun it for a while. I would weaken before it did. No, it would be better to fight it here.

All those thoughts, and others, circled my mind in the time it took us to execute this brief dance. I surveyed the ground, looking for some sort of advantage.

I feinted forward and it sidestepped. I ran to a tree with a dead branch and began to crack the limb off with the idea of using it as a club.

With my back turned, the Reaper team charged.

As I expected.

At the last moment I collapsed toward its legs. The Reaper with the eyes didn't communicate the move quite fast enough, and they tripped and went headlong into the bole with the dead branch, striking with a resounding thunk.

Still rising, I tore the Reaper tied on the blinded one's back. I gripped it by the bottom of the torso and cracked it against the stump of a downed tree, the way some men will kill a snake by grabbing by the tail and cracking it like a whip. It hissed and shrieked and yowled.

The blinded one followed the sound, and I hurled the torso off into the woods. It spun crazily, its arms thrashing, and it fell with a crunch of leaves and brush. The blinded one ran past, and I struck it with my belt-wrapped fist with all the power I could put into the punch. It sprawled forward, and I leaped on it, got the belt around its neck, and planted my foot on the back of its neck. Then I hauled on the belt, putting my back into it as the bargemen used to say on the Missouri, until I heard cartilage crush and bones break.

With the legged one dead, it was an easier matter to hunt the other down and do away with it with my sharpened shovel.

It is strange, but when I take a life, even that of a neck-wrung chicken, I feel a moment's kinship with the creature. A dead human sets me wondering what his mother once dressed him up in for the wintering ritual of Thanksgiving. Yet dead Reapers evoke nothing of pathos, just relief that there is one less deathdealer supporting the Kurian Order.

As I looked down at the dead duo, it occurred to me that I might have more in kinship with them than I knew. Neither of us was human. We were both easily recognized, even from a long way away. For the foreseeable future I would have a Reaper's lifestyle, operating at night and hiding out during the day.

I started to disrobe it while the body was still limp and easy to manipulate. Reaper cloth was usually a valuable commodity, the first thing stripped off a dead one on the battlefield or ambush point. Usually Southern Command's bloodthirsty madmen, the Bears, claimed the lion's share of the substance.

The Reaper cloth, usually slick as oiled fishing line to the touch, felt rough in my hands, more burlap than silk. Taking a handful, I tested a piece, and it tore apart as easily as a workman's dungaree material.

Clearly it wasn't the usual bullet-stopping weave, obtained from some unknown source (rumored to be in the Southwest or Mexico).[*] Perhaps the Kurian or Kurians actually running the Coal Country were poor in whatever constituted wealth that allowed them to trade for more Reapers and garments to protect them in their dangerous duties—which seemed strange, considering the importance of coal to the richer surrounding principalities and the efforts made to keep it flowing.

Still, they looked like Reaper robes, sized for near to seven feet

---

[*] The rumors Ahn-Kha had heard were true. See *Valentine's Resolve*.

and with a heavy hood that could be pulled down to hide the face. On close inspection, however, my feet would give me away. Reapers, for all their size and strength were surprisingly light—designed that way, I imagine—and there would be no way my rowboat-sized tracks would be taken for a Reaper's. Still, it might serve at a distance, and how many locals, seeing a Reaper head down a side road at night, would be inclined to follow to check out its boots?

You learned very early in the Kurian Order to keep out of a Reaper's business. Any interview or interaction could end badly.

I surveyed myself as best as I could. My shoulders were perhaps a bit too broad, especially with my disproportionate—to human tailoring—arms. I tugged down the robe a bit, then decided to add a second underneath, wrapping the hood around my neck like a scarf. With the first pulled out and down, the hood came down across my eyes perhaps a bit too much—I could cut eye slits or try to fashion some sort of visor or sunglasses.

"That was amazing," a voice said from the darkness.

I spun. It was Longliner, lately rescued from the van. He must have broken with the others shortly after I left them and followed me. It was an impressive feat in the dark, but then sometimes my fur does gleam in a little moonlight.

"Why didn't they kill you?"

"I'm on their team."

"Why would you wish to go to work for the Ordnance?"

"It's better than here. Easy to get to Chicago or Ontario. I'm a good-time guy. If they can set someone like you up, why not me?"

He looked at the bodies, so pale they almost shimmered in the dark.

"How'd you get the better of them?"

Easily, I thought. They'd had their bells seriously rung by the coal-dust explosion. If only we could arrange for every fight with the Reapers to start with the overpressure of a major explosion.

Longliner looked at me in a sidelong fashion. "I bet it's some brain voodoo that screws with their connection to the Old Man."

I had no idea how a real Kurian agent would reply, so I elided the confidence of one long used to wielding power—something I'd only seen—with the much more familiar caution of an operative in a hostile land.

"I have no idea what you are talking about. For your own safety, it would be wise not to imagine further."

"I'm clean; I'm clean with that. I'll forget everything I saw here."

"For a price, I suppose," I said.

"One you can afford. Maybe I should say, one you can't afford to turn down."

"I'm ready to listen," I said. "But not here, now. Let's put some clicks between Number Four and us, before they sort out what went wrong. They already know that at least I escaped."

"If the Old Man or whoever was properly plugged in. These mountains mess with them.

"I'm ready to help. Which way?"

"Downhill, toward civilization. You carry the torso."

"Shit, why do you want to bring that?"

I grunted in answer. It took an effort on my part to turn my back on the opportunistic little toad and throw the larger corpse over my shoulders.

We reached water and sheltered downwind from a highway

bridge. The bridge was unguarded; a good sign. If the Order had information that we'd escaped the explosion, it would be reasonable to assume that a trooper car at least would be keeping an eye on the crossing.

A riverbank at night is a raucous place. With the water falling to summer levels, the flow had been reduced to a good-sized creek and there were endless rocks for the water to splash against. Frogs were in good voice and the bats were out, with their barely perceptible yeeks.

"Maynes Point is just across the river," Longliner said.

"Glad you know where it is. Go and get us some food. Something fresh for now, and dried or preserved for later."

"I'm not leaving you until we have some kind of understanding," Longliner said.

"I'll make you this deal. Do what I say for the next three days and I'll give you the general outline of my mission. If you help me with it, I will get you out of the Old Man's reach. You may go to the Ordnance, if you like. As for your employment there, I can promise you nothing, though there are many who will be grateful if you help this mission to succeed."

"Deal. Back with the groceries in an hour. You want me to steal them?"

"I want you to get them without attracting attention. If they could not be missed for a few days, that would be ideal."

It occurred to me, watching Longliner pick his way across the river rocks and slapping mosquitoes (they bothered me, too, at the ears and around the eyes) that it would be easy for him to betray me to the authorities. I don't pretend to have any great perspicuity in reading humans, but it seemed most of the younger Quislings in this principality were looking for a way up and out. Maybe the shabbiness of this baling twine and the whitewashed towns and coal-dusted rail stations beneath the silent, uncaring mountains drove the ambitious toward cleaner fields. Or it could be that if your name—or your spouse's—wasn't Maynes, it was a foregone conclusion that you weren't going that high.

Longliner on a Short Leash

He returned with a cook's apron knotted into a bundle around some pieces of fried chicken, some still-warm biscuits, an entire platter of Jell-O molded into an elegantly scalloped shape, and "coffee" in a plastic Thermos.

"I raided a church basement kitchen. It's pregnant-teen support night."

"What is your story?" I asked. "Why this, why now?"

"I've heard stories about the agents. We have an ex-agent churchman here, Apolio. Colonel Apolio. He lives at the White Palace. Political executive counselor for the Militia Officer Union and honorary fire marshall. He's a bit goofy; every now and then he gets a brain-backfire and comes out with a real landslide of cussing. They don't let him go to the Maynes family services. There the priest is, talking on about hopes for mankind and the new world of designed thought, and someone starts yapping shitfeast cocksnake and all that. That's the story the district fire captain told, anyway."

I toasted the flesh on a long flat-head screwdriver from my tool belt, wishing I had some chunks of sweet heartroot to add to the kebab.

"He talked about being an agent?"

"Not directly, just said that the Kurians can take a good man and make him a 'veritable demigod.' At first I thought he'd started into cussing, but then he told me what demigod meant. This was right after I got a commendation for turning in Robert Kenzie for selling a television. He gave the award and took me to lunch after.

"Anyway, I asked him about the Powers and he said he couldn't talk about that. He wouldn't do anything—boy did I beg him, I'm telling you straight. Finally he said that you had to live it to understand. I asked him to train me or whatever, and he said if they thought I'd be a good one, they'd get in touch with me.

"They never did. I did become a Youth Vanguard leader and they gave me some counterintelligence training, me and a few others for a summer at a place near Baltimore. Really great, but there were these coastal types with their New York and Boston accents and three-turn ties. Still, they didn't ruin it for me, and the Church gave me an assignment at Number Four, just reporting on the usual conversations and whatnot. I had to do evaluations on everyone every year, even the director, which I liked, knowing something the director didn't."

"I'm surprised you're telling me all this. What if I were part of the Resistance?"

"A Grog in the Resistance. Yeah! As if those backwoods swampies would breathe the same air as a stoop, beg pardon."

We ate for a while. He hardly touched the chicken, leaving it for me.

"What's your opinion of your fellow men?" I asked.

"Most of 'em aren't fit for chicken feed. Church has it about right. The cream rises to the top; then you use that to make sweeter cream. Repeat, generation after generation."

"Have you produced your own cream?"

"Was that a dirty joke? You are full of surprises, friend."

His use of the word "friend" both pleased and frustrated me. I was pleased that he considered me such, but frustrated at the deception. I prefer to be open and honest with both friends and enemies.

"I meant the next generation. You're old enough to have started a family."

"Physically, yes. But I'd like to be a little more established. Sure, the Church can always hook me up with some homemaker, but it would mean different work and I want to make my mark. Not that I don't enjoy a night's churning."

I wondered, but I was no judge of human desirability any more than this fellow would know that most of the males of my kind looked for long, delicate fingers, silky arm hair, and eye size as measures of classical attraction. In the more earthy terms of a pure rut, a nice wishbone shape to the small of the back and legs will catch my eye, and that in turn brings up memories of my mate and family, so I will return to my camp-side meal with Longliner.

"Did you get the usual set of enhancements?" I asked. It was a shot in the dark, but I'd often heard that the Kurians change their agents just as the Lifeweavers helping the resistance "tune up" their Wolves, Cats, and Bears.

"I've only had the first course. There were six of us, lined up in long white shirts, with the Archon himself giving us a sermon and then performing the ritual. He gave me something that looked like a marble. Rougher surface on the tongue. He said it would taste like candy, but it reminded me of pine-tar soap.

"I swallowed it. It gave me a headache. A headache I couldn't have thought possible. If I'd had a gun, I might have shot myself."

I wondered if he'd just received a sugar pill. When I was on the Gulf Coast of Louisiana in the sixties, the Gray One details I'd led had sometimes gone turtle hunting for our human officers' soup pot. I'd watched a few hatchings of sea turtles and seen the mad scramble of the little green turtles for the safety of the surf, harried the whole way by birds, crabs, and even dogs. The Kurian Order sometimes reminded me of that process—they released masses of fresh-faced recruits into the wild, and then sifted the best of what survived for advancement.

"So what's next?" Longliner asked.

"I need a better weapon," I said. "I've an idea of where to get one."

Getting My Gun

The church at the Youth Vanguard academy was much as I remembered it, save that it was dark, with a ceiling that vanished in shadow, taking much of the hanging banners with it.

Longliner and I crept in through the open front door. A pile of blankets, each with some kind of alarm tag on it that would sound if one tried to remove it from the church, lay neatly folded in a basket, and there were a few travellers slumbering in the pews.

The rifle was still in its locked glass case, roughly at the height of a coffin on display. I should have just smashed the glass, grabbed it, and run. But the glass of the case was so perfect, not a sign of a ripple or a bubble, glass the quality of which you rarely see in anything post-2022 . . . I couldn't bring myself to destroy such perfection. Besides, I did not want to awaken those slumbering in the pews.

So I settled down on my back and worked the underside of the case with the heaviest screwdriver I had.

Creeeek! and a lance of light divided the church. "Who's there?"

The old drill sergeant followed the muzzle of his pistol through the door leading to the church school with a quick step so as not to frame himself in the light of the hallway.

Ahh, the old fellow would be prowling the halls.

I attracted Longliner's attention and pointed him toward the old fellow. "Pull rank if you must," I muttered. "Just don't make any threats we can't carry out."

Longliner approached him with hands up and they were soon engaged in an animated conversation. The young man had talent. I could see why the Church chose him.

Now that I held it in my hands, I could truly appreciate the care that had gone into its creation. At the core of the rifle was an old .50 caliber sniper weapon. A small amount of metal had been filed away and a substantial amount of wood added, along with an elaborately braided leather sling. I could still see a few hairs knotted into the sling—whoever had used this in action had collected human scalps.

Wood had been added to the stock to make it better fit a Grog-sized frame. The sling had the short strap/long strap arrangement with an extra ring in the middle so it could be used as an aiming aid as well as a carry.

The original optics had been removed and replaced by a forward-mounted "scout sight." It was about the size of a pocket monocular. It allowed you to scan with your eyes, or use the rifle's iron sights for quick firing. If you chose to use the 4x magnification, you simply looked down the side of the barrel. The lens was big enough that you didn't have to press your eye to it.

Next, I had to acquire some .50 shells. I had a fairly good idea of where to do that.

It was a cool summer night, cloudy, and I suspected it would rain lightly. The air had that wet smell.

The fire station was about three-quarters garage. The rest was a

two-story building with a little observation and training tower supporting the radio mast.

The fire stations buttoned up tight at night, especially this one. I
had heard someone had thrown a bunch of dynamite through an
open second-story window—one of the firemen had been able to pop
the detonating caps off the fuse before it exploded.

For my weapons I chose my old short-handled shovel. I tied a
backup knife around my neck with a leather thong.

I drained some motor oil out of one of the ambulances parked
outside the fire station into a garbage can lid. It stank like turned
cooking oil. Who knows how many times it had been filtered and
recycled?

Nevertheless I stripped and spread it thickly all across my body.
In a close fight like the one I hoped to start, I didn't want someone
getting a hold of my forearm hair. The motor oil had the added benefit of darkening my fur, not that the moon was giving much away
tonight. Then I cleaned my palms on some convenient bark.

I inspected the building's security. No cameras, but then again
this was a small-town fire station, not the Atlanta Gunworks. I inspected the utility conduits and decided that they would serve as
access to the roof.

I swarmed up the electric lines. The rain had slackened into
something only a little heavier than a mist, easily blown by the wind
so that the millions of delicate reflections in the security lights of the
firehouse looked like dust.

The tower seemed unoccupied, but just in case I checked. There
was a locked cabinet up there. I ripped the padlock clasp out of the
wood, muffling the sound with my hands, and found a small radio

and a lever-action carbine familiar to viewers of old Westerns. I checked the caliber. It was just a .22, useful for rabbits or intimidation.

Unfortunately, using the same technique wouldn't work on the roof access door, which was well locked on the inside with only a bare handle in the wind and weather. There was a greasy outlet for the kitchen ventilator—far too small—and an old and long-defunct air-conditioning unit covered with roof-patching material.

The last, and noisiest option, was the skylight over the garage area. Inspecting it, I was pleased to see that the glass was in disrepair—two panels were missing and had been replaced by boards and tarp. The points of the nails that secured them had been driven through the window frame. It would be a pleasure to destroy such shoddy work.

I looked into the garage. An ambulance, fire truck, and armored bus rested inside, ready to go at a moment's notice. There was room for another large truck, but judging from the stains on the floor and placement of equipment, there was one ambulance out or on loan to another station. A light burned in the reception office at the main door, which had a window looking out on the minimally lit garage.

It would be a fair drop to the top of the bus parked under the skylight, perhaps two body lengths if I hung from my fingers before dropping. Some think that because of our arms, we have an apelike ability to swing from tree to tree and perform acrobatics. To tell the truth, I don't like heights.

I tore out the wood covering the missing panes. It was easily done as there were nails in only one edge.

As I nerved myself for the drop, I shifted the knife and shovel to my teeth. Theatrical, I know, but had they remained shoved into my belt, I might have stabbed myself. I swung over the ledge, hung from the fullest extent of my arms, and dropped.

I landed on the bus like the proverbial ton of bricks. The metallic thump was like a mortar going off beneath me. Sure that everyone for blocks around had heard it, I rolled off the bus opposite the office.

A fireman sitting by a dispatcher's phone slumbered in a comfortable chair that tilted back. I quietly wrung his neck as if it were a chicken's and hid the body in a janitorial closet.

I explored a set of stairs leading to the dormitory and private rooms. All seemed quiet, though a toilet flush caused me to press myself into an alcove in the main hall that had an industrial-sized washer and dryer. I saw a mild presoak for delicates that I could probably use to get the oil off my skin and fur.

Judging by the sizes of the rooms, there were perhaps as few as eight or as many as twenty firemen in the Beckley station on this overnight.

I found the arms locker, but it was wired in such a way that I decided it would set off an alarm if I opened it without punching in a key code (unfortunately, no one had written the code inside the plastic cover, as so often can be found thanks to the lazy owners of such systems). I left it for now.

Following the exposed conduit sheath, I came to the main electrical junction box for the building and the garage. There was a large red lever on it. I turned the main breaker off, then used the shovel to break off the handle. Emergency lighting flashed on, fitfully. More than half the spotlights failed to function.

Typical KZ attention to detail.

Power outages were frequent in most KZs, especially at night when it would least be missed for the performance of maintenance.

Now, for the killing.

I took the stairs three at a time, shovel in my right hand and the knife in my left. At the top of the stairs I met my first Beckley fireman, moving toward the staircase, supporting himself and feeling his way along with a hand on one wall, blinking in the darkness as he headed to the garage and occupied office to discover what had happened.

I buried the knife in him, then used the shovel to push him out of the way.

Next I burst into a dormitory. About half the beds were occupied. There were shouts and I heard the clicking of someone hitting a light switch.

From my side, the fight was an easy one. I simply lashed out at anything that moved with the knife or the sharpened shovel. When a body dropped, I stomped on it. I don't believe I made any sounds other than breathing, though there were numerous cries and confused shouts from the Beckley firemen.

I threw one body through a connecting wall—one would think a fire station would have more robust construction—and followed it through into the next room. There were two in there, but only one tried to fight; the other had to be pulled from under his bed.

In the entire fight, I only received one serious wound. A woman stabbed me in the ribs with a sharp pair of scissors. She was dead before I realized I was fighting with a female, but on later consideration I decided that if she passed all the examinations and tests in order to be one of those who dragged the elderly, sick, and halt off to their deaths, who was I to deny her a place with her comrades.

Finally, the fire station was quiet, save for the sound of my breathing and the steady drip of blood here and there into pools. There was one hiding in the showers—I saw a pair of ankles, probably female, as I quickly rinsed my hands and feet and put a cotton dressing on the scissors stab—but left that one alive. It never hurt to have someone spread the tale.

I decided it was safe to crack open the arms locker. I had my choice of fire axes to use, and I broke it open with two swings of the biggest axe. I found a short machine gun with a hand-finds-hand grip-magazine of the type favored by Georgia Control officers and helped myself to all the ammunition I could find for that. I also took a full-length battle rifle and a shotgun. Between that and the big .50, I had enough to get started.

On a whim, I took a permanent marker from the office and etched an icon that looked like a reversed, inverted "L" on the inside of the arms locker. The symbol is used by a tribe of Nebraska Gray Ones that were long enemies of my people—it denotes a revenge killing.

That would puzzle whoever was investigating it. Perhaps they'd think the murderers had begun a word game of hangman and done nothing but put up the gallows before being interrupted.

I loaded the shotgun, pocketed some extra rounds, and threw the rest of my prizes in a sleeping bag and headed out the door.

With that, I went out and joined Longliner. He'd produced transport, a big sort of three-wheeled motorcycle with two tires in front for steering and a fat drive tire in back, like a wheeled snow machine in a way.

"I thought for sure you'd never come out again," Longliner said.

"Then why did you wait?" I asked.

"I figured if you were killed, I'd put some rope burns on my wrists and say I was your prisoner. Tell them all about you."

The boy, oh, how would some phrase it—the boy had balls.

"What's that machinery?"

"That's a Cobra. Faster than an ATV, and almost as rugged."

He revved it, a pointless, silent exercise with an electric engine. The hardwired programming prevented a rider from wasting energy on burn outs. "How do you like it?"

"How do you know how to work it?" Too late, I hoped that didn't sound suspicious.

We stood, looking out over the ugly scar on the torn-away hills and the mining gear, trucks looking like toys in a child's sandbox from this height.

"Well, Longliner, time to be on your way."

"Aren't you going to give me a letter or something?"

I almost felt sorry for him. He'd wrought considerable evil when he'd plunged Number Four into violence against the Order, but then it was surging back on the regime in unexpected ways. Time would tell whether he'd triggered a rogue wave or a tsunami.

"Tell them you need to speak to the Special Operations Department. Give them this code word: 'spoonbread.'"

"You may take the Cobra. I've always been more comfortable on my legs."

"Nah, I have a feeling you're going to need it. I'll steal a bicycle somewhere."

"Use that talent of yours sparingly. But you can help me further by lighting a few fires on your way out, from a distance. Just something to divert attention."

"I told you, it doesn't work so well from far away. Whatever it is has to be really inflammable."

"All the better. You'll be able to see it from a distance, then."

The Cobra had an interesting recharging system. A sort of metallic-and-rubber shepherd's crook was clipped in two pieces to the back. There was a good deal of naked wire in the Coal Country. You simply screwed the two ends of the "staff" together, plugged it into a power converter about the size of a loaf of bread, and hung the crook on any live power line—with a spark and a faint crackle of ozone, so it was something that attracted attention, unfortunately. The machine did the rest. There was also a plug that you could put into an ordinary wall outlet, but those were harder to find accessible and slower to use.

"I'll be out of the territory soon. Sure like to know what you have in mind. Don't see how you can do much on your own."

"I still can't discuss it."

He seemed a lucky fellow. He'd probably make it to the Ordnance. What would they make of him? The fire-starting trick was too deft for them to waste; perhaps he would get his dream of training as an agent.

So began a strange six weeks of my life. I crisscrossed the Coal Country several times, silently going up and down jeep trails in the lush, windblown hills, using the rifle and my own abilities. I shot perhaps once every two or three days. I didn't snipe individuals, I saved my bullets for machinery. The Coal Country could afford to replace a few firemen or troopers. What it could not afford was a loss of productive equipment.

I had to kill on two occasions, both times when breaking into a garage to destroy fireman vehicles under repair—and the machine tools used to repair engines. I had tried to knock the guards unconscious, but that sort of thing works best in movies. In practical life, they topple over and twitch as bowel and bladder empty and respiration fails. Several guard dogs also met their demise in a more direct fashion, with a crossbow I fashioned out of a leaf spring and an old rifle stock.

It was a matter of an hour's work with an acetylene torch to render any engine unfit for future service.

I survived by taking to brush, or holding up in a remote attic, grain elevator, or abandoned cell tower used by the Reapers. Reaper nests are not the most comfortable, usually it is a blanket or two thrown over a piece of foam from an old couch cushion, but it served as a hideout from dawn to dusk, giving me a chance to work on my gear and plan the next strike.

My greatest coup, while operating alone, was the very satisfactory destruction of three mining vehicles, two earthmovers and an excavator, which had been incautiously parked under a cliff so they had to be guarded on only two sides. I obtained some explosives from the mine office and planted them above and brought down a substantial chunk of hillside on them.

Replacing entire ambulances and mining site loaders was an expensive prospect for the Maynes Conglomerate. They were having a bad coal year because of Number Four and events elsewhere, despite labor drafts to increase production. Only one currency had any real value in the Kurian Order, and that was from living human beings. For the first time, the Coal Country lost something other than miscreants and social outcasts to "repurposing."

At this, the embers of revolt smoldering all over the Coal Country heated up.

Accusations have been leveled at me, since, that I was responsible for the deaths, as I was the one doing the damage that resulted in levies of vital aura being sent to the Georgia Control and elsewhere to replace the machinery I was wrecking. That is between my conscience and me. Few of those making the accusation ever lived under the Kurian Order or supplied any kind of other idea for its destruction, other than "spontaneous" and "organic" uprisings of those trapped behind the fangs and claws of the Reapers.

I've also been accused of deciding, on my own, that the Coal Country should be plunged into revolt, rather than letting the locals make up their own minds. I assure you, it would not have been difficult for the people of these coal-filled mountains to turn me in, if they'd so desired. A furry creature the size of an outhouse gets noticed, moving from one valley to another, even if it's only by boys and girls out fishing for a supplement to the family supper.

The Coal Country Kurian made his worst mistake, however, when he decided to clear the hills of the mountain people. They expected nothing of the Kurian Order save the right to be left alone, and when carriers full of troopers and firemen suddenly pulled up to either side of their valley, deploying horsemen and bicyclists to empty their settlements and carry off whomever they could catch, they made a bitter and resolute enemy.

My War Begins

I don't know how long I could have carried on my one-Xeno war. Winter would cut down on the nuts and berries and fish I could gather and make getting around more difficult. I might have retreated into Kentucky and started up again next year, if the temptation to bargain for a legworm ride back to the Mississippi didn't prove too strong, that is. In any case, a chance meeting cut it short.

A small fire had heated a couple of cans of beans and WHAM!, and I'd just smothered the small fire over a couple of foil-wrapped potatoes I'd buried under it as my breakfast, when I heard an approach to my camp. If they'd meant to backshoot me, they probably would have done it while I was framed by the firelight.

"Want some beans?"

They showed themselves, two adults, male and female, and a boy. Each adult had an infant strapped across the chest, wrapped in a sort of blanket roll of thin insulating material. They looked haggard, except for the boy, who held a squirrel rifle with a water-bottle silencer in his arms, cradling it like a ten-year veteran Wolf.

The man had a long-stem pipe and a long-barreled pistol in his belt; the woman two knives, a big butcher model and a small paring or skinning version. They had the wary, foxlike look of hill people.

"Want some beans?" I repeated.

The boy produced a spoon quickly enough, but the mother held him back until the father nodded.

"You're that Golden Eel."

"Yellow, maybe, in the right light. It's only poetry to call my kind 'Golden.'"

"Well, that's what I heard you called. Slippery enough and lots of teeth. Thanks for the hospitality."

They sat down and produced small pannikins from their bundles. They politely waited for me to decide how much I wished to share. I divided the beans and WHAM! into four portions, pushed a couple extra chunks of meat into the portion for the (probably) nursing mother, and distributed the food.

They ate eagerly. "Nothing like hot food," the boy said.

The woman turned discreetly sideways and took the infants for nursing. The father took a gallon plastic water container out for her and held it so she could drink easily at intervals.

The mother produced a bag of hard candy. She gave one striped treat to the boy and offered another to me.

I shook my head. "Thanks, I'm not much for candy."

He extracted a sample of the recent output of the Maynes photocopier, unfolded it, and passed it to me. It wasn't the latest password, but a wanted poster with my identification photo with the cropped-off ears. I was worth twenty thousand dollars and a house on Maynes Mountain, it seemed.

I glanced at the reverse side. Someone had drawn a crude map of a trail west.

"There's a bad spot for Reapers on the fifth leg, just before the Kentucky border," I said. "Picked up some bodies there."

"Oh, they're mostly operating around the mines and railroads these days. Showing themselves, even in daylight, to scare off saboteurs."

"You'll want something to trade in Kentucky," I said. "They're a good bunch, but sharp dealers."

"We have about thirty yards of silk folded tight," the father said. "Plus there're a couple of old gold coins my father saved for his escape. He never made the try; died of a broken pelvis in a rail accident. With the troopers scared to go out in less than a squad size, we thought we'd try our luck."

"I've no particular destination. I'll give you a ride tomorrow."

"You're not on your way to Hopkins Hollow?" the girl said through a mouthful of beans. "They've been looking for you. Looking for you in a good way, I mean."

"Not sure I've heard of that."

"It's not on the maps."

THE HOLLOW MEN

Hopkins Hollow was owned by the MacTierney clan. They were, in fact, distantly related to my old "partner," but I did not find that out immediately. The Hopkins family had been gone for decades before the Kurians even showed up, but they never changed the name because tradition and common use meant more than family ego.

Pre-2022 it had been touched by a road, but a washed-out bridge turned it into another of the many jeep trails crisscrossing the Coal Country on disused roads and rail lines, marked by old post boxes covered by creepers and filled with squirrel scat.

A stream ran through it year-round and a largish open meadow was the divide between the MacTierney clan and the Bilstriths. Other than water, they shared every bounty that came their way. If the MacTierneys slaughtered a pig, they invited the Bilstriths over to enjoy roast loin, and the Bilstriths would then insist that the Mac-Tierneys use the Bilstrith smokehouse. Weddings and births to one clan or the other were celebrated as if they'd happened at home, and there was an unspoken rule against intermarriage between the two groups—though from what I observed, a Bilstrith's first sexual explorations were usually with a MacTierney and vice versa.

It was a little piece of saddle country between three higher hills, two to the south and a third to the north. The MacTierney clan had the wider south end for its plots and pastures; the "neck" to the north was under another group, the Bilstriths.

"Hell, it's the Guerilla Grog from Number Four," a boy whooped as I approached.

A sparse-haired, hawk-nosed man who introduced himself as "Old Leslie" showed me around. "You picked the right day to come; a hog has met its fate." Old Leslie's accent was noticeably different from that of the other hill people, even to my inexperienced ear, drawling as opposed to their gentle modifications of vowels, adding an "ah" sound where possible: "Ahhh dooon't riiightly knoow" against "Ah doan't ratley know."

He'd fled another revolt farther south, escaping up the spine of the Appalachian Mountains until he landed here. It turned out he'd worked in a rum distillery as a boy, and he added that experience to the family's own somewhat famous still. Now "MacTierney White Whiskey" was the closest thing to a famous label that you could get with moonshine. He'd become a local favorite as a toastmaster for gatherings, having a remarkable memory for names and incidents.

"That's Kemper Bilstrith there. She's run the family since her husband died in the 'fifty-eight fevers. He married in, took her name. Curious, eh?"

He pointed out a man in a shovel beard with bright red suspenders with polished brass fittings. "That's Red MacTierney, more or less the head of the MacTierney clan, but he looks at it as more a ceremonial post and defers to the heads of household for most everything.

He's eager to meet the giant Grog that put the whole of the Coal Country into a revolt."

"I followed my own instinct for what seemed the right thing to do," I said. "I think everyone was ready to turn on the Kurians; I just happened to be here when the moment came." I find that statement very easy to remember; I have repeated it many times since then.

"Reminds me of the snakebit preacher. You ever heard that one, big fellow?"

"No."

"Well, in these hills there's still a strong Pentecostal strain. Don't know if you've heard of them, but on occasion they prove their faith by handling serpents, because God decides when the asp bites—and the righteous don't get bit. So this preacher fellow was famous, when the mood was upon him, for giving his whole sermon with a snake or two draped around him. Sometimes they'd crawl right inside his shirt and go to sleep, as a matter of fact.

"So one day, one of his parishioners has a cousin visiting from a couple of watersheds away, and the visitor wants to see a man so favored by the Lord that venomous serpents go to sleep in his shirt. At first, the preacher joked that it was because his preaching was so boring, it put man, babe, and beast alike into a slumber. But his parishioner and the visitor insisted, so he went and got the snakes out, picked them up, and sure enough, he got bit right off.

"'Serves me right,' the preacher said. 'I should remember that it's only safe to pick up a snake when God tells me to. Doing what man asks me to do requires prudence and judgment.'"

Old Leslie laughed, and then indicated all of the members of the group:

Caspin and Deed MacTierney, the hard men of the MacTierney clan. If they felt cheated or wronged, they attempted to right it, civilly and quietly if possible, but right it they would. Between them they'd killed five men.

V. Scott Mallow, a drifter who joined up because he wanted to fight the Kurians.

Jebadiah Bilstrith, one of the best hunters in Virginia. A bowman, he used his weapon—which had a reel—to hunt or fish.

Glassy, the lone female. Just "plain old mean." Her weapon was a knife.

The Neale brothers (Rod, Able, and Mercy) were from a nearby county and were good friends to the Bilstriths. They were shotgun men and great judges of horseflesh. "They're horsemen, through and through. They can ride any animal anywhere."

Old Leslie himself—a survivor of the Charlotte revolt in the Georgia Control, he had fled to the Coal Country to hide out.

"I'm a durn good shot, if I don't say. I can make you some reloads for that big .50, if you care to give me your casings."

Mancrete—a huge bear of a man, with a hook for a right hand and a machine pistol for his left. "Uses taped-together magazines."

"Ten men? Against the whole Coal Country?"

"They're ten of the best men in the mountains. The way we see it, we're not at war with the Coal Country. This is a feud with the Maynes clan.

"We have someone on the inside, too. He sends messages to one of the Bilstrith gals who works for the telecom. She gets on the phone, a line they don't know about that goes across half the county, and passes word.

"We were hoping you'd join us. You've dug coal, hiked the hills, risked yourself for us like you were kin—even killed one of those Ghouls I hear. All that's left is for you to sample our white whiskey."

I sampled.

I wasn't their leader, I was more of an interesting (and intimidating, I suppose) addition to the cadre. My knowledge of the land couldn't match theirs, but I had years of experience in surviving and fighting against the Kurian Order. Nevertheless, the rumor somehow got going that these men were my retinue. I suspect it had something to do with the fact that I was the nonhuman of the bunch. "That hairy yellow Grog and those men" became "that hairy yellow Grog's men" and so passed into history. But let the record show that the MacTierneys and the Bilstriths were fighting for weeks before I joined them.

GOOD-BYE TO LONGLINER

As a side note, at about the time of the Hopkins Hollow barbecue, Longliner crossed the Ohio River and entered the Northwest Ordnance. Of course, the password I had given him, and the SOD group were both out of my imagination, but he was more than ready to cover his disappointment by relating everything he could about me and the Coal Country to the authorities in the Ordnance.

Those in the Ordnance, who had already suffered some small loss at the hands of David Valentine and me, expected that where I was, my David was also operating.

His arrival may have been akin to the clap that starts the avalanche. The Northwest Ordnance (for those of you who don't recall, it was a Kurian mix of Pennsylvania, Ohio, and parts of Michigan and Northern Indiana) was already vexed with the difficulties in the Coal Country. The Maynes Conglomerate had bought a good deal of heavy equipment from the Ordnance, and a few new Reapers, arranging to pay off the purchase with a steady stream of coal over a year. The Ordnance had received only a handful of the expected overflowing barrel when the flow slowed to a trickle, far less than the Ordnance would need to keep its factories going and provide electricity for the coming winter.

With the Coal Country badly in arrears, a pleading message arrived from the Maynes family. They needed another loan of equipment to make up for some unexpected losses and accidents. The Maynes financial whiz suggested a "rearrangement of terms" and possibly even the shipment of a certain number of "repurposed" citizens. Without fresh equipment, the Maynes Conglomerate argued as follows:

WE WILL BE UNABLE TO MEET THE NECESSARY COAL SHIPMENTS ARRANGED AT THE PITTSBURGH CONFERENCE. THEREFORE IT IS IN THE INTEREST OF US BOTH TO COME TO AN AGREEMENT AS QUICKLY AS PRACTICABLE. WE ARE READY TO SEND NEGOTIATORS; WE SUGGEST HUNTINGTON AS THE LOCATION FOR NEGOTIATIONS.

The Northwest Ordnance saw an opportunity. With the Maynes team clearly in dire need, and with the Ordnance in a strategically enviable position, bordering the Coal Country to the North and West, they could solve their coal problem, gain control of a vital resource, and establish themselves as a northern rival to the Georgia Control all by striking a single heavy blow. The Coal Country had troops enough to manage their population, but nothing like a military force capable of resisting a major invasion.

They promised the Coal Country a pair of train shipments carrying everything needed. What they received were two trains swarming with Moondagger zealots.

The Ordnance played a rather simple trick on the trusting Coal

Country logistics people. After the cargos were verified and loaded onto Ordnance trains, the trains pulled out from their depots. Somewhere near the border, the freight cars filled with mining equipment and transport and gasoline and such were swapped out for freights loaded with the vicious Moondaggers. To guard against anything happening to the trains, the entire rail line had troops stationed along it to hurry the freights along in safety. Moondaggers dressed as ordinary rail guards waved from their cupolas as the invasion trains rocked by.

Longliner even led a team of operatives in to infiltrate Charleston and raise a disturbance that could be conveniently suppressed by the Moondaggers.

Military historians of the Kurian era agree that this was the apogee of the Moondagger skill at arms. But along with the well-executed insertion came the same old brutality to the local populace. It was not unique to the era, sadly, but probably the best remembered.

However, the Georgia Control considered the Coal Country a minor province. They were the Maynes family's feudal protectors, as things worked in the Kurian Order, and they were an important component in the ticking, self-lubricating machine of the Control. For all the difficulty in getting coal up to the Ordnance, even the Maynes family knew that the Control must be fed black ore first. The Control, having already been called for help in quelling the sporadic acts of violence and industrial sabotage, had troops already shuttling north in the beetle-like, swollen VTOL helicopters familiar from the many press photos of the Georgia Control's elite Tarheel Rangers. Thanks to their air-mobile capability, while the Ordnance had no difficulty seizing the main population centers and transport network in the north, the coal mines themselves came under the Control.

What all the parties to this carving up of the Coal Country forgot was that the Maynes family, corrupt and incompetent as it was, was at the very least local, with blood going back generations before the Kurians. While they accepted the relatively bloodless Maynes regime for decades, rule from Atlanta or Columbus would not be suffered for long.

But all this was still to come, within a few weeks of my barbecue in Hopkins Hollow.

It was my first time out with the Hollow Men. (I'm told this could be interpreted as a literary reference, but it was unintentional—though come to think of it, Eliot's "eyes I dare not meet in dreams" line applied to Mallow, and when we rode at night, we could be aptly described as "shade without color." Some of the hill people called us at first "the Hollow Men," even though a woman and a Golden One rode as part of the company, "violent souls" regardless.)

The Cobra was parked back in Hopkins Hollow. I rode, instead, on a two-wheeled cart pulled by a strong roan thoroughbred that had a knack of kicking up gravel into the driver seat. Old Leslie held the reins, giving me a chance to admire his driving and giving Glassy, who rode beside, a chance to glance at his fine profile. The back of the cart contained our food supply, some white whiskey for anything from antiseptic to amiability to water purification to bribes, and a few improvised land mines.

Even in a party as small as this, there were already groups forming. The MacTierney brothers and Jeb Bilstrith kept to the front and consulted one another on the ride. Behind them came Mallow leading the trio of Neale brothers, and we followed in the cart with Glassy. Mancrete, large enough to be a group himself, rode behind the cart. Glassy joked that he was there to scavenge any apples that rolled out of their basket.

The plan, as I understood it, was for Glassy and Jeb to plant the mines on the road going north from Marlinsburg, which supported a trooper barrack. The troopers, who occupied the surviving half of a demolished high school, had the luxury of a very hard-to-get-at car park in the auto shop surrounded by enough fencing and wire for a prison (much of it pre-2022, the students in this town evidently needing to be kept safe from the residents, or perhaps the reverse).

The rest of us would shoot up a fortified gas station just outside of town, as though raiding gasoline. That would draw the troopers, who would hopefully lose a truck or two to the mines. The hill people also knew that it was easier to fight the machinery of the Kurian Order than the men. So many trooper prowlers, New Universal Church clergy transport, and fireman vans were lost that the remaining had to be pulled into the towns and put in well-guarded motor pools. This meant they couldn't be deployed quickly to the more rugged areas of the Coal Country, which also meant that, especially at night, we owned the roads and could move at will.

The ambush we executed at Blue Run on old Federal Route 35 was a typical example. The long-coated gunmen deployed atop a vertical limestone cut a good forty feet above the road. To even reach us would mean running along the road for better than a quarter mile in either direction.

We caught a relief convoy on its way to the border trooper station at Point Pleasant. The troopers there stayed in the country for thirty days or so, trying to stop arms and other contraband coming in from the legworm clans in Kentucky, then returned to the urban areas for two months of lighter duty. The longer we could extend their tour at Point Pleasant, the less inclined they'd be to leave their fortified garrison watching the rivers and hunt for guerillas in the mountains.

We'd laid down an explosive strip in a gravel-filled divot in the old road; it was powerful enough to take out an armored car. My work in the mines had qualified me to be the explosives expert of the group. Our detonator was an unreliable relic, so I'd also rigged a trigger, just in case the detonator couldn't create the voltage to set off the charge on the plastic explosives.

Two armored buses, an armored car, a tow truck, and an SUV with a machine-gun mount provided the main body of the convoy, with a vanguard of two trooper cars and two motorcycles running ahead. It was a typical escort for the period. We hadn't dared to try a convoy this large before, but the geography of thirty-five in this spot was to our advantage.

Both trooper cars roared over the mine strip. They ground right over the gravel without result. A motorcycle followed, motor blatting. Dust shot up in an instant whirlwind, followed a split second later by the report. The bike spun slowly in the air. The rider, arms gyrating and legs bent up his back, cartwheeled into the roadside trees and was swallowed by the green with hardly a rustle.

The trooper cars put on a burst of speed and raced down the

highway to Point Pleasant, perhaps to summon reinforcements or just to escape the fire we were now pouring down the limestone cut.

The explosion had blown out the gravel in the roadbed, leaving a deep, meter-wide trench between the two lengths of asphalt. The armed SUV struck it and flipped nose-over, putting a quick end to the gunner. The first bus had better luck; it crashed to a halt of blown tires. The bus behind managed to avoid hitting the lead, but it went off the side of the road and ended up on its side, a great gray elephant felled by nothing more than a soft shoulder leading to a deceptively overgrown ditch.

The troopers tried to deploy out of their vehicles, but under our guns and advantage in height, it only meant more bodies scattered on the road and shoulder.

My companions were the most careful shots I have ever served with. They aimed—but did not fire—more often than not. The exception seemed to be the Neale brothers, who employed their shotguns as if they were noisemakers just as much as weapons, whooping and shooting in the air when no target offered itself.

I struck the fuses on two satchel charges I'd made out of old coal sacks and sent them whirling down to the stricken buses, where they exploded in a more satisfying blast of destruction than my failed mine strip.

At an order from MacTierney, we pulled out. I stayed behind with my long rifle to discourage pursuit, but my thirty minutes of lead time for the Hollow Men presented me with only one target, one of the survivors from the bus who attempted to get to the SUV's machine gun. I missed with the first shot, but I was close enough to encourage him to return to the safety of the bus's bulk.

As darkness fell, I picked up my rifle, casings, and bedroll that I'd been using as a chin rest, and I departed for the green hills, feeling a little too satisfied with the day's work. We'd soon be matching ourselves against a far greater threat than the poor half-trained troopers.

THE DREADCOATS ARE COMING

I believe our raids changed the balance on both sides. Ordinary townspeople turned into overnight guerillas, knowing that violence could be blamed on us. The description of men in long coats with a hulking Grog among them, appearing out of nowhere, striking, and retreating again, was an easy-enough image to describe such that the troopers and churchmen had witnesses lined up, ready to provide alibis for their own and blame the violent acts on us. We would have needed helicopters and doubles to be everywhere our attacks were reported to occur.

Where we did strike, we always seemed to have local teenagers showing up to cover our tracks, collect our shell casings, and warn us where there were patrols and stillwatches placed on the roads and trails. I was constantly amazed at what they could accomplish. There's something about youths of eleven, twelve, or thirteen that makes authorities hesitate to clap them in handcuffs and run them in, I believe.

The Maynes family warmed up their photocopier again. Now we had a new name, the "Dreadcoats." It was modified by the phrase "so-called." The long riding coats of the MacTierney brothers and Jeb Bilstrith had inspired the name.

REWARD REWARD REWARD

$50,000

For information leading to the CAPTURE or provable KILLING of enemies of our peace and prosperity, the so-called Dreadcoats.

Among these is the yellow-haired Grog known as Hickory

whose reward will be included as a bonus

for his CAPTURE or provable KILLING.

"How come old Hickory here gets a special mention?" Mallow asked. "I've killed more'n he has."

"They're still mad at him for Number Four," Old Leslie said.

"The Dreadcoats are coming! The Dreadcoats are coming!" Glassy said.

Amused at our growing notoriety, we experienced endless examples of "aid and comfort" from the Coal Country people. Fathers, sons, and not a few grandfathers and grandsons dug up and restored weapons that had long been hidden for this moment. At first, the acts of resistance were similar to the kinds of things that had been going on since the massacre at Beckley: tires slashed; fires set; graffiti scrawled on church buildings, Maynes Conglomerate businesses, and fire stations. With the Dreadcoats (and their increasingly notorious "Yaller Grog") ambushing collection vans and shooting up the firemen and Coal Country troopers, organs of the regime could scarcely enter some of the smaller mountain towns without being met with gunfire from hedges and attic windows.

I am not sure when the exaggerations began about the size of "my" army. It wasn't an army, and it certainly wasn't mine. It could be that the Maynes family, in explaining to its creditors the reasons for the slowdown in coal, lied about our size and the scope of our attacks. It could have been wishful thinking by the rumormongers, who were eager for good news and hope. If a wild-haired Grog was leading a dozen men, no doubt it would soon be a hundred. With a hundred practically in existence, a thousand was not out of the question. And so on. If the rebellion wasn't waxing strong, why the Moondaggers? Why the Tarheel Rangers?

So the news of a rebel army in the Coal Country began being broadcast on the Resistance radio, and common knowledge became historical fact. To this day there are histories of the war for liberation that put the strength of the Coal Country rebels at seven to nine thousand.

That incident kicked off what became known in the Coal Country as the Bloody October. Violence was met with reprisal, which begat more violence, murder in compound interest.

The Moondaggers carried out most of the killings. It was highly unusual for the Kurian Order to just kill without harvesting the aura, but the Moondaggers seemed exempt from having to conserve the energies the Kurians needed.

Worse, they carried out the executions in public. They beheaded their enemies using an axe in the time-honored fashion. To say this was strange to the Coal Country people would not even begin to describe it.

We witnessed the end of one in a little crossroad town just south of Charlotte. Four bodies, looking like unfinished mannequins waiting for a missing piece, lay on a flatbed tow truck. A second tow rig had a sport utility vehicle painted with the Moondagger logo, with four very flat, cut-up tires.

A local boy who'd found us on a dirt bike explained: "They came through, two motorcycles and this big car. Stopped at the bakery and just cleaned them out—not just the finished stuff but also the flour and butter and eggs and lard and whatnot. Couple of us threw eggs at the motorcycle riders, since they wanted eggs badly enough to just open up a door and take them. They took off after the kids, and that was when Mr. Dalgren—that's his body there, in the checkered shirt—took out his buck knife and went to work on their tires.

"They were dragging Pem O'Dowd out of the bakeshop by the hair and arm, taking her to the car, when they saw the damage. Their captain or whatever got so mad when he saw the tires that they sat poor Pem in the gutter and just shot her in the back of the neck.

"Now they're hauling Robbie Gaines up to the axe," the kid said. "He doesn't even live in the town. Must have come in to visit, and look where it got him."

"Do you have a shot?" Deed MacTierney asked.

I had a Moondagger who was issuing orders to the others in the sights of my long gun. His beard was cut into a sharp triangular shape, giving me a nice sighting post at the center of his chest. "Do you want me to take it?" I asked.

"No," MacTierney said. "They'll just take it out on the locals. We'll have to think this through."

We learned a good deal about the Moondaggers that terrible October. We learned that they didn't care for women, except as mobile, laundry-scrubbing uteruses ready to produce the next generation. They saw themselves as favored by the NUC and the Kurians, and therefore it was their duty to reproduce themselves with increased numbers by whatever method available.

Even worse than the murders in these hills were the outrages against women. They would not touch virginal girls; everyone else was reservation game.

The families started hiding their daughters if they happened to be in Moondagger territory. This led to further outrages, for if there were no women about, the men made do with whatever they could get their hands on, "whatever" being teenage boys.

These outrages only heightened the rebellion. We had more and more Coal Country troopers acting as informants about Moondagger patrols and operations. The main fireman armory in Charleston was opened and looted in an overnight operation that netted our rebellion hundreds of thousands of rounds of ammunition, explosives, and machine guns fresh from the factories of the Georgia Control. For the first time, we were able to fight on something like equal terms.

ENEMY OF MY ENEMY

The Moondagger patrol died well.

We caught them in the crossfire of two captured machine guns after simple wire-control charges took out the first and last vehicles in a five-car column moving into the mountains out of Charleston.

I cut the machine-gun fire and picked up my heavy "Grog gun." One Moondagger had taken cover behind the armored side door of the gray-green-painted transport. I put a shell through the door and the gunner.

We called on them to surrender, but they roared defiance out of their barrel chests and heavy beards. We held the high ground and the fire lanes. They fell one by one to single shots.

We laid them out in a neat row together and covered their faces with plastic sheeting and packing material. The Dreadcoats and a few part-time guerillas divided weapons and ammunition into "carry off" and "destroy" piles.

There was a recoilless rifle tube in one of the transports, and three wooden boxes of .75 mm shells with close-quarter and enclosed space charging. It could destroy anything short of a freight train or tank, or open an access point in a fortified building. I tested the weight and wondered if I could rig it for fire from the shoulder. It did not seem like a difficult job; here was already a shoulder-pad notch for the gunner aiming the weapon.

"Wait! Wait!"

I paused.

"Thank you. You have no idea how expensive these interfaces are to replace, especially since that purge in Ohio."[*]

"You misunderstand the position of the Maynes family. It's bread and circuses in these hills, my Golden One. The Maynes clan forms a convenient locus of interest and discontent.

"That's one of the reasons we tolerated Joshua's erratic behavior. It made for hot gossip. If the people were busy hating him, wondering how he could get away with all he did, they weren't thinking at the level above the Maynes clan."

"You're from outside. You don't care about the people here."

"You do? A Kurian?"

"I don't see why a Kurian couldn't become fond of a particular people. It may surprise you to know, however, that I was once as human as . . . the next fellow. I was about to say you, strangely. Talking to you, it is easy to forget your species. You sound like a very large man, probably a bass baritone singer, with a bit of a head cold."

"You're the elder Maynes."

"Give that ape a Kewpie doll! What gave it away? Me giving it away? Are all your kind so slow?"

"This is not the most pleasant conversation I've ever had."

---

[*] An Ob-Gyn who had been careless in her choice of boyfriends was arrested and removed from the Xanadu facility. She had, however, left a "poison pill" behind in the form of a loyal nurse, who arranged for the accidental destruction of several years' worth of viable Reaper embryos. Reapers became almost impossible to replace in the northern half of Eastern North America for several years thereafter.

"I'm smart, not pleasant. The two have nothing to do with each other. The pleasant ones most all died in 'twenty-two."

"May I make a modest proposal?"

"If you can do it without twitching so much as a claw."

"We could arrange for a truce, of sorts. Between you people and the legitimate government of the Coal Country. I don't care for the Tarheel Rangers crawling all over the mines, looking for excuses to send miners off to the Control, and the Moondaggers the Ordnance has introduced are even more loathsome."

"On that we are agreed," I said.

"How does this sound: I will provide you with Maynes family security vehicles, uniforms, even identification. Weapons, ammunition, even explosives. In return, you will let the coal flow freely and limit your attacks to the Moondaggers and Tarheels."

"Then we go back to killing each other once this is all over?"

"From the inside, the Kurian Order is anything but, buck. It's a mess. The only truly successful ones are either so small a single Kurian runs it, or a place like the Georgia Control, where they've subcontracted running the show out to a few trusted humans. I believe they're doomed. A few have fled your planet already, assuming this final effort to work an understanding out with the Lifeweavers comes to nothing."

"You would switch sides that easily?"

"I don't love them. I just didn't see the point in dying, and they relieved me of that burden. Again, I didn't have to like them."

"Why don't you think you'll fall with the rest of the Kurian Order if it does go?"

"I know people. I used to be one, after all. Everything's negotiable; you just need something of value to the face across the table."

"I have one condition."

"Name it."

"This interface as you call it comes with us. A Reaper in the party might prove useful if our identity is ever questioned. I also might need to communicate with you. The phone service around here is terrible."

He nodded in assent, and I found myself an ally of a vampire.

Coal Country Calls for Help

I requested, and received, Joshua Maynes Vee Three's converted bus for the Dreadcoats. We also requested an SUV with a couple of light motorcycles attached (they rode on the back, roof, and fenders like saddlebags) and an armed pickup with a recoilless rifle for some extra firepower.

Mallow and Bilstrith were both against a truce with the Old Man. Mallow believed it to be a trap; Bilstrith thought that the Dreadcoats were just being used to carry out the dirty work the Coal Country couldn't manage to do on its own.

We checked the vehicles for explosives, received our passwords and some identity papers—MacTierney was our liaison with the Maynes clan, so perhaps there was some communication between the hill people and the White Palace even before the massacre at Beckley and the Coal Revolt began.

"A curious fellow came through. Ex-churchman. He's working with the resistance now. Said he sensed that the Kurians were worried about things here."

"Sensed? Sounds worse than the snake handler from Old Leslie's story," Rod Neale said.

"He speaks and you believe him. You wouldn't think a man as

old as he could be traipsing around the backwoods on his own and still look neat as a pin, but he managed it. He must have incredible health."

"Or he's not who he says he is."

"Occam's razor: the simplest explanation is usually the correct one."

"I sent out word. We need anything they can send us. Guns, men, even valuables we could trade."

"We'll get a few radio messages of support. If we're real lucky, we'll make the resistance shortwave news broadcast from those guys with the accents in the Baltic. First language of freedom . . . yeah, but it sure sounds like a second language when you use it."

"Yeah. But we won't see a bullet or hand grenade."

"Crossing Kentucky isn't the easiest thing, you know. Or running down the mountains across Pennsylvania. You ever done it?"

"I crossed Kentucky," I said. "You are right. It would not be easy. The Kurians are very possessive of that railroad and the area around Lexington."

Perhaps support from Southern Command or the Green Mountain Boys would appear. Perhaps even both, as a Lifeweaver-guided balance to the Moondaggers and the Tarheel Rangers.

"Well, the fact of the matter is that unless they show up right soon, it won't matter. At the rate the Moondaggers are killing people or dragging off girls, the Coal Country is going to be a few mines and their workers guarded by the Tarheels, and a bunch of empty little towns."

"If we don't have an army to fight them . . ."

"Perhaps we do not need one. It seems to me we already have all we need. Wasn't it Napoleon who said that when two opposing armies are in close proximity, a dogfight will start a battle?"

White is a popular color in West Virginia. I am told one of the best eateries in Charleston is a floating, white-painted bar and restaurant called the Float.

It was popular with both the Moondaggers and Tarheel forces. Even when they were in civilian clothes, it was easy to tell the difference between the forces by their facial hair. The Moondaggers wore full beards for the most part; the Tarheels elaborate sideburns and mustaches.

Word had gone around that there had been a fight at the Float a few nights ago, when the Moondaggers, who maintained all-male forces, accosted a pair of female Tarheel helicopter pilots.

"Which of the two is the more volatile?"

"Hard to say. Those men from the Carolinas will get into a brawl quickly enough, but the Moondaggers will kill at the drop of a hat."

"Then it's the Moondaggers."

Glassy went into the bar to try to buy cigarettes, and she came out with a Tarheel beret hidden up her skirt.

We found one of their trucks parked outside the bar, and Glassy kept watch while Mancrete and I went to work on it. By the time we'd finished, it looked like it had passed through a robotic digestive system. We left a Tarheel beret sitting on the dashboard.

Two Moondaggers appeared, one helping the other, who was ill. I decided that a refreshing swim in the Kanawha River was in order.

MYTHIC ARMY

The destruction the Moondaggers and the Tarheel Rangers inflicted on each other was minor but very real. The local commanders knew what was happening and did their best to dial down the emotions of their men.

Dealing with the reality on the ground in the Coal Country was one matter; reporting to their respective superiors in the Ordnance and the Control was another. They might be blamed, or worse, they might be ordered to start carrying out full-scale warfare against their opposite numbers.* They explained the murders and losses as being the work of guerillas.

Operations analysts on both sides worked the numbers and arrived at a guerilla army close to five-thousand strong. My best estimate of our numbers in the field at that point was between two hundred and seven hundred.

The other freeholds had their own agents in both headquarters, so they saw the same assessments the Kurian Order compiled.

The Dreadcoats deserved every line of their mistaken reputation. For their numbers, they did damage beyond anything you could

---

* There is evidence the Moondagger commander demanded exactly that, a "free hand to deal with all enemies of whatever uniform," as he wrote back to Columbus.

expect that a squad-sized (later a company) team short of a mob of Southern Command's Bears might accomplish.

We had more volunteers than we could handle. We armed the best ones with captured weapons and sent them to the mountains to be trained by clans like the MacTierneys; the others we asked only to pass information about enemy strength, movement, and intentions.

With our ranks swelled with volunteers from the hill people and town, we forced the members of the Kurian Order back into their garrisons. We also received a few deserters into our ranks; even a Moondagger shaved off his beard and joined us. Some left as quietly as they came, after a few weeks of rough living on poor food. As I recall, the Moondagger stuck, and became quite the connoisseur of MacTierney White Whiskey.

We didn't have the ability to train them. All we could do was pair the new recruits with a veteran and hope that the elder could keep the younger alive until he learned how to shoot from cover and find food on the march.

Still, there were many deaths. The Tarheel Rangers knew how to fight guerillas; they spotted us with their aircraft, pummeled us with light artillery, then brought in helicopters full of men to mop us up. All we could do was try to bring down a helicopter here and there with machine guns.

One thing was certain. Only a trickle of coal was leaving this section of mountains, mostly by truck. Now that we had some real explosives, we were bringing train traffic out of the mines to a standstill. They simply didn't have enough manpower to guard the lines and fix what we wrecked.

We were always very careful with enemy bodies. We arranged

them, neatly, covered at roadsides of major thoroughfares with whatever identification and documentation we could find intact.

Our own dead were treated with a little less reverence. I passed through towns where they were hanging from traffic lights at the main intersection. Sometimes they weren't even our own dead. The Moondaggers would lose six and then grab the first eighteen Coal Country men they could find and execute them, using the ratio that one Moondagger equaled three ordinary men.

We baited a trap for the Moondaggers, expecting just such a raid. We had some of our new men pepper a Moondagger patrol—a lucky shot killed one of theirs.

The nearest village was a five-building-wide spot in the road that didn't even qualify for a community center, just a roadside market with an emergency reserve of twenty gallons of gas and twenty gallons of diesel under lock and key.

The Moondaggers liked to travel in groups of SUVs, roaring up the little roads in fast-moving, almost bumper-to-bumper convoys. Sometimes they would drive two or three abreast when they could, filling the road with radiator grille and tire. The sight was as terrifying as a charge of Cossacks with drawn sabers, I'm here to tell.

We did our best to wreak havoc in the wake of the Moondaggers pursuing the Southern Command forces over the mountains and into Kentucky.

I fear we made things difficult for the legworm clans, because we heard from civilians that the Moondaggers were outraged by our little pokes and jabs and blamed the Kentuckians for them. The standard Moondagger reprisal was three deaths for every one in-flicted, and though we were inflicting the deaths, the Kentuckians were paying for our actions.

I did manage to catch up with my friend David Valentine before he disappeared into the bluegrass. It was good to see him alive, al-though he'd obviously seen many miles and endured further priva-tions and injuries since our good-bye beside the big black Lincoln from Xanadu. As that conversation was recorded better elsewhere,* all I will add is that I returned to the Coal Country doubly sure of the justness of our cause and our ultimate victory. Military forma-tions like the Moondaggers never last for long; they make more en-emies than they can destroy in their temporary victories.

---

* *Fall With Honor*

A Suspicious Cease-fire

The Tarheels quit the Coal Country in the winter of 2074–75. The trickle of coal flowing out of West Virginia had been replaced by some fresh surface mines in Tennessee, so there was no longer a point to the loss of life. If the Moondaggers wanted to keep their hand in the beehive for a few trains of coal a month, they were welcome to it.

We were bringing fresh horseflesh up into the mountains when I heard of the approach of forces from Southern Command and the Green Mountains. At first I had difficulty believing that anyone would have the nerve for such a high-risk, potentially low-reward operation.

There was an oddity to their arrival, though. The ex-churchman whom I'd been told about at the Hollow never showed up again. Either he'd finally fallen to bad chance or, for some unknown reason, he'd been removed from his duties of communicating with the Coal Country.

Later, I learned that a simple trick had been played on the freeholds that were coming to our aid. The Moondaggers got a hold of a Golden One and set up a fake resistance camp near the border with Kentucky.

By the time we learned of the ruse, the Green Mountain Boys and Southern Command were already the victims of one nasty surprise when an alleged welcoming barbecue turned into a slaughter of their senior officers.

The Moondaggers executed their operation admirably. They even went so far as to get a Golden One to pose as me, as the Coal Country guerilla army was known to have a Xeno in it, though whether I was the commander or a lucky mascot was a matter of opinion.

The assisting forces guessed the ruse and executed an admirable midnight withdrawal.

With the forces of Southern Command and the Green Mountain Boys departed, the Coal Country enjoyed a glorious fall season of celebration. Men shook hands and backslapped on the street; young people just walking in the same direction stopped, kissed, and proceeded for a few blocks holding hands before parting on their separate business; everywhere there was music and dancing. Spontaneous parties would form where two or three musicians found a comfortable public place to sit with their instruments. In a few minutes others would gather to listen or dance and some old-timer would extract a flask from his back pocket or her purse and libations would be passed around.

Usually fall is a season of dull wools and nylon shells, but not during that brief, happy spell.

I had seen the liberation of the Ozarks and the Dallas–Fort Worth Zone. Those were raucous affairs, fireworks and bonfires punctuated with horrific sights of vengeance against Quislings and churchmen.

In the Coal Country, the celebration resembled a vast family re-union under the auspices of some fantastic boon. Old differences were forgotten and the division between those who worked for the Kurian Order and those who suffered from it blurred and vanished. Of course, some churchmen fled, and there were directors and man-agers of the Maynes holdings who decided to "get while the getting was possible" and escape with every portable valuable they could wrap their hands around.

"Good riddance," more than one Coal Country native shouted into the burned-oil exhaust of a stressed, departing engine. "Don't come back now, y'hear?"

One beret-wearing grandfather, seventy if he was a day, led a little procession of family west.

"Where're you headed, old man?"

"Hope it's not far!"

"Kentucky. My father's there."

"Your father. Hooooly shit."

"We're a long-lived family. Hale and hearty, as you can see. I fully intend to walk eleven more miles today, and we've already put four behind us. See that brat back there?" He winked.

"Why now, just when life's good?"

"They might let Arkansas go, but not the Coal Country."

"They'll take their revenge. The Kurians prefer a knife in the dark to a Guernica."

The old man's worlds circled over me like turkey vultures.

They could celebrate in the towns, but there was still fighting to do. The Georgia Control still had garrisons at the largest mines and rail depots. Coal still flowed south and east to the Kurian Order power plants.

If the Coal Country controlled its own mines, they might just be able to negotiate a neutrality, as Kentucky did, selling a certain amount of legworm meat in exchange for its independence.

The Curtain Falls

We heard of wars and rumors of wars. What exactly happened to the Green Mountain Boys none could say at that time. The Moondaggers claimed that they'd cut them down, forced a surrender, then executed the remainder outside of Harrisburg on the grounds of an old country club golf course near Carlisle. Supposedly five hundred men lie in three sandpits. The Green Mountain Boys said they'd bloodied the Moondaggers' noses at the Battle of Conodoguinet Creek and then headed back north to winter in their windy mountains.

In Kentucky, the Moondaggers pursuing the Southern Command forces (who had much farther to go) made the mistake of acting in their usual high-handed fashion with the legworm clans. They rode through the bluegrass in their usual fashion, taking women and girls for breeding purposes. The squabbling Kentuckians, who had cousins and in-laws scattered among the clans, switched over from wary neutrality to active resistance as soon as they heard the news.

The Moondaggers, more used to slaughtering farming collectives who've taken up pitchforks than facing a highly mobile enemy who ride and shoot from their preteen years, began to bleed from a hundred paper cuts. The Kentuckians settled for shooting down scouts and picking off broken-down truck crews from supply convoys, but eventually any army will run out of scouts and logistical drivers if you kill enough of them.

It was a simple ambush, or so we thought. There's a section of train track on a grade near the Kentucky border, just before it descends again to Big Stone Gap.

Pulling up railroad track, if you've never done it, is taxing but satisfying work. I always felt as though I was ripping the Kurian regime out of the soil by the roots, leaving wounded earth that would soon heal and turn green.

We were overconfident. A series of single-engine planes had been circling over the Pikeville population. We guessed someone there had seen us—or more probably, me—and reported guerilla action to the Knoxville garrison of the Georgia Control, which was burning precious aviation gas searching for us. The garrison wasn't having any luck; it widened its pattern and gave up before the morning was over.

I was still pulling up ties when we heard the train whistle. We hid ourselves. A coal train rattled up the tracks. Easy prey, we thought, except it was moving more slowly than usual, at a marathon runner's pace, with a couple of engineers riding the nose to examine the tracks for signs of tampering. They spotted our tampering and hit the brakes.

Still, we could take out the engine. MacTierney gave the order for rocket-propelled grenades. I put a bullet into a machine gunner behind sandbags wired atop the engine.

The train screeched to a halt before it reached the damaged section of track. Coal dust flew and we heard the hail-like rattle of ore hitting the bottoms of the gondola cars.

The coal filling every other car was just a thin layer held up by canvas and two-by-fours. The shipment was a sham.

Hundreds of scratched, filth-smeared ravies victims poured out of the gondola cars as they were tipped sideways, unloading the living cargo heedless of injury—the diseased ones would be mostly dead in a few days anyway, and those with enough faculties to keep themselves alive would spend the rest of their lives like wild animals.

We fell back, going up the service road that ran parallel to the tracks. The ambush train continued to drop mortar shells on us until we were out of sight. The noise and explosions drew the ravies victims like flies to a corpse.

"There's a quarry—open ground to hold them off. For a while, anyway."

It seemed the best of nothing but bad choices.

An old sign read VULCAN MATERIALS—MIDSO. A MAYNES CONGLOMERATE PARTNERSHIP.

It was a gravel and cement plant, at least it had been recently. There were a couple of big machinery buildings for processing ore and an aluminum-sided office building up on big concrete blocks with about four feet of clearance. There were a couple of rusty and patched trailers near the open-scar quarries, and one heavy yellow loader. A big water tank, intact and full, was the main attraction to the place. It would make a good observation point and would provide us with water, at least.

Some of the mechanics managed to get the loader going and used it to haul the trailers up to the office, where they were scavenged for food and retrofitted with some of the office building's aluminum siding for defensive loopholes. We made a little triangular fort like a fat pyramid with an unusually wide base and the two trailers as its sides. We had an endless supply of cinder blocks to plug gaps and put against the outer walls.

We sent out two scavenging parties to find supplies of food. Ominously, one never returned.

It was a frosty night of horrors.

We had been expecting a few bands of ravies victims. We were miles from any real population centers and well off the road. Of course, ravies bands did tend to gather, attracted to one another's calls, but the bands rarely grew very big; they moved at so many different rates, they tended to break and reform and break again, only to be briefly attached to a new one, like oil drops spilled on water.

The plan was to beat them back with thrown rocks, sharpened poles, and reserve gunfire for emergencies, as gunfire would attract others. On the nearby roads, all we had met were groups of two to four. We should have let the disappearance of the scavenging party be a lesson to us.

"Screamers, like a swarm of ants!" the lookout at the water tower shouted.

I used my arms to vault up onto the roof of one of the trailers. The night was dark and it was difficult to see. "Everyone, we need your guns. To the loopholes!"

We didn't have any of the usual equipment that would aid in night fighting. Two police spot lamps were it. One flickered on and

washed over a blob of pale figures coming across the gravel-bed expanse of the cement plant's clearing. They were widely spaced and
frantically moving, reminding me of the baby turtles I'd watched on
the Caribbean beaches hurrying to the surf before the birds and crabs
could get them.

The first few shots were just blind fire at motion in the darkness.
Finally a shot told; a figure caught by the spotlight leaped in an off-
balance imitation of a jumping jack, fell, and didn't rise again.

I put the battle rifle to my shoulder and joined in the fire.

We could never have defended against a mix of ravies sufferers
and Reapers.

There must have been some remnants of the Twisted Cross still
operational. The general in Omaha had had several working trains
filled with men in their isolation tanks who were animating Reapers
they had been matched with.

I'd learned rather too much about how the Twisted Cross operated
near Omaha. They needed their isolation tanks for animating their
Reapers, and that was very heavy equipment, like moving around six or
seven soaking bathtubs at the very least. The roads of the Coal Country
were in no condition for such a heavy rig, unless it was a tracked tank, so
they must have moved by rail, as they had in the Midwest.

I managed to find the train. It was too well guarded, waiting on
a siding with machine-gun positions all around and a flatbed-
mounted antiaircraft gun (not that the rebels had any aircraft, but it
would make short work of any kind of improvised armored vehicle
that might be used to approach the train) for a lone Golden One.
There were dog handlers and motorcycles and ATVs waiting to deploy against guerillas.

Still, I had a small supply of explosives—my own double-sized suicide harness, which I'd never bothered to wire onto myself. Keeping to
wooded cover and off the road flanking the rail line, I travelled a couple
of miles up the track and placed my explosives in a cut, wiring the switch
under one of the rails where it was sure to be pressed. A very close examination would discover the mine, of course, but disabling the engine
would mean some kind of blow had been struck by the Coal Country
against those who'd selected us for eradication.

The rest of the story has become a legend of the wars. I've heard
the song written about our little Coal Country army and the ravies
outbreak. About how, in our last extreme, the men placed explosives on themselves rigged to a timer that they had to reset daily (or,
more simply, unlock or break the harness holding the explosives to
their bodies) to keep the bomb from going off. If you went out of
your head with ravies, you had at most twenty-four hours of racing
around and shrieking before it blew you to bits, assuming you
didn't thrash your way out of the harness.*

The song is more popular west of the Mississippi than in the Appalachians. I believe no one in the area cares to be reminded of the
outbreak.

I left the Vulcan Stand, alone again. For a while I moved south,
thinking that if the disease were to take me, I'd rather it did so in an
area where the Georgia Control was setting up operations. Twelve

---

* At least one failed. There is a "self-destruct" harness in the Resistance Museum in Atlanta. Apparently whoever
was wearing it removed it by hooking it on a sharp rock and cutting it off in the style of a bear scratching its back
on a tree.

hours passed, and I had no signs of trembling in the muscles or head-ache (beyond a low-level foggy one caused by fatigue). I slept for six or seven hours with my head against a fallen log on a bed of pine branches, and I was surprised to wake up again in control of my faculties. I recited a few lines from the Rhapsodies, and they came out at the volume I expected, my voice steady and clear.

There's no question I was bitten and scratched, both pretty badly. As we'd learned that others had caught the virus from bites and fingernail scratches,* and I looked like I'd been through a threshing machine, the only conclusions were either that I was immune, at least to this strain of ravies, or that the virus took much longer to present in a Xeno.

The stillness of the Coal Country disturbed me. The only living things I met were livestock—mostly chickens and nimble-looking goats—and household pets, and they stayed well shy of me. Once I thought I heard an observation plane, but it never appeared over the ridgeline that obscured the sound. It may have just been an ATV or motorcycle in the distance with the acoustics of the hills playing tricks.

---

* The vector for transmission by scratch seemed to be either the specimen's own fresh blood or virus-containing fecal matter caught under the nails. Ravies sufferers scratch themselves anywhere there are hair follicles, often until they draw blood.

To the White Palace

When those who experienced it describe this kind of devastation, it's common to see "I passed through dead lands" or similar constructions. The land wasn't dead; the people had been destroyed. The land would continue to thrive, to cover its scarred mountains until a new generation came to collect the coal waiting beneath these hills.

I did not feel any more alone than I usually did; I am almost always among those who regard me as a stranger. The usual birds and squirrels inspected me from the surrounding trees. The jays shrieked and the squirrels chattered angrily.

The bites and scratches could still kill me. They'd become infected, and eventually the discomfort roused me out of my grim trudge, my last trip east to the White Palace, so that I walked into an empty New Universal Church building in search of iodine and dressings.

In the last extreme of the ravies outbreak, some of the locals had sought shelter there, by the look of it. They'd made a good, if desperate, guess—if a vaccine against the strain were to arrive, it would be distributed by the church dispensaries. Nothing brings folks home to their Kurian god-kings like the threat of violent, insensate death, I suppose some in the Order believed.

They'd waited, and they'd died, waiting, probably unable to believe that the Kurian Order would just abandon the Coal Country. Of course, they'd done nothing like abandoning it. They'd just burned off a diseased crop, the way a farmer would burn a field full of scabby wheat.

I found a few corpses in there, a mixture of wounded and a suicide scattered here and there in the corners. Why the suicides chose corners I couldn't imagine—some last human impulse for safety?—but that was where the bodies were resting. There were no churchmen, just a single woman in a pewter-colored New Universal Church nurse's habit: "scrubs" with two extra-long scarves to go over the hair and mouth, if necessary.

You could ignore the corpses. They mostly looked like drop piles of laundry, if you just glanced across the pews of the dark meeting hall. The smell wasn't quite so easy. I made it to the little medical offices, broke open a barred window, and took a deep gasp of fresh air. Rather than remain among the bodies, I grabbed some dressings, alcohol, some scissors and a few other necessities and went out the back door. I disturbed some starved-looking dogs tearing into a pile of corpses laid outside the back next to a two-gallon can of gasoline. They looked like ravies victims, probably euthanized by the nurse inside early in the epidemic during their fruitless wait for an antidote. They'd never got around to burning their dead.

I found a better use for the gasoline. I chased away the dogs, then made a pile of the waiting corpses on the church altar and set fire to them.

Once the church was truly alight, I found a rooftop spot to watch it burn while I rested. The fire brought no one save, I suppose, moths.

The windows went first, crashing and splintering noisily; then the roof came down, pulled down by the weight of an ancient air conditioner. For a few dazzling minutes, sparks rose in the sky like souls pulled to the infinite rhapsody.

I dozed after that.

When I awoke, the church was still smoking. Its steeple, or rather a part of it, still stood, a black finger pointing accusingly toward the heavens. I hope it's still there, to be honest, to remind people that death can fall from the clouds, without warning, changing everything.

The White Palace was missing a few windows. It, too, had suffered from fire, though the damage was limited to some blackening like misapplied eye shadow rising from the frames.

I observed it from my old bus shelter for thirty minutes. I saw no signs of any patrols, no ravies victims.

The White Palace looming empty affected me more than I would have been willing to admit at the time. Here, at least, the Kurian Order should have had a skeleton crew of key personnel, but it looked as though I would find nothing but skeletons, judging from the bodies I found in the main parking lot—a hasty evacuation had been in progress when the ravies sufferers showed up. There'd been some kind of battle, and it looked as though the diseased had been shot down.

I heard a few ghostly noises from the attic during my quick tour. Perhaps a few of the Maynes clan had concealed themselves up there in hopes of a restoration of the old order. That or their spirits were saying hello to an old hireling.

The White Palace had won one of the earlier rounds, then.

Some of the vehicles were still serviceable; in fact, someone had stocked up my former employer's converted minibus for a long trip. I wondered how far over the Kentucky border it would get me before gas or tires gave out.

To complete my witness to the flow of history changing here in the Coal Country, I still had a question or two. I decided to seek my answers up in the quarry.

It was in the hills behind the White Palace, beyond the old golf course and the bridle paths. I'd heard it mentioned now and again as the destination of the Reaper-fodder in the Coal Country. If nothing else, I could mark the location of bodies. I gauged the sun as I approached; I had only a brief time to talk before the early winter twilight descended.

The quarry was a sort of horseshoe-shaped indentation in the hillside where limestone had been cut at some point. A pond, swollen with the winter weather temporarily into a lake, lay in the center of the horseshoe, lapping up almost to the sheer walls of some parts of the cuts. Mossy boulders with black and dead growth indicating the high-water mark stood like islands in the lake. I wondered if, during the worst of the summer heat, the lake shrank to a mud hole. How many bones were exposed?

A little dock extended out into the lake not far from the path I used to approach the quarry. A rust-flecked bucket and a tangle of fishing line waited in the cold afternoon breeze. Did someone fish here for a dinner? What sort of Gollumesque* lurker would want corpse-fattened catfish lurking in the lake?

"Show yourself, Maynes," I shouted. "I give you my word on the graves of my ancestors and children, that I will not harm you, directly or indirectly. I only want to know."

The Reaper with the missing lower lip stepped out from the tumble of rocks on the far side of the lake. It looked even more fleshless than usual.

"I'll be more comfortable with my shotgun on my lap, if I'm going to be speaking through that," I said, extracting my gun. "My promise still stands. I won't hurt your surrogate, either."

I sat down, at least twenty feet clear of the water. Who knew what might come surging out of that dead pool. The Reaper in a combination of wading and walking came around, passed the dock, and approached.

"That's close enough," I said while it was still out of jumping distance. I wished in vain for a Quickwood stake. "Thank you for speaking to me."

"you are the first person i've seen in days," the Reaper said. A little saliva ran out of its mouth when it talked, thanks to the missing lip.

I tried to summon some of Maynes's sardonic bravado. "Were you expecting bathers in the middle of winter?"

"the firemen have not come," the Reaper said.

"Have you not kept up on current events? The firemen are mostly dead, fled, or hiding behind as many locked doors as they can manage."

---

* An allusion to an underground gangrel creature created by the twentieth-century fantasist J. R. R. Tolkien.

"i do understand there's been fighting. i have not dared send my mouthpiece down to the white palace. has it been occupied yet?"

"Only by hungry raccoons," I said.

"pity. this used to be such a pleasant part of the country."

"You are the first Maynes? The judge from the Old World?"

"i am."

"So why are you speaking through a Reaper?"

"it is a privilege granted to few. i have become an immortal. as an immortal, it's wisest to deal with mortal man through surrogates."

I had been told such things were possible but only half believed it. The general of the Twisted Cross had been far more useful to the Kurian Order than I could believe this living waxwork ever was.

"Do you sometimes go out and ride horses in the middle of the night?"

The Reaper blinked and yawned. Had Maynes briefly broken contact? "it's one way to get around the coal country. safer than you would think. until the troubles started, i rarely saw anyone but trooper cars out. i suppose you saw me during one of my rides."

I found myself wishing I'd steered straight into him that night. Maybe that would have just hastened all that had happened since.

I turned and walked away, putting the shotgun over my shoulder. Quick steps followed. I swiveled the gun so it pointed directly behind me and fired, then spun.

I'd caught the Reaper in the shoulder, but it was still coming. I emptied the shotgun into it. No effect.

It was on me and crushing, biting. I managed to wiggle one arm up under its chin. The lashing tongue struck me about the face, drawing blood. One eye suddenly went blurry.

My other arm, around its waist just below the ribs, held it fast as I pushed back, back. I reset my feet to get more leverage. It began to thrash back and forth like a snake.

With a *kraak!* the Reaper's back broke. I dropped it and it flopped around like a fish, the legs working at counter-purpose to the upper torso. It kept folding and opening itself like a living jackknife.

I kicked it in the ear to get its attention. "You broke the agreement, Maynes. I'm not about to be harvested. Not after everything you've put me through."

I'd dealt with enough snakes in Nebraska to know what to do with this cripple. I found the biggest boulder I could heft from those littering the quarry and returned it to the spot where it was still thrashing around. It had managed to turn its torso completely around.

"Speaking as one of the few surviving employees of the Maynes Conglomerate and Mine Holdings, I hereby give notice," I said, and flung the boulder down on the Reaper's head. It made a satisfying crunch.

The elder, or should I say eldritch, Maynes had offered no last words. Perhaps he was already in flight from whatever abode he inhabited near the quarry. I could only hope that one of the remaining ravies sufferers would come across him before starving to death. It would be a nice piece of irony, though I doubted Maynes had anything to do with spreading the virus in his own territory.

When the rest quit flopping, I rolled the boulder off the corpse.

Reaper cloth did not breathe and was prone to getting moldy if wetted, but it was warm and stopped bullets admirably for the weight. I disrobed the avatar and rolled up the cloth. I could at least get a nice short-sleeved tunic out of it.

I probably should have spent the night looking for Maynes. There was the chance that he had a Reaper in reserve—though if he did, he should have been spending his time riding its back for asylum in another Kurian Zone. The Georgia Control and the Ordnance would want yet another scapegoat for the catastrophe in the Coal Country, and this time a few directors and members of the Maynes family wouldn't do.

Blinking as my vision tried to adjust to the mixture of blurry from the damaged orb and clear from the remaining, I could only hope it was a cold, dark winter to the north, and the Georgia Control's factories were cutting back on production thanks to lack of energy.

As to the disposition of the Coal Country, had we won anything? To anyone with sense, it was a bloody, gainless shambles. But it did bring the Resistance to the doorstep of the once-placid East. The area between the Georgia Control, the guts of the Kurian Order, if you will, and the brain in the Northeast with all of its New Universal Church colleges and training centers, with the central nervous system around Washington in between, had been thrown into a state of panic such that they'd gone to the extreme of sewing a virulent new strain of ravies to clear the mountains.

But my sense was that places like Hopkins Hollow would survive. Ravies worked best among defenseless civilians, tightly packed in urban areas. The independent mountain families were self-reliant, well armed, and scattered. Without a series of operations such as the one we suffered at the Vulcan Materials site, even the Georgia Control couldn't pacify the area without devoting almost all of its known troop strength to the heavily wooded hills, cuts, and valleys.

I'd come out of it alive. Time would tell if the damaged eye would heal; otherwise I supposed I could easily fashion a Reaper-cloth eye patch.

My favorite time in the Coal Country woods was the golden hour before sunset. The sun would pierce the woods and run in shafts, turning everything it touched to gold. Wildflowers inclined their faces to it, children eager for a father's touch. Even the birds seemed to quiet at that hour (unlike the first hour of daylight, when they would try to outdo one another in raucousness). Not only was the sun's golden beauty pleasantly relaxing—for me it was hygienic. Humans cannot appreciate the cleansing warmth of sun on fur, almost as good as a long hot soak, and certainly better in that you did not have to wait for your fur to dry.

I did my best thinking in this hour and the twilight thereafter. A quiet walk in the woods would often puzzle out a problem in just this way.

Had I lived up to my own moral code? A close examination would show that I failed on a number of ideals. But abandoning an ideal just because you fall short is a road back to an animal existence. Having spent time as a Quisling, I could now have a little more sympathy for the men and women who accepted, or even sought, those roles when I fought them in the future.

I was heartily sick of fighting, but the fight had to go on, or all the deaths of this account become nothing more than a collection of unfortunate incidents, one Xeno memoir of a dreadful time.

One man would understand. I would go west and see if I couldn't pick up the trail of my friend David Valentine. Shared burdens felt lighter.

By this time the record of my experiences left little extra room in the old waterproofed bag that served as a pillow. I cannot remember exactly where I acquired it—while rooting through an attic looking for clothing that would fit, I believe—but it served me well and I have it to this day. I believe it was meant for boating or fishing.

I, like many of my kind, have a poorish memory. However, if I keep a little memento or draw an icon or a few picturesque words to remind me, a great deal of it comes back. Most people have at least heard of the cognitive experiments performed by Shyun on the Gray Ones—cold in conversation, they could not describe a rifle they used daily for a month, but showing them a bullet for the weapon or a paper target they'd hit with it opened the floodgates: how it shot in bad weather, cleaning routine, sighting quirks. Most educated people these days can identify Shyun along with Pavlov as a famous behaviorist and give a rough description of the experiments.

My own memory is a little better than that, but if I can aid it with a few words or a memento—I still am in possession of my Number Four work ID—my memory is exponentially improved.

Originally, these notes were to be presented to the intelligence services of Southern Command to give them a better idea of conditions in the Coal Country. I'm still not convinced they have merit beyond that, but with memories of the Kurian Order beginning to fade, other generations may find them of interest.

Looking back now, most of what is published on the Kurian era divides the Quislings from the Resistance with a thick shining line. Families were either one or the other, and in cases of division, neither camp speaks to the other. It was not so simple, each Quisling and Resistance fighter washed into the other like a salt marsh where a river meets the ocean. The most zealous Resistance fighter wasn't above doing a little black-market trading with the collaborators. Even Quislings ready to receive a brass ring, certifying them as an ally of Kur and immune from the fear of the Reapers, were known to act to save lives, at risk to themselves.

I can think of several Resistance members I loathed and a few Quislings I respected, even admired. Even in the Coal Country I enjoyed the company of some in the White Palace. I encountered intelligence, devotion, and ability in the Kurian Zone—and I would not care to weigh too heavily the difference between their qualities and our own in the Resistance.

Allow me to end this brief digression by wondering in letters if our need to have the Quislings depicted in the blackest possible terms has anything to do with the treatment of captured Quislings at the end of and after the war.

The other goal of this memoir is to reclaim my own name. I've been labeled "the Grog who led the Coal Country rising" so many times that it galls. My friends in the mine, who stood together when it would have been so easy to walk out, or those citizens of Beckley who just wished for some promised cookware to feed their families, need to be remembered more than one aged, grizzled Golden One with wobbly teeth and a droopy eye. Like all the most persistent untruths, there is a tiny kernel of accuracy—I was in the Coal Country, and I was the most recognizable figure wherever our guerillas were fighting.

I hope my account has proven to be of value to those, both laymen and professionals, interested in the Kurian Order and events in the second half of the twenty-first century. I now close this portion of my memoirs and ask not for pity or admiration, calumny or honor, but only understanding.

APPENDIX

The Coal Country Revolt and the Decline of the Eastern North American Kurians

The preceding memoir presents a unique, firsthand view of events in the Coal Country in the key years of 2073–2075, written by a skilled observer with no motivation to either cover up certain events or make more of them than history requires.

The Coal Country revolt was, for decades after the fall of the Kurian Order, a mostly forgotten affair, appearing only tangentially in accounts of the ill-fated Operation Javelin or in Buckman's substantial *War Diary of Green Mountain Boys*. Only an analysis of records kept by the Kurian Order functionaries, mostly archived either by the Georgia Control or the Baltimore Kurians who supervised what was left of Washington DC, revealed its importance to the overall Liberation.

If the reduction in coal production was noted at all in the first wave of histories, it was noted only briefly: "The Kurian-allied Maynes clan's mishandling of its zone resulted in a brief takeover by forces of the Georgia Control and Church-led Moondagger Paramilitaries. The East and Southeast suffered some electrical shortages over the next decade until other sources of coal were opened up, frequently resulting in blackouts and brownouts in the midday and overnight hours." So reads the dryly informative (but excitingly titled) *Tithe of Blood: The Complete History of the Kurian Order.*

Numerous frantic reports from the Georgia Control and the seaboard between New York and Florida tell a different tale. Coal was widely used to generate electricity, of course, but it also heated apartment buildings with only irregular supplies of other fuels. More important, it was used, rather laboriously, to create gasoline. The gasoline shortages experienced by the Georgia Control make for exemplary reading for anyone anticipating having to shift blame or CYA. The Georgia Control, the manufacturing dynamo for the entire eastern half of the United States, almost ground to a halt without gasoline and diesel for its trucks, much of this gas and diesel being generated using coal.

The directors of the various energy-dependent concerns complained loudly and in triplicate of the decrease in production, perhaps fearing a visit from the Reapers. Universally, they blamed first the lack of gasoline—it had been in short supply with the loss of the Texas and Oklahoma pumps—and then the cutbacks to electricity that idled what work they could get done without fuel in their tanks.

The Georgia Control's military remained effective—briefly. They received their gasoline first, followed by key aircraft at the airports, followed by the police and fire forces (who now and then ran short, sharply limiting their effectiveness). As the fighting ground on in Kentucky and the Transmississippi, their weapons and vehicles began to go idle from lack of spare parts and munitions rather than fuel. The Kurian Order slit its own throat with its prioritization of oil. In desperation, they restarted a couple of the offshore oil pumps in the gulf, but it was still a long, pipeline-free trip up to the Macon and Atlanta hubs from the coast.

GLOSSARY

BEARS—The toughest of the Hunter classes, Bears are famously ferocious and the shock troops of Southern Command, working themselves up into a berserker rage that allows them to take on even the Reapers at night. They are also famous for surviving dreadful wounds that would kill an ordinary man, though how completely they heal varies slightly according to the injury and the individual.

CATS—The spies and saboteurs of the Hunter group, Cats are stealthy individuals with keen eyesight and superb reflexes. Women tend to predominate in this class, though it is a matter of opinion whether this is due to their bodies adapting better to the Lifeweaver changes, or the fact that Cat activities require the ability to blend in and choose a time for acting rather than using more aggressive action.

GOLDEN ONES—A species of humanoid Grog related to the Gray Ones, Golden Ones are tall bipeds (though they will still sometimes go down on all fours in a sprint) mostly covered with short, faun-colored fur that grows longer about the head-mane. Expressive, batlike ears, a strong snout, and wide-set, calm eyes give them a somewhat ursine appearance, though the mouth is broader. They are considered by most to have a higher culture than their gray relations. Their civilization is organized along more recognizable groups, with a loose caste system rather than the strictly tribal organizations of the Gray Ones.

GRAY ONES—A species of humanoid Grog related to the Golden Ones, the Gray Ones have hair that is shorter than their relatives, save for longer tufts that grow to warm the forearms and calves/ankles. Their bodies are covered in thick gray hide, which grows into armorlike slabs on some males. They are bipeds in the fashion of gorillas, with much heavier and more powerful forearms than their formidable Golden One relations, wide where their cousins are tall. Unless organized by humans, they tend to group into tribes of extended families, though in a few places (such as St. Louis) there are multitribe paramountcies controlling other tribes in a feudal manner.

GROGS—A nonspecific word for any kind of life-forms imported or created by the Kurians, unknown to Earth pre-2022. Some say the term "grog" is a version of "grok" since so many of the strange, and sometimes horrific, life-forms cooperate; others maintain that the term arises from the "graaaaawg!" cry of the Gray Ones when wounded or calling for assistance in a fight. In most cases among the military of Southern Command, when the word "Grog" is used, it is commonly understood to refer to a Gray One, as they will use other terms for different life-forms.

HUNTERS—A common term for those humans modified by the Lifeweavers for enhanced abilities of one sort or another. Up until 2070, the Hunters worked closely under the direction of the Lifeweavers in Southern Command, but after so many of them fled or were killed during Consul Solon's incursion, the Hunter castes were directly managed by Southern Command.

KURIANS—A faction of the Lifeweavers from the planet Kur who learned how to extend their life span through the harvesting of vital aura, the Kurians invaded Earth once before in our prehistory and formed the basis for many vampire legends. Although physically weak compared to their Reaper avatars, Kurians are masters of disguise, subterfuge, and manipulation. They tend to dwell in high, well-defended towers so as to better maintain mental links with their Reaper avatars. Face-to-face contact with one is rare except for their most trusted Quislings. Some have compared the Kurian need for vital aura with an addict's need for a drug, especially since the consumption of vital aura sometimes leaves the Kurian in a state of reduced sensibility. Most Kurians live life on simple terms: are they safe, do they have enough sources of vital aura, and how can they gather a large supply and keep it against their hungry and rapacious relatives.

KURIAN AGENTS—The Kurian answer to the Hunter class, Kurian agents are very trusted humans, often trained from early childhood to use psychic powers similar to those of their masters. There are reports of Kurian agents able to assume the appearance of other races and genders, confuse the minds of their opponents, and even read minds to uncover traitors.

LIFEWEAVERS—A race thought to have populated some nine worlds, modifying or creating an unknown number of life-forms. They appear to be some form of octopus crossed with a bat, equally at home in the water or gliding between treetops. A faction of Lifeweaver scientists on a planet called Kur created a schism when they began to use the vital aura from other living creatures to extend their life span. Soon open warfare broke out. The Lifeweavers were successful in keeping the Kurians confined to Kur for millennia, but they managed to break out and invaded Earth and an unknown number of other Lifeweaver-populated worlds in 2022, our time.

LEGWORMS—Long centipede-like creatures introduced to Earth in 2022 that reach lengths of more than forty feet and eight feet of height or more. They are a useful but stupid creature, able to bear heavy loads, but they can only be urged to move at a pace above a walk by a skilled rider and constant prodding. The chewy flesh from around each one's hundred clawlike legs is high in protein and edible, barely, and the skin from their eggs makes a tough, breathable form of leather that is a valuable trade good if harvested before the newly hatched legworms consume it. They lay eggs in the fall and become sluggish and torpid in the winter when they gather together en masse to shelter their eggs.

LIFESIGN—An invisible signature given off by all living organisms, in proportion to their vital aura. Reapers can detect it, especially at night, and are able to home in on humans from miles away. It is possible for a human to train herself to reduce lifesign through mental exercises or meditation, and it is possible to camouflage lifesign by hiding in densely wooded areas or among large groups of livestock. Earth and metals do tend to block it. There are some who maintain that a sufficient quantity of simple aluminum foil can conceal lifesign, especially if one keeps one's head properly wrapped, but empirical evidence is lacking, since individuals who try to sneak past Reapers relying on layers of foil rarely return.

LOGISTICS COMMANDOS—A branch of Southern Command that concerns itself with acquiring difficult-to-obtain supplies, mostly medicines and technology. It does this by purchase, trade, and outright theft. It is common for veteran Hunters to go into the Logistics Commandos as a form of retirement from fighting.

MISKATONIC (THE)—A fellowship of scholars devoted to studying the Kurian Order and categorizing Grogs. While the Miskatonic contains its share of academics, there are also "field" people who accompany Southern Command's forces to act as advisers and record evidence. Researchers at the Miskatonic have developed more effective weapons for killing Reapers, mostly thanks to the discovery of Quickwood and its derivatives.

MOONDAGGERS—A religious military order that fights for the Kurians. The order was created and is closely directed by a branch of the New Universal Church that is more patriarchal and theocratic than the typical churchmen. Famous for their brutality, the Moondaggers were key to putting down the revolts in the Great Plains Gulag in 2072. They were nearly destroyed, however, when they resorted to similar tactics against the legworm ranchers in Kentucky from 2075 to 2076.

NEW UNIVERSAL CHURCH—A religious order of trusted Quislings who help manage the spiritual and intellectual needs of the human subject populations in the Kurian Zone. Much of their time is spent rationalizing the deaths of those taken by the Reapers and keeping the human breeding stock quiescent. Higher-level churchmen are often trained by the Kurians in similar psychic skills as those used by Kurian agents.

QUICKWOOD—An olive-tree-like plant that acts as a catalyst in a Reaper's bloodstream, freezing it in place and killing it quickly. The only drawback to Quickwood is its rarity, as the small supply that Southern Command managed to acquire was virtually destroyed by Solon's Forces, though some seeds were saved and a few plants now thrive in the wild and in controlled and defended environments. The Kurians are working on modifying their Reapers to be immune to Quickwood, but for now the Reapers deal with a Quickwood wound by a fast self-amputation, if practicable.

QUISLINGS—Humans who work for the Kurian Order. There is a great deal of dispute as to what exactly constitutes a "Quisling," but usually someone at the bottom rung of the social ladder who follows orders is not considered to be actively supporting the Kurians, even if he happens to drive a collection van for the Reapers. Quislings are more commonly held to be those actively working for their Kurian Masters in pursuit of immunity for themselves and their families. Quislings who do great service in the name of their Kurian lord are sometimes awarded a "brass ring" granting immunity from the Reapers to themselves and their immediate family.

RATBITS—A short-lived Kurian experiment to create a rodent with a higher concentration of vital aura, possibly as a replacement for difficult-to-control human populations. They are approximately raccoon-sized and combine the features of a rat and a rabbit. They have a level of intelligence that is measurably close to that of a human child in grammar school. They were bred in a vast expanse of Texas Hill Country known as "the Ranch," but they resented being harvested as much as humans did, and they escaped into the wild, eventually forcing the abandonment of the Ranch.

REAPERS—The avatars of the Kurian Order, Reapers are very powerful humanoids that form the basis of most of our vampire legends. With only a vestigial reproductive system and a simplified digestive process based on the consumption of blood and a small amount of flesh, Reapers are fast, strong, and deadly, particularly at night when the connection with their Kurian Master is strongest. They are strong enough to tear through metal doors and hatches, can jump to second- or sometimes third-story windows, and can run as fast as most cars can move on all but the best-maintained roads. Hunters find Reapers most vulnerable during daylight hours, when the Kurian connection is weaker, especially directly after a feeding, when the Reaper is sleepy from the blood intake and the Kurian is lost in the sensations of the transfer of energy.

TWISTED CROSS—A military faction of the Kurian Order, the Twisted Cross uses trained humans to operate fighting Reapers in a manner similar to a Kurian Lord's. The Twisted Cross activities in North America were stillborn when the Golden Ones revolted and destroyed their base in 2067. There are reports of more successful Twisted Cross military formations operating around the Black Sea and in Southeastern Europe and Asia Minor, the Asian Subcontinent, and Japan.

WOLVES—The great guerilla fighters of the Hunter class, Wolves are famous for their endurance, sense of smell and hearing, and ability to operate without logistical support. They can cover a good deal of ground in their all-day runs, often evading even mechanized opponents.

VITAL AURA—The energy created by all living things, but enriched and refined in sentient, emotionally developed creatures. Thus, a human will have much more vital aura than, say, a much heavier cow or pig. This energy is what sustains a Kurian over his extended, and seemingly limitless, life span.

Geographical Notes

Freehold—Any area in active resistance to the Kurian Order. Every man, woman, and child in a freehold tends to be familiar with the use of a variety of weapons essential for securing their homesteads, and highly motivated to keep out of the clutches of the Reapers. Freeholds vary in size, but the largest ones in North America are the United Free Republics in the Transmississippi and the old Quebec/Maritime provinces of Canada.

Kentucky Free State—A freehold comprising much of the old state of Kentucky, minus much of the bluegrass region, some parts of the Jackson Purchase, and the area around Louisville and with the addition of Evansville, the small industrial city in Southwestern Indiana and some of the more mountainous sections of Northeastern Tennessee. Previously it was a quiet, neutral territory where the legworm ranchers grazed their giant creatures. Thanks to the heavy-handed actions of the Moondaggers in pursuit of Southern Command's formations from 2075 to 2076, the Kentucky revolt broke out and resulted in the formation of the Army of Kentucky. It, with the support of a single Southern Command brigade in the western half of the state, managed to break away from the Kurian Order and form a freehold.

GEORGIA CONTROL—A Kurian Zone known for its high-quality weapons and trade goods covering much of the old Southeastern United States. Unlike most Kurian Zones, management of this region is left to Quisling "directors" who keep the Master Kurians fed through meticulous record-keeping of the health, productivity, and reliability of the human population. Their world is one of gruesome and remorseless "bottom lines."

GREAT PLAINS GULAG—An ill-defined region running roughly from South Dakota to North Texas, Eastern Colorado to the Ozarks. It is a patchwork of Kurian Zones, mostly made up of fortified farms, mines, and oil and natural gas fields, with Nomansland in between. The Kurians there are mostly a passive problem for Southern Command, but they react to any attempts to take over territory with scorched-earth tactics and depressingly thorough slaughter of civilian populations. It is also one of the Kurian Zones with the widest gap between the freedoms and lifestyles enjoyed by the privileged Quislings and the subject labor force.

IOWA RINGLANDS—A Kurian Zone almost completely devoid of Kurians, the Ringlands are a collection of vast, rich, and highly productive rural estates given to brass ring winners from all over North America. They have a small but well-trained military known as the Iowa Guard and a superb education system for training the next generation of Quisling leadership. Young men and women brought up in Iowa are often chosen for the best positions in other Kurian Zones when their ring-winner parents encourage them to move out and earn their own rings.

KURIAN ZONE (OR "THE ZONE")—There are many different flavors of Kurian Zones, but they all have a few things in common. The remote Kurian Lord and his Reaper avatars are at the top of a pyramid of power. Below them are a few trusted Quislings and the New Universal Church high officials directing a slightly larger middle layer of functionaries and police. Kurian Zones tend to have only small groups of well-armed soldiers, relying on club-wielding police, mercenaries, and special travelling military cadres like the Moondaggers to protect them.

MIDSOUTH ZONE—A weaker Kurian Zone comprising Memphis on the Mississippi, Nashville, and the areas in between. It is considered an ally of the Georgia Control, maintaining its independence by providing military assistance to the Georgia directors now and then.

NOMANSLAND—Any area not part of a Kurian Zone or a freehold is generally considered Nomansland. This can include stretches of useless, postapocalyptic wasteland inhabited only by a few bandits or dangerous Grogs to the bigger Grog lands of St. Louis and the northern half of Missouri. Frequently, headhunter gangs roam across Nomansland areas, looking for runaways from the Kurian Zone to return for bounty or sell to the highest bidder.

One mistake the unwary make in venturing into Nomansland is assuming that there is little chance of meeting a Reaper. Kurians who wind up on the losing end of a power struggle or ambitious offspring of a powerful Kurian can sometimes be found in Nomansland zones, trying to incorporate that region into the Kurian Order or simply hiding out from powerful enemies.

NORTHWEST ORDNANCE—A collection of old rust-belt states around the Great Lakes, excluding Chicago and Wisconsin and including some bits of Southern Ontario. The Northwest Ordnance is viewed by the rest of the Kurian Order as something of a "sick man of North America," and jealous eyes are watching it from all directions, waiting for it to fall so that its more valuable parts and populations might be divided up.

SOUTHERN COMMAND—Not so much a geographic region as a military command and operational zone, Southern Command was one of the first networks of military resistance formed after the Kurian Invasion in 2022, and in pure manpower is the largest. It maintains contact with other freeholds and formerly cooperated with them when possible, but after several disasters and reverses in the last few years, it has adopted a "defensive stance," concentrating on better defending the United Free Republics against Reaper and Grog incursions and training.

UNITED FREE REPUBLICS—Once considered one of the bright spots of North America, the UFR has retreated into a well-guarded neutrality. The United Free Republics had a tumultuous birth, when the collapse of Consul Solon's Transmississippi, which had overthrown the Ozark Free Territory, caused a ripple effect in the surrounding Kurian Zones, especially in Texas. After ridding themselves of Consul Solon through a mixture of luck and planning, the Ozark Forces plunged into Texas and Eastern Oklahoma in response to uprisings there, managed to surround and then occupy Dallas, and plunged south into parts of the Rio Grande valley. Shortly thereafter, the United Free Republics entity was formed, somewhat along the lines of the old states of Arkansas, Oklahoma, Missouri, and Texas. Military reversals led to new elected leadership and a new direction for UFR's military arm, Southern Command, but most believe it is only a matter of time before the UFR manages to link up with the freehold in Colorado and the newly organized rebels in Kentucky.